BOOK ONE OF A

THEO NEWTON

SERIAL

DESTINY

MARK P. SMITH

This novel contains quotations from the American Standard Version (ASV) of the Bible, which is in the public domain.

Publisher: Independent Publishing Network

ISBN 9781805179535
First published in Great Britain in 2024
First Paperback Edition published in 2024
First Printed July 2024.

FIRST EDITION
FIRST PRINT

theonewtonnovel@icloud.com

X and Instagram @TheoNewtonBook

Dedicated to my late Father who passed in 2018, he was my hero. And to my son, my superhero, who battles each and every day. Inspired by my childhood admiration of the British Decathlete Daley Thompson.

PROLOGUE

The story of '*us*', of human origins is complex. It is a tale with twists and turns, made from discoveries and mysteries, of ancestors and cousins. It spans millions of years and several continents, from the ancient forests of Africa to the frozen caves of Europe.

For a long time, archaeologists and anthropologists thought they had a clear understanding of how humans evolved from our apelike ancestors. They traced our ancestry back to a species called '*Homo erectus*', which lived about 2 million years ago and was the first to use fire and stone tools.

They believed that Homo erectus gradually gave rise to another species, '*Homo heidelbergensis*', which lived about 600,000 years ago and was the ancestor of both modern humans and Neanderthals.

They assumed that Homo heidelbergensis split into two branches; one that stayed in Africa and evolved into Homo Sapiens, and one that migrated to Eurasia and evolved into Neanderthals. They thought that Homo Sapiens emerged in Africa about 200,000 years ago and later replaced or interbred with Neanderthals and other archaic humans around the world.

But this story has been shattered by discoveries and new technologies. Fossils, DNA, and ancient artefacts have revealed a much older, more complex, and messy picture of human evolution.

They have shown that Homo sapiens did not just appear out of nowhere but were the result of a long and dynamic process of genetic and cultural exchange with other hominins. They have shown that Homo heidelbergensis was not a solitary species, but part of a diverse and variable group of populations that lived across Africa and Eurasia.

They have shown that Homo sapiens did not simply replace Neanderthals and other archaic humans, but coexisted and interacted with them for tens of thousands of years.

They have shown that Homo sapiens were not the only ones to develop sophisticated behaviours and technologies but share them with other hominins who also had their innovations and adaptations.

The evolution of Homo sapiens is more complex than we had come to realise, a jigsaw with many missing pieces and many confusing shapes, many of which continue to elude us. A puzzle that provokes our understanding and invokes our curiosity.

But what if the story of Homo sapien evolution is more mysterious, much more complex, and far-fetched than could ever be realised. What if the entire human story needs to be rewritten?

This is the story of us.

How we came to be us, but crucially, what comes next for us.

This is the story of one man.

One man who unites us, but also diverges from us.

The One who will usher in a new age for Humanity.

CHAPTER 1 CREATION

MAY 25 2000 6:23 A.M.

And God created man in his own image,
in the image of God created he him
Genesis 1:26 ASV

Theodore Newton, paced back and forth down his hall passage, stopping only to peer through a single clear pane of glass in his otherwise frosted front door.

He was deeply pained and visibly upset. Of Jamaican descent, he had a broad, powerful stature, he stood 6 ft 4 inches, looked around 200 pounds, an athletic build. His slightly crooked nose suggested he had been involved in some serious fights in his life. His face while still young, looked tired and bruised, suggesting that this 24-year-old was at the very least a semi-professional boxer.

Theodore had been up all night, waiting for his love, his wife Isabella to return home. She wasn't answering her phone, nor responding to her SMS messages. She should have finished her shift at the hotel around 11:30 p.m. and home by 12:15 a.m. She would only have to walk for a minute or so to get to the bus stop, then wait for the bus for a quarter to the hour. It wasn't the last service of the night, so unless cancelled, there was always a later bus.

He kept going over in his mind, the varying scenarios of what could have happened to her, with each thought he was getting progressively more agitated.

What about the baby, '*my god the baby*'. Isabella had joyfully informed Theodore, that they were expecting only a couple of weeks prior, she was around 6 weeks pregnant, estimated due date of January 3rd 2001. Before his mind could spiral down another upsetting train of thought, he was sharply brought back to the present by a loud bang.

He hurriedly opened the door to find a short, slim build, middle-aged man, balding, but with some grey hair mixed with his natural brown colour. He was smartly dressed, except for his tie which needed adjusting.

Theodore stared intently at the man, who, aware of how distressed the owner looked, assured him in a caring but authoritative manner.

'Theodore, **don't** panic, I have called in a couple of patrols, they are going to the hotel and will retrace Isabella's steps, one of the units will go through the park, in case she decided to walk. We **WILL** find her"

Theodore embraced the man, tears slowly rolling down his face.

"Thanks, John, but, I should be out there man, if anything happens to them!"

John Richardson was a Detective Inspector with the Metropolitan Police. He had served with Theodore's father, Levi Newton; until he was killed in the line of duty by a young male in a stolen car.

Stepping back from the embrace, John questioned what he thought he heard "Them?"

"Yeah..sorry, you don't know yet. Isabella is pregnant, about 6 weeks"

"Congratulations, Levi would be so proud" he grabbed the hand of the soon-to-be father and shook it.

"Thanks! John, it was a surprise, I tell you, but things feel... they feel so good, you know. Then this."

"Keep Calm. We **WILL** find her. She will be ok, you have my word. I have to get to the station but **STAY** here, a patrol will visit, you have to stay, in case she comes home, ring me if she does."

John gave Theodore a final embrace, then grabbed his hand, giving it a shake, he turned to the front door and left.

#

Police Officer "This is Juliet Kilo Romeo Seven, requesting medical despatch, Broadacre Park, Dunthorpe. Beech Terrace entrance, we have a white female, aged mid-20s, with signs of vomiting and possible concussion."

Isabella Newton was slumped on a park bench in Broadacre Park, when she was discovered by a passing early-morning runner, shortly after 6:30 a.m. It was thought she had been waiting for her bus, but it never arrived, deciding a cut through the park could be easier, as she could catch another bus from Park View on the other side of the park.

However, she never made it through the park. She had a sudden onset of dizziness and felt extremely tired, she sat on the park bench and that was the last she could remember.

She couldn't recall what happened after that, not even vomiting.

#

Still exhausted and drifting in and out of consciousness, Isabella was now in a hospital bed in a side room. A nurse was carrying out observations of Isabella's vitals when Theodore entered.

"Is she OK? Is she awake?" Directing the question to the attending nurse. Now at the bed, Theodore leaned over Isabella and kissed her forehead, she was clammy, her eyes remaining closed.

"I guess you are her Husband?" Theodore nodded

"She is tired, her vitals look normal, we have her on IV fluids. The registrar is on the ward." Theodore stared at the nurse waiting for more "I will get the Reg when they are free, she will have a chat with you. Is there anything I can get you? Tea or coffee, toast even?"

"No, I'm OK, thank you, she will be ok?" Motioning in Isabella's direction, the pained look returned to his face.

"She is tired, the Registrar will answer your questions"

The nurse left the room. Theodore placed his left hand on Isabella's right cheek as he leaned over and kissed her forehead again, she let out a slight groan but remained sleeping.

Theodore walked around the bed and picked up a green plastic chair in the corner of the room and next to the window, placing it alongside the bed with the window behind. He sat down and held Isabella's hand.

"Isabella, darling, please wake up. Show me you are ok"

Isabella lay there breathing gently, her chest rising and falling slowly. Her hand was warm, unusual for her, she always had cold hands, something she teased Theodore with when the opportunity presented itself. Often, she would surprise him, by lifting his training vest or t-shirt, grabbing him, and placing her icy hands over his warm chest or back. Secretly he loved it, but he would never let on.

He liked that he was vulnerable to her, intoxicated by her, and in love with her. Without realising it, Theodore had drifted off to sleep, unsurprising, as he hadn't slept all night. He was crouched over, resting his head in his crossed arms, his right hand still holding Isabella's warm hand.

It was the sound of voices in the room that woke him, temporarily disorientated with a fuzzy, still tired head, he took a moment to take in where he was. He glanced over to Isabella, his hand still holding hers. She was still asleep.

Casting his eyes towards the doorway, he noticed the clock on the wall, it was 12:23 p.m. There were three people in the room, the nurse from earlier, a slim middle-aged woman and a young male who looked irritatingly fresh-faced, but must have been around the same age as himself.

"Hi, I am the Registrar on duty, my name is Dr Williams and this is Dr Kumar. You are Isabella's Husband?"

Theodore responded with a tired nod as he stood up from the plastic chair. His legs, stiff and aching from sitting on the hard, poorly designed plastic chair.

"Yes, I am Theodore, Theodore Newton, Isabella's husband"

Dr Williams continued "We have taken blood from Isabella to check for any infection markers. Her oxygen saturation is normal, her blood pressure is slightly elevated, nothing out of the normal. I have requested an ultrasound, as I believe she is pregnant. It is a little early, in her pregnancy, but I like to be proactive. Give her a thorough M.O.T. so to speak..." Dr Williams paused and looked at Dr Kumar "I will be frank with you erm.. Mr Newton. I am a little concerned she has slept this long. There are no signs of concussion or any obvious lacerations on her head. She does appear fit and well. Can you confirm if she was on any medication you are aware of?"

"No medication, no prescribed medication. She has started taking some vitamin supplements, for the pregnancy, that's all I'm aware of"

"Good, Thank You. Do you mind if we do a more thorough check of her? To eliminate causes"

Theodore gestured towards Isabella, nodding he was in acceptance.

Dr Kumar grabbing the stethoscope and ophthalmoscope, proceeded to listen to Isabella's chest. After a minute of moving from Isabella's lungs to her heart to her upper abdomen, he then proceeded to look in her ears, nose, mouth and eyes. All the while Isabella didn't stir.

Dr Kumar moved away picking up the folder from the bottom of the bed and began writing. Dr Williams and the nurse meanwhile, pulled back the bedsheets. The registrar, starting with Isabella's feet began to examine for any bruising, swelling, cuts or discolouration of the skin, anything of significance.

Upon examining Isabella's lower belly and upper groin, Dr Williams let out a *'Hmmmm'* and looked up to Theodore then turned to Dr Kumar.

"What do you make of that?" Gesturing to a tiny red scratch three to four inches below the belly button. She continued "Has Isabella had any recent surgeries, been waxed, had any notable accidents, anything you can think of?" Looking up and directing the question directly to Theodore.

"Nothing, No operations. She hasn't mentioned any accidents. She isn't one to pay for a wax. What do you see?"

Dr Kumar now examining the wound "It looks like a tiny incision, maybe a week post-op, keyhole perhaps?"

"It does look like it doesn't it, it's healing well, whatever it is, the scar will be barely noticeable, but it's something." Dr Williams responded.

Theodore was now looking concerned his voice shaking "Are you saying someone has operated on her?"

Dr Williams quickly responded "She has a small cut, which hasn't been sutured, it looks like a very well-executed keyhole procedure, but it may be nothing. Her blood results will show us if there is a spike in her CRP markers, indicating any infection."

"Do you think this could have happened this morning? Be the reason why she was found collapsed?"

Dr Kumar chipped in "It's unlikely that this was done today or indeed in the past couple of days. The healing is well established. But we can't rule out that it's not a contributory factor for her presentation"

"We will send Isabella to Ultra-sound, just to make sure everything is ok with the baby." turning to Dr Kumar she continues "We can't X-ray, there is a risk to the foetus. While I am hesitant, we could do an MRI and an EEG, to rule out any seizures. The blood chemistry may give us more of an idea."

Dr Kumar interjects "Do you think an MRI is necessary?"

Dr Williams gave a respectful look to her colleague "You are correct to raise your concerns. But in this instance, I suspect it is required"

Turning back to Theodore, Dr Williams explained what she had discussed with her colleague and that she would be back a little later, suggesting that Theodore try and get some more rest or at the very least, something to eat.

Theodore watched the medics leave the room as he slumped back into the hard plastic chair. He turned his gaze onto his wife. She was just the same as before, breathing gently, eyes closed, still sleeping.

He considered grabbing a bite to eat but thinking about it, his stomach was in knots, he was hungry, but wasn't in the mood for food. Pulling out his phone he began to compose an SMS message to Detective Inspector John Richardson,

'Isabella is still asleep, spoke with the Dr, they are doing tests. Has anything come up from where she was found? Let me know. Thanks T'

Theodore placed his phone back in his pocket, stood and turned to look out the window. It was a bright day, the view from the 4th floor of the Darling Memorial Hospital, presented him with an outlook over the main car park, then of a busy main road, houses which backed onto a large open park with expanses of playing fields and the occasional cluster of trees.

As he scanned the horizon he noticed an aeroplane passing overhead at altitude, no contrails in wake. For a moment, he thought he had seen a bright flash below the aircraft, maybe a couple of thousand feet lower, almost like a reflection from the sun, but it disappeared as quickly as he had thought he had seen something.

The nurse returned to the room with a coffee.

"I know I didn't ask you, but here is a coffee, I didn't know if you take milk and sugar, so I guessed."

She placed the cup on the mobile side table, together with a small packet of digestive biscuits.

"Thanks"

The nurse nodded with a sympathetic glance, turned and left the room.

Theodore must have nodded off, the half-drunk cup of now cold coffee was placed on the window sill, together with an empty packet of biscuits the nurse had provided. He raised his head and glanced at Isabella who, at some point woke as her hand was holding his.

"Isabella, it's Theodore"

She let out a murmur but her eyes never opened. Looking at the clock on the wall it was now 2:53 p.m. He began to rise from his seat when the door opened, and the nurse and a porter entered.

"Mr Newton, the porter will take Isabella down for her scans, you are welcome to accompany her or you can stay here"

"Thanks, I'll go"

The porter, who identified himself as Paul, released the brakes from Isabella's bed and proceeded to manoeuvre the bed out of the room and down the corridor to the ward exit.

It was another long and tiresome experience for Theodore. Mostly sitting, on more hard plastic chairs. At one point when the waiting area for the ultra-sound had no one else waiting, Theodore did a few stretches to loosen up. He even considered doing a few calisthenic exercises, but the idea was quickly dismissed when Isabella's name was called.

Then when waiting for the MRI, which was a buzz with people coming and going, he decided to do a set of press-ups, more because he thought that he would be interrupted during his set by Isabella's name being called. It never happened, he received a few cursory looks from those in the waiting room, mostly followed by unapproving tuts. He didn't care, he felt anxious, pent-up and sick of waiting around.

They must have waited for quite some time before Isabella was eventually seen for the MRI. It was 5:39 p.m. by the time they returned to Isabella's room. She didn't stir once.

It wasn't long after they had returned, that the nurse entered.

“Mr Newton, sorry I never did introduce myself, I’m Joanne Matthews. I will be finishing my shift soon, the evening staff will be taking over. I will do a final set of observations before I hand over, is there anything I can get you?”

“Thank You, Nurse Matthews, Joanne?”

Nurse Matthews nodded in approval, he continued

“I am fine. I will stay for a while longer. I need to change and grab some of Isabella’s things from home. Is it Ok for me to stay with her tonight?”

“Unfortunately, you can’t stay on the ward overnight, you are welcome to stay in the waiting area outside of the ward, there are vending machines there. Visitor times end at 8 p.m.”

“Thanks, Joanne, I best go home now and return with her things. I am fine waiting outside the ward. Have there been any results from her scans?”

“Not yet, I will be honest, It’s unlikely you will get any updates until the ward round in the morning, but if you check in with the nurse on duty when you get back, they will ensure they let you know if anything changes. I am back on shift tomorrow at 7 a.m. Try and get some proper sleep.”

“Thank you, nurse. I suppose I will catch you tomorrow”

“Please, call me Joanne” The nurse turned and left the room.

Theodore bent over and kissed Isabella on the forehead and whispered into her ear.

“I love you. I won’t be long. I want you awake when I get back”

Theodore left the room and headed home. Still very anxious but less so than earlier in the day. At least for now, he had his Isabella back.

#

Theodore arrived back at the hospital with 15 minutes to spare, it was 7:45 p.m. He was carrying his gym bag, a black branded holdall. On arriving at Isabella’s room he was surprised to see she wasn’t in her bed. His heart began to race.

“Teddy”

Theodore turned to see Isabella, holding onto a nurse for support. He stepped towards her offering his arm for support, but instead of grasping it, she let go of the nurse and embraced Theodore. The pair would have remained locked together if it wasn't for the nurse who insisted that Isabella return to her bed.

He was now very much relieved to see his wife awake.

"Izzy, thank god, how are you feeling? What happened?"

"Teddy, I'm ok, I feel a bit woozy like I've been tranquillised, I'm not too steady, fortunately, Emma here was able to keep me on my feet"

Theodore turned to the nurse "Thank You, Emma, have there been any results?"

"Not yet. As Isabella said, I'm Nurse Hays, but I am ok with Emma. We won't get the results back quite yet. I know you have just arrived and you'll want to catch up, but we have strict rules, visiting hours end at 8 p.m., so you have to be quick. I am sorry"

"I understand"

The nurse left the room.

Isabella with a wry smile on her face "How are you Teddy? I bet you have been worried"

"Worried! She says. I've been beside myself. Johnie Rich will tell you." Her giggling stops as she responds

"You didn't drag John into this? Did you?"

Theodore "This? What is this? You were missing. Not answering your phone. Not replying to t.." Theodore hesitated, realising it wasn't her fault, before continuing "You won't believe how worried I was, for you and the baby"

"Was my big soft Teddy Bear worried?"

"Izzy, this is not the time to joke. Of course, I was worried. Do you know what happened? You were found in Broadacre Park on a bench"

“This is it, I don’t fully remember.” Looking at Theodore with an unsure look, she continues “I left the hotel. Walking to the bus stop as usual. I got there at 11:35 p.m. no buses passed me before I got to the stop. I waited for the bus, and by 11:55 p.m., I figured it wasn’t going to arrive. I knew if I got to Park View, I could catch the number 18 bus at a quarter past midnight, so I went through the park. But this is where things get blurry.”

Theodore “They said you had been vomiting. Did you fall? Bang your head?”

Isabella “Not that I can recall.” She stopped to think before continuing “I.. I started to feel faint, uneasy, not sick, I don’t think, more lightheaded, like I had been spinning around and unbalanced. So I think, I sat on a park bench. That’s all I can remember.”

Theodore “One of the doctors I was speaking to earlier, a Dr Williams, said that you have a small puncture wound, a little below your belly button. They wondered where it came from!”

Isabella “A puncture wound?”

Lifting her gown, she examined her belly area, “I can’t see anything”. Theodore pointed to where he had seen the wound, but all that was now there was a tiny scratch, barely visible.

“It’s almost gone. It was more of a scar, the doctors said it looked like a post-operation wound, like a, what was it they called it?”

“There is nothing there now, just a little scratch. I don’t feel anything. Very strange. Is the baby ok? Did you tell them I am pregnant?”

“I didn’t tell them, I guess they read it in your medical file. They think the baby is ok. They did an ultrasound, an MRI and an EEG. We will get the results tomorrow, but the radiographer did seem happy with your ultrasound scan…” Theodore paused for a moment “Keyhole surgery! That’s what they said the wound looked like, but a week post operation with no stitches”

Isabella was taken aback by what her husband had divulged "Wait a minute? I haven't told anyone but you that I am pregnant. It won't be in my medical file. How do they know? And an MRI? Thats unusual? Why did they do an MRI? Is that safe for the baby? I know an x-ray isn't safe, but an MRI?"

Theodore was displaying frustration that he didn't twig on earlier "I don't know. I will check with John, maybe he mentioned it, I told him this morning. They never explained why. I never questioned it. They said it was safe. They are the Doctors, I suppose they know what was best. You were pretty unresponsive."

A single tear rolled down her cheek "You are right, but still. I will ask them. Teddy if they have hurt our baby. I will KO the bloody doctor"

"Oooh Izzy, steady now. Keep the boxing in the ring. We will get answers." He gently squeezed her hand "Can I get you anything?"

"I could do with a King Bombay Bad Boy Pot Noodle. I'm starved. And a bag of crisps. And some chocolate."

"Well Izzy, as it happens" Theodore proceeded to pull several items from his holdall. A change of clothes, a pale pink dressing gown. A few cosmetic and wash items. A pair of fluffy slippers and some food items including a pot noodle, a big bag of crisps and a multipack of Yorkie chocolate bars.

"Oh Teddy, you are brill. Thank You. Now give me a kiss and bugger off before you get wrong"

"Do you not want me to make the pot noodle for you?"

"I think I will have that a little later. Give me the crisps and that kiss."

Theodore lent over Isabella and they locked lips for a moment.

Isabella pulled away "I do love you. And Thank You"

"I love you too. I will be in the waiting area if you need anything."

"You don't need to wait. Go home and get some sleep. I'm OK, honest Teddy. Please."

Theodore looked knowingly at Isabella, he could read her pretty accurately now. After 9 years together, they knew each other's little mannerisms, their expressions and noises. If she said she was ok, she was ok. But he wasn't going to go home.
John lived a few streets away. He was going to see about crashing there for the night.

CHAPTER 2 REST

MAY 26 2000 8:19 P.M.

Come unto me, all ye that labor and are heavy laden,
and I will give you rest.
Matthew 11:28 ASV

Theodore Newton, not wanting to arrive unannounced, had the courtesy to ring John Richardson just moments before arriving at his front door, asking if it was OK to crash at his for the night.

John, as his godfather, had an obligation and a promise to Theodore's late father Levi, to watch over him, they were the last words that Levi uttered to his partner. It was never an issue, John adored Theodore, like the son he never had himself.

In the immediate aftermath of the death of Levi, John took in Theodore and looked after him. Until shortly after turning 17, Theodore was ready to return to his own home. An only child, he had not known his mother, a Brightwell Island native, she gave birth to him in Jamaica but did not want him.

Levi, wanting a fresh start, moved with his son to the U.K. Having served with the Constabulary Force in Kingston, he joined the Metropolitan Police and so making the transition to British life easier. Levi however, was not alone, a few of his relatives emigrated onboard the '*Empire Windrush*', unfortunately, they were no longer alive to support Theodore. He had lost touch with his extended Jamaican family, many of whom, had chosen to find opportunities elsewhere in the British Isles.

John was divorced, approaching 5 years. The loss of his partner and best friend had taken its toll on all of his relationships, but most of all with his wife, he took to drinking, becoming dependent. As a result, he was temporarily suspended from work in the Police Force. His superiors offered him a choice and so he opted to check into a retreat to deal with his addiction and sought professional counselling.

He was 4 years sober. Theodore, being the wise and caring soul, like his father, helped John through his recovery, grieving together. It was John who encouraged Theodore to find a focus and to get into boxing, occasionally sparring together when work allowed.

Theodore used the life insurance from his late father's payout to establish a gym and boxing club, investing together with a couple of his boxer friends. With his dad's pension and police '*death in service*' payment, managed to navigate through his difficult start to adulthood, giving him financial independence.

Without John, to guide him, he could have set off in a different direction, the influences of London life a powerful and intoxicating mix.

Theodore went to thump on the door, but John pulled it open before his fist could land.

"How is Isabella? How long has she been awake?"

"How did.." John interrupted, guessing what was coming

"Give me some credit, firstly, you would still be at the hospital, you would be in the waiting room at the very least, but more likely, twisting some poor nurse to let you stay with Isabella. And how could you forget that I am a Detective Inspector for Her Majesty's Police Force!"

"You rang the ward, didn't you? You wanted an update. Don't pull that DI crap on me, you old bugger"

"Ha! Less of the old, I may be in my 40's, but I'm not past it. Do you want to go? The gloves are in the garage. Come on! No? Ha ha." the joviality helped lighten the mood before turning to a more serious matter "Seriously. How is Isabella? The nurse did say she was awake, but didn't have anything else to say."

Theodore "She was awake when I got back to the ward, nipped home for some of her things. When I got to her room she wasn't there. I panicked, but before I could let my heart race away, she was back in the room, she had to go to the loo. She is well, all things considered, tired, and a bit unsteady on her feet, I think she is doing OK. She had bants, so she isn't all that bad."

John found himself laughing again "Bants? I try to understand you young-uns but, that's a new one on me!"

"Bants! Really? Banter. It's something Izzy and I use. Thinking about it. I can't say I notice anyone else using the word."

"That's because they don't! No one does! But she is well? What did the doctors say? Any results yet? Sorry. Do you want a cuppa? I don't have anything stronger, you know" John shrugged his shoulders apologetically.

Theodore read the shoulder shrug for what it meant "Hey man, never say sorry. Never explain. At least not to me. I'll happily have an Earl Grey if you have one or a coffee."

"I remember when your old man told me about when he gave you your first cup of Earl Grey. Ha Ha, hilarious"

Theodore laughed "I never. I mean never understood back then, why he put half a spoonful of sugar and half a lemon juice in it. It was bloody awful. Funny, as that's how I now take it. And one day, when Junior is ready, will do the same thing to them."

John still laughing "A-ha ha, what goes around comes around. You are your dad's son. He would be proud." John continued "So test results? anything?"

"They are saying the results should be back tomorrow. The Doctor seemed quite thorough. Did an ultra-sound to check the baby. An MRI and an ECG or was it an EEG? Anyway.."

John interrupted "An MRI is unusual, it's not usually a routine procedure. Sorry carry on."

"Anyway, I mentioned this to Isabella. She seemed concerned, as they knew about the baby, but until this morning only the two of us knew. She wants to know how they knew. Did you happen to tell them?" John with a puzzled look answered

"The first I contacted the hospital was this evening. Maybe they had some indication, from a test perhaps?"

"I don't know, maybe. They noticed a small mark, a little way below her bellybutton. They said it looked like it could have been a small, what was it they said." Theodore had to stop and think. "A microsurgery thing, but it looked a few days old and didn't have any stitches"

"Keyhole?" John suggested

"That's the one. Keyhole surgery, they said looked similar to what it would look like maybe a week later. But when I mentioned it to Izzy, she had no clue, weirdly, when she checked it herself, it was just a scratch. Like it had healed in a few hours."

"Interesting. A fast healing mystery procedure hmmm." John considered what his friend had revealed before continuing "From a policing perspective. Unless the tests reveal something and the hospital officially suspects foul play, there isn't much else to go on. It may not even be a police matter"

"I suspect you are right. But it is bizarre. I'm now aware of how hungry I am. You ate?"

John with a wink "I ordered pizza, the second after you rang. It shouldn't be long"

Theodore smiling appeared more relaxed "Good man. Can I ask for one more thing? Am I ok to take a shower?"

"Towels are in the airing cupboard, don't adjust the temperature on the shower. It's taken me ages to get it spot on, a tiny turn and it's either too hot or too cold. I've warned you."

#

Theodore returning to the kitchen after freshening up, was in an upbeat mood "That shower. You need to get a plumber"

John, with a smug look "Adjusted it did you? Told you!"

"I like my showers cool. It went from hot to freezing with a minor adjustment. That shower doesn't conform and needs to be ripped out. It's a health hazard."

"I did say. Replacing it, well it's not a priority. I'm thinking of moving, to something smaller. I've been looking at the apartments on London Road. They are nearer work. Modern. Clean. Suits a guy like me."

Theodore was surprised at John, knowing how much work he had put into modernising his home "Expensive. You afford one of those?"

"If I stop buying you pizza. Tuck in"

The pair spent the next hour eating pizza and catching up, the TV was on in the background, a sports highlights show was on.

John "How are you feeling about the idea of becoming a dad?"

Theodore thought for a moment, trying to consider his emotion after what had occurred that day "Excited. Scared. Happy. Worried. I wish Dad was here."

"He would be proud of you. He did a great job raising you by himself. Follow his lead and you will be OK. You have a fantastic career. I am sure Isabella will want to spend time with the baby, is she thinking of giving up working at the hotel?'

"We haven't really spoken about it. But, if she wants to stay home, I will support her. We don't need the money. I do have a great Job."

"How is work going at the moment?"

"We are expanding into Scotland, we have investment to open gyms in 4 new locations. I will be scouting out the shortlisted sites soon. Exciting times"

John continued the line of questioning "How many gyms do you have now?"

"Seventeen. 4 in London, a couple each in Manchester and Birmingham. Liverpool, 2 in Wales, pretty much everywhere that matters."

John patted Theodore on the shoulder "That's great, you have expanded incredibly fast. Don't know what made me think of it, I can't remember if I ever asked you, but did Levi, sorry, your dad, show you his card trick?"

Theodore started to laugh "Show me! Every day as far back as I can remember"

John is eager to know more "Did he ever teach you it? Reveal how he did it. He would NEVER NEVER.." Theodore's laugh gets louder as John continues "..let on how he did it. I will be buggered if I could work it out."

"Hey, man. I asked. My god, did I ask, beg, plead? I even agreed to do the dishes, washing, and clean my room for a month to find out. He wouldn't let on."

"That's a shame. I really wanted to know that one."

"That's the thing, it's bizarre. He never taught me the trick. But I think I can do it. I tried it on Izzy a couple of times and I got it right. Beginners luck. You have a deck?"

John in disbelief "NO. You kidding me?.." Laughing he continues "Remember. I can take you, if you are leading me on" John winked "I have a deck, let me get it." John stood from the kitchen table where they were sitting and went into another room, returning with a pack of cards. He opened them and shuffled them. Did a bit more shuffling of the deck under the table so that Theodore couldn't see anything. Before bringing the deck back into sight, he paused, looked at Theodore and glanced around the room looking for any reflective surfaces.

"You are one paranoid cop. You know that. **I CAN'T SEE** the cards." Theodore began to laugh at his friend's paranoia.

"You cannot blame me for being a bit cautious"

John placed the deck of cards facing down on the table.

John indicated to the pile "Go on then, amaze me, what is the top card?"

Theodore smirked, looked at the ceiling and closed his eyes.

"Come on, your dad could do this in 10 seconds."

"Don't rush me..." John started to make a tick-tock sound. Theodore glared directly at him but he quickly turned his look to a broad smile as if by some divine intervention, he now knew the answer.

"10 of Diamonds" Theodore announced. Just as John started to reach out and grab the card Theodore continued "Wait. That's the bottom card in the deck, the top card is the Jack of Hearts"

John let out an uproarious laugh "This should be good. Your dad only did the top card. Good luck son. If you are wrong. You owe me £15 for the Pizza." John put his arm out. Theodore nodded and took the hand of his friend and shook it.

"Deal my friend. Are you serious about those apartments? You have put a lot of work into this place. Besides, at this rate, you won't be able to afford it with all the pizza you will be buying me."

John reached out grabbed the top card and turned it over exposing the face.

"No way." He picked up the whole deck and turned it over exposing the bottom card. "I don't believe it. I'll chalk that down to beginners luck. Hang on. Your dad told you surely?"

Theodore was laughing more at the amazement that he got both cards correct.

However, Theodore turned more serious now answering his friend's question "No John, he never told me"

"Well. It has to be genetics then. That's a gift you have there. How did you do it?"

"I honestly don't know. I was going to guess. But then when you commented about my dad being faster, it brought over a wave of emotion and I could see both cards, like exactly as we are seeing them now. I said the 10 of Diamonds first as that was the card on the deck, which I thought was just turned over and placed on top of the deck, but the cards were slightly out of alignment so I could make out some of the cards beneath, also turned over. I figured it had to have been the bottom card, the Jack was next to the deck on its own, I assumed the Jack was the top card."

John in disbelief "Amazing. It sounds to me, that you are talking about premonition, are you honestly telling me, you think you were looking at the revealed cards before they were revealed?"

"I guess so. But I could only see them once you mentioned my dad, as if emotion played a part. Better call Peter Venkman, aye!"

"If you start thinking about marshmallow men, you let me know" he winked again "I'm trying to recall if your dad was ever emotional. Who am I kidding, he was cool as ice. Rarely ever showed much emotion on the job"

Theodore thinks about his dad "He could show emotion, often when asking for the 3rd time to clean my room. And what's with your eye, John? It keeps winking at me" Theodore winked back "I'm beat. I'm going to call it and get some sleep."

"Finally. For a minute I was wondering if you were like your old man and didn't sleep. You know where the guest room is.
I'll be getting up at 5 a.m. Early start tomorrow."

"I'll try and get up then, but you know me. Never have got used to getting up early."

"Ha Ha. We will call this baby training 101. You have a lot to learn in the next 8 months. Night Theodore"

#

The morning arrived all too soon. Both of the friends had experienced an unsettled night. Sleep eluded them, except for fleeting moments which returned them to a state of trying to get comfortable, but their minds wouldn't rest, something of the events from the prior day troubled them.

John showered before heading down to the kitchen, the smell of fresh coffee filled the air. John enters the room and sees Theodore sitting at the table holding a mug of steaming black coffee, he appears away in thought.

"Morning. How did you sleep?"

"Hey John, I didn't hear you come down. Not well. I drifted off a few times, but sleep evaded me. My mind was on the go, but for the life of me, I can't remember what was troubling me. How about you?"

John moved to the coffee pot and poured himself a mug of coffee before stirring in three large spoons of sugar "The same. I learned not long after joining the force, that If I wanted to stay a Police officer, I would need to manage my sleep, to switch off from the horrors that I encounter each day. But the technique I learned, well it failed last night"

Theodore was concerned for his friend "What was troubling you?"

John thought for a moment "I was thinking about that, what did you call it.. a keyhole incision, that you said Isabella had. You mentioned that it had healed impossibly fast. That reminded me that Levi, your dad, experienced something similar. Not a keyhole injury. He was stabbed in the shoulder by a career criminal, a dangerous chap, name of Harry 'Big Snake' McKay, trying to make a run for it. Anyhow, your dad gave chase, man how he could run, I haven't seen anything like it, he should have been in '*The Games*', he rugby tackled 'Big Snake', but Snake managed to get to his feet first, pulled the knife and lunged at Levi. He escaped."

"Dad never told me that story"

"Probably because he was ashamed, he didn't think of it as one of his finest moments. But the damnedest thing, even though the knife went in quite deep leaving a 3-inch cut, within a couple of weeks it was completely healed leaving just a scar"

"I remember seeing the scar a couple of times when I was a kid, I asked him what it was, but he said it was nothing. He always deflected when I brought it up. Makes sense now."

"But then last night, you pulled off the same card trick your dad did. Maybe emotion plays a part in it. But there are other things, I just need to piece it all together."

"Other things?"

"Yeah, as I said, I will need to piece it all together. I had better head to the station. It is still early. Feel free to use the gym in the garage. There is a spare front door key hanging in the passage, post it through the door when you have locked up"

"Thanks, Have a good day. Oh and let me hear these 'Other things' when you have pieced it together"

John winked as he left.

CHAPTER 3 DEVASTATION

MAY 27 2000 7:49 A.M.

For I know the thoughts that I think toward you, saith Jehovah, thoughts of peace, and not of evil, to give you hope in your latter end.
Jeremiah 29:11 ASV

Theodore spent almost an hour using Johns's free weights, then, the hour after that, on the treadmill doing some easy cardio. He showered and changed into fresh clothes he had packed in his holdall, before heading out the door.

On his way to the hospital, he stopped off at a fast food outlet, ordering amongst other things, a foot-long breakfast sandwich and a large salad, comprising a third of mixed beans and pulses and a third of boiled egg and ham. Breakfast and lunch sorted.

Passing along the corridor at the entrance to the hospital, Theodore grabbed a couple of magazines for Isabella, some chocolate bars and two coffees from the shop.

Isabella was already awake when Theodore entered her room.

"Hey. You're here early."

"Hi, beautiful." He leaned over Isabella and kissed her forehead. As he pulled back she grabbed his shoulder and kissed him gently on the lips. He continued smiling "Hello. You slept well?"

"I barely slept at all. I wasn't tired. I feel amazing. Full of energy" Isabella glowed, her eyes were bright and she was alert.

"Wow. That's great, so you are feeling better? I stayed at John's last night. Used his gym before coming here, I was planning on getting here early, but since John lives so close, I figured it would be a good call."

"How is he?" Isabella asks

"He is OK. A little stressed. He is thinking of moving to those new apartments on London Road, now he has the house all fixed up. He has done a really great job. Except for the shower, haha. That shower" Isabella's ears perk at hearing of John's intentions

"Oh really. They look fantastic. From what I have seen passing on the bus. I quite fancied looking at those."

"About the bus. Don't you think it's time you had a car? I know you don't mind getting the bus and the little walk. But.." Isabella interrupted "I agree. I have been thinking about that myself. I quite fancy a Mini, something small."

"Well ok. I have to say, I was expecting some Izzy pushback on this. Save the environment. Save the planet."

"You mock me, sir!"

"I do no such thing. And to prove I am your Knight in shiny armour. I bear gifts." He pulled the foot-long sandwich from his bag.

"Oh, my good knight. What feasts have thee, on this fine spring morn? Kneel before your princess, so I shall gaze upon thine splendid footlong" Chuckling she continued "And I think you will find its 'Shining Armour', not shiny!"

"Aren't they the same thing? Command it, oh princess and I shall fall upon one's sword. Yeah, I can't pull it off can I"

"No my dear, you cannot. But you will do for me."

"Half of that is mine, by the way, I got it from that place on William Thatcher Street that you like. And I have a Latte for you. Extra hot and two sugars."

"My good knight. For I shall make you a Lord..." Theodore laughing interrupted "I think we are done with all that knights speak. You win"

Isabella just chuckled as she took a bite from her breakfast sandwich.

Theodore pulled up a chair next to the bed and the pair talked. Mainly about the future, preparing for the baby and getting the house sorted. Talk even turned to buying Johns's place, if the price was right, it was in a better part of the city, nearer the hospital and the hotel, should Isabella want to keep working. A park was close by and St Josephs School was considered the best.

There were so many positives. They lost themselves in conversation.

#

It was almost 11 a.m. when the Doctors doing the ward round entered Isabella's room. Dr Kumar was in attendance with the consultant, Mr Jenkinson and Nurse Matthews. Dr Williams, the registrar from the prior day, wasn't amongst the group, instead a lady wearing a grey suit, who was never introduced, nor did they introduce themselves. She sat in the corner of the room and just observed.

"I am Mr Jenkinson, the consultant on duty today, I believe you know my colleague Dr Kumar. I specialise in Neurology, specifically in Neuro-oncology."

Theodore turned and looked at Isabella, she was already holding his hand, but her grip tightened. The consultant continued

"Looking at your blood results. Well, I'm not one for holding back, they are inconclusive. We don't detect any signs of infection markers. That's not to say there isn't anything viral, we will need to run additional tests there. What makes it inconclusive is, well we usually test a sample, if it yields a result for something, we test again. And at this hospital, a third time. Two of the three tests yielded the same negatives across the board. However, one test did reveal CEA or Carcinoembryonic Antigens, they were above the 2.9 nanograms per millilitre of blood threshold. These are not necessarily identifiers of the potential presence of cancer, but together with other results can help paint a picture. But be mindful, I am not saying you have cancer. Further tests are needed and as I have already said, two of the three tests we performed showed no sign of the antigens."

Isabella shook slightly and with hesitation spoke up "So that's good. I may need more tests, but It might not be cancer?"

"There is more. On your point, indeed, it might not be cancer, but I will stress **MIGHT NOT**. As you state, we do need to carry out further tests. However, when were carried out the MRI scan we encountered. How should I put this? Well, we identified a foreign item in your Uterus. A very thin cylindrical object. Now an MRI would, through tissue contrasts, show indications of tumours, we did not see any at this time, that is not to say this will change, we will just need to be vigilant. But this foreign object is, well, quite bizarre. I believe Dr. Kumar here, together with Dr. Williams, observed a laceration on your stomach. I wish to examine the area, If I may."

Isabella, eyes red with tears rolling down her cheeks nodded as she looked at Theodore for comfort and reassurance. Knowing his wife well, he knew it was his turn to speak up.

"Do you think someone inserted this foreign object into her?"

"That is what we are assuming. I am sorry. There is more to inform you. There is a possibility that the foreign object could interfere with the foetus. We do need to carry out a further MRI scan to determine the risk, to both yourself and the foetus."

Isabella whimpering "Do you know what the object is, what it is made from?"

"That is inconclusive, unfortunately. Since parts of it are opaque, we assume it is a form of metal, however, not all of what we have imaged is opaque. To be honest Mrs Newton, we do not know what it is. It is very small. It was only because we were trialling new computer-based identification methods, that the object was detected. Put it another way to answer your question, Mr. Newton, it is narrower than a standard syringe needle used for keyhole procedures."

Theodore trying to comfort his confused and distressed wife, looks around the room, trying to make eye contact with anyone offering some form of support, his gaze lands on the mystery woman in the corner of the room. She stares back, expressionless, emotionless, then stands and leaves the room, leaving Theodore perplexed.

"Izzy, it will be OK, we will get to the bottom of this. I'll ring John, and give him an update. Mr Jenkinson, please, in your best medical opinion, Izzy will be fine, won't she? And the baby, it will be fine?"

"I understand that what we have presented here could be considered as bad news. Hence Mrs Newton's emotional state. But this is a highly unusual presentation. We don't have a great deal of facts. We need to repeat the blood tests. Dr Kumar here will attend to that right away. Once those are done. We will carry out a further MRI scan, however, I do need to point out the risks to the child.

An MRI could cause the foreign object to shift or move, that is, if it is indeed a metal be it ferromagnetic, paramagnetic or diamagnetic. However, the response to the MRI could give us an indication as to what we are dealing with.

I am sorry and I do hate to be the bearer of bad news, but I haven't finished."

Theodore shocked at hearing that the Consultant was finished couldn't hold back "Sorry? What you just said is, well it's plain gobbledegook, but there is more. What the hell man."

Isabella, in a state of shock, yells "TEDDY. Please." He grabs her arm and rubs it, trying to offer some form of apologetic support.

"We also detected traces of a yet unknown blood group in your blood sample. When we ran a blood typing test, we expected to see a known blood group, for you Mrs Newton, we expected to see blood group O as per your medical record. But while some of the sample results did indicate antigens on the red blood cells, they did not conform to known blood groups for antigens. Your results at his time, are a mystery."

Isabella, now more composed, calmly asks "How will any of this impact the baby? Please tell me. I need to know"

Dr Kumar speaks up for the first time "Honestly Mrs Newton, we do not know. This is all quite unusual and to be honest, none of us have encountered any of this before. It's actually quite.."

Mr. Jenkinson interrupted Dr. Kumar "quite easy to perform additional tests to target where clear errors have been made. Dr Kumar, If you will, can you please examine Mrs Newton"

Dr. Kumar indicated that he wished to examine Isabella. Theodore stood and walked around to the other side of the bed and took Isabella's hand. Nurse Matthews helped Isabella pull the bed covers back, then pulled her bed gown across to expose Isabella's stomach.

Dr Kumar examined the area in question "There is no sign of the laceration. Not even a scar or red mark. It has completely healed"

Mr Jenkinson incredulous "That's impossible. Nothing heals that fast. Are you sure you observed what you are claiming?"

Nurse Matthews spoke up "Four of us, we all observed a distinct laceration to the skin, approximately four inches below the belly button, it was clear as, well day. There was a definite cut"

Dr Kumar nodded "I agree, there was something there." Theodore found a break in the conversation

"When my wife and I took a look last night before I left, sometime around 7:50 p.m., the cut had reduced to a red scratch. Still clearly defined, definitely there." Isabella nodded in agreement.

"Well Mrs. Newton, you are becoming a more and more mysterious case. Thank You all. Dr. Kumar. Please, see too what we have discussed. Mr and

Mrs Newton, we will keep you informed as to whatever we find." The consultant concluded.

The medical staff left the room. It was on his mind the whole time, but Theodore had to say it "He was a charmer. Do you think he is a little autistic? No bedside manner. What is ferromagnetic, para-thingy or the other one? Did we need to know any of that?"

#

The rest of the day was uneventful. Waiting around for tests. Sitting on hard plastic chairs, except for Isabella who had a slightly more comfortable wheelchair, while she could walk, it was hospital protocol to ensure she was allocated a wheelchair. The couple talked, trying their best to avoid discussing what they were both thinking. They reminisced about their past and the days when they first met.

They were not long back in the hospital room when Nurse Joanne Matthews entered. She looked upset. Isabella sensed something was up.

"Joanne, is everything ok?"

"Sorry, yes. No. I shouldn't say anything, Mr Jenkinson, he, Argh, he makes me want to scream."

Theodore agreed "He does have an interesting bedside manner"

"Very cold I should say. Robotic almost" Isabella added.

Nurse Matthews continued "But that is not all. Dr Williams handed her notice in with immediate effect. She won't be coming back."

"Wasn't she the Doctor that was here yesterday?"

"Yes. She handed her resignation in, I don't know why. I liked her, she was one of the more friendly Doctors around here"

Isabella put her arm around the nurse to offer support

"Sorry to hear that."

"I just need to take some observations. You are good people. I am so very sorry." Isabella and Theodore looked at each other, perplexed. Theodore spoke up "Is there something we should know? About Izzy?"

“The Consultant will be here in a minute. Let me get your blood pressure, Isabella. I need to clean myself up. I am sorry.”

Nurse Matthews hurriedly carried out her observations and just as quickly left the room, leaving the couple irritated. Isabella who was sitting on the side of the bed started to cry. Theodore stood her up and as he embraced her, whispered words of comfort, she was shaking, he could read between the lines and Nurse Matthews's behaviour was troubling.

It was at that moment that a group of people entered the room. Mr Jenkinson, Dr Kumar, The Mysterious Woman wearing grey from earlier, a different nurse and an unknown fifth individual.

Mr Jenkinson began “Mr and Mrs Newton. We have had a chance to look at the results from today’s tests. What we have to announce is still very new to us, so I will apologise now if I do not make myself fully clear, this is, to be honest, because we haven’t managed to understand fully what is going on..” Mr Jenkinson was interrupted by the 5th individual, speaking with an Indian accent.

“I am sorry for interrupting Mr Jenkinson. May I introduce myself? I am Professor Madhani. I am a Professor of Genetics with a particular specialism in blood, I work at the Dunthorpe University Hospital Research Centre. My colleague here made me aware this morning of the unique test results that appear to have been observed from you. We consulted on the results, but I wanted to see for myself. So I have personally been involved in your second set of test results. My associate here” Professor. Madhani looked towards the direction of the woman in grey “I asked to be here before I arrived. Mr Jenkinson If I may”

Mr Jenkinson raised a hand to gesture “Certainly. The floor is yours”

Acknowledging his colleague he continued “Thank you. We have identified a rare form of Leukaemia. It appears to be at the very very early stages of development, this is why the results were previously inconclusive. We will, of course, start treatment. You have options to consider.

But secondly and quite unusually, your blood itself. Leukaemia, of course, is a blood cancer, which affects the blood-forming tissue in the bone marrow and lymphatic system.

However, while we expected to see your O blood group, we have discovered your body, and this may be related to leukaemia, does appear to be rewriting its blood group. However, this is a previously undocumented blood group and does not conform to the known blood groups A, B or AB, or indeed any of the much rarer groups we have seen. We do need to do more tests and further research. With your permission, we would like to study your blood further."

Isabella again and understandably so, was in tears "What does this mean for the baby?" Theodore was now sitting next to her holding both her hands.

The Professor continued "I will let Mr Jenkinson explain, but from the point of view of your blood group. We do see a blood group change when the patient is the recipient of a bone marrow transplant, however, from what we know of your medical history, this is not the case?" Isabella shook her head. "Then there are other instances of Chimerism, that is when there are two genetically distinct cell populations in an individual. This is usually the process that follows a bone marrow transplant, but it could occur naturally, our research in this area is very poor. The third and most plausible explanation is pregnancy, if your baby has a different blood group to you, your blood could change, but if this is the case, we haven't seen a response this vigorous so soon in a pregnancy."

Theodore could see Isabella was confused and had a distant gaze "Is this blood change dangerous to Isabella or the baby?"

Dr Kumar offered his opinion "It is too soon to say. We need to devise a study and monitoring procedure. Carefully observe and prescribe, but I would be negligent to say that there were no risks, to either yourself or your baby. Mr Jenkinson?"

"Thank you, Dr Kumar. From your ultrasounds and second MRI, we have determined that the cylindrical object that we observed has, unfortunately, been absorbed into the foetus."

Theodore in shock "**WHAT**? Is the baby ok, what does this mean?"

The consultant continued "We don't know. We don't know what the object was, how exactly it came to be there, what it will do for the viability of the foetus.." He paused and for a split second appeared to show empathy "My apologies, your baby. We have options for you, which we will discuss when you have processed this sad news."

Isabella trying to process this devastating news "Can I be alone, please? I cannot take this. **PLEASE**" Isabella was screaming, the tears flooding down her face, her eyes red. She had visible lines of pain as if she had aged 20 years with the news.

Her husband joins her, a tear slowly rolling down his cheek

"I am sorry. This is difficult for us both. Especially Isabella. If you could give us a moment"

Mr Jenkinson glanced around the delegation before responding "Of course. We will put together our proposed steps and we will go over that tomorrow if you are ready, but we do need to move quickly. In the meantime, if you need clarification on any point, Dr Kumar will be available to answer any questions."

The group left the room. Isabella stood and walked to the window. Theodore motioned to follow, but Isabella put out her hand indicating for him to stay. She stood motionless, gently sobbing as she gazed at the world passing by. The May sun was shining but grey skies were approaching from the distance. Isabella knew that dark days lay ahead.

CHAPTER 4 LOSS

EVENTS TO DECEMBER 26 2000

The thief cometh not, but that he may steal, and kill, and destroy: I came that they may have life, and may have it abundantly.
John 10:10 ASV

Theodore's heart was racing, he was in agonising turmoil. The joyous moment he had been waiting for was almost upon him, but at the same time, it was tearing his heart apart. He wished he could look forward in time and see the outcome of the choice Isabella and he had taken.

Over the past eight months, the couple had talked about the future. Some very long and very serious conversations, always extremely emotional, sometimes angry, but more often, close and peaceful.

Halfway through her pregnancy, Isabella was told that there was a fifty-fifty chance that she may not survive the full term and to be prepared for an emergency caesarean section. The issue was that her body was finding it harder to heal itself, the main concern was blood loss. She had opted for a less aggressive form of chemotherapy, this would give the unborn child the best chance of surviving but would present the greatest risk to herself.

Theodore while looking forward to being a father, couldn't contemplate losing his love. Early on in her pregnancy, he begged Isabella to consider terminating the baby. The early indication for Isabella was an abortion gave her the greatest chance of surviving the Leukaemia. She did not prescribe to the medical opinion. Theodore, while it broke his heart supported her. It was after all her body, her life, her choice. Her greatest argument was that they could have aborted, but, she could still lose the battle against cancer, so Theodore would have lost twice. Or that both she and the baby could survive. Have faith was her mantra.

It was at this halfway stage of carrying the baby, that finally the results were back on the mysterious blood group that had been discovered. Analysis confirmed it was a new and previously unidentified blood group. Initially code-named *'Blood X'*, it was short for Xeno. Reluctant, Isabella and Theodore agreed for foetal blood sampling to be carried out.

During the risky procedure, the specialist practitioner inserted a needle through Isabella's uterus and into blood vessels in the umbilical cord attached to the foetus. They successfully managed to sample the Child's blood which came back as *'blood X'*. But this wasn't the most fascinating discovery.

Within the unborn child's blood were antibodies for diseases that Isabella claims, she had never had. On examining the blood of the child, antibodies for chicken pox were discovered, however, never having had chickenpox, those same antibodies were not present in Isabella. Her medical record confirmed that she had never been vaccinated against the disease.

The discovery of the *'blood X'* and antibodies came as a confusing revelation to the medical team, on the one hand, the placental function seemed to be working, as the antibodies from the child did not pass to the mother, but on the other, it wasn't working as the foetal blood appeared to be mixing with Isabella's blood.

At seven months of full term, the prognosis for both Isabella and the unborn child was a 10% chance of survival. The chemotherapy treatment had started well, there were indications the leukaemia was being reversed, but, the cancer became more aggressive and started to spread beyond being a blood cancer. Isabella's main organs had become infected.

At eight months of full term, the advice was an immediate c-section, the baby wasn't developing as expected and there were indications that the placenta was breaking down.

The medical team caring for her were now sure that neither the baby nor Isabella would survive beyond this point. But Isabella refused. She wanted one last Christmas with her Teddy at home.

Advising against home leave, the hospital eventually relented and allowed her to go home for 24 hours.

She spent most of Christmas Day asleep on the sofa, Theodore was massaging her feet whenever she was awake, it comforted her, and the pain of her body shutting down became but a memory.

For a couple of hours, while she slept, Theodore had '*simply*' decorated the living room with some Christmas ornaments and a basic decorated tree.

They told each other how much in love they were. Isabella managed to laugh, and Theodore cried. They had previously talked about names for the baby, but they could not decide. They had considered Levi, but Isabella had never met Theodore's father, they considered John, he was after all godfather to Theodore, but Theodore considered him more an older brother and it seemed, too normal a name, not befitting of the Newton's ancestry of more uncommon names.

Isabella didn't know her parents' names, they we young and immature, so gave her up for adoption as a baby, a bond that she shared with Theodore, whose own mother gave him up. She spent her childhood moving from foster home to foster home. While there were some loving and protective guardians, none of them provided her with the loving connection a parent and child should have, she was never adopted.

While asked several times, at various hospital appointments, they agreed they did not want to know the gender of their child, so in the end, Isabella settled upon one name each for a boy or girl and made Theodore promise it would be the name for their child.

She requested if they both didn't survive, she wanted the child christened, even though they no longer believed, she wanted to be buried with their baby. If the child lives but she didn't she wanted to be cremated.

At 2:13 a.m. on the 26th December, an Ambulance was called. Blue lights flashing, sirens off, they raced to Darling Memorial Hospital, Isabella had to be resuscitated a couple of times. Her body was about to lose the fight. They arrived at the Hospital at 2:35 a.m., Isabella was wheeled straight into the Operating Theatre.

Theodore sat alone in the family room. A now lukewarm cup of black coffee, that he was given on his arrival, was still in his hand. The pain lines were all too evident on his face. His eyes were red, a tear slowly rolled down his cheek.

It was 3:12 a.m. when the door to the family room opened, Dr Kumar and Nurse Matthews entered, followed by the hospital chaplain, Father Simons. Theodore looked up, glancing at each of their faces for any indication of positive news, there was none, and his heart sank as he braced himself for the news.

Dr Kumar, his demeanour full of sorrow had the duty of passing on the news "I am so sorry Mr. Newton. We did all we could. Isabella has passed. She was at peace before we began the caesarean procedure. We tried several times to resuscitate her" He paused. Theodore was shaking, his eyes red trying to hold back the tears.

"The baby is being cared for in neonatal, he needed some assistance breathing but is doing well on his own now. He weighs 4 pounds 1 once, which is a little below the average weight, however, it's not too concerning, as he is being well cared for. Again I am so so very sorry for your loss. Do you have any questions or need anything"

Theodore glanced up, wiping his eyes "A boy?.." He paused and let out a small pained laugh "I have a son!" Tears rolled down his face. It was obvious to those in the room that he was in torment, his emotions were heading off in a mix of directions from agony to joy and then sorrow, anger, and surprise, it was all too much, he didn't know what to feel.

He was numb, did it matter that he had a son now? How should he feel about the boy when he has just lost his wife, his love, his Izzy? How could he take a child home, how would he cope, how could he raise him? But the child was his sole responsibility, it needed protecting, but how, did he fail to protect his Izzy? His mind was circling through the same thoughts without end, with no specific emotion attached to how he should be feeling.

"I am the hospital chaplain, Father Simons, I don't know if your wife or yourself are religious, but I am here to offer support and guidance at this sorrowful time" the calm and almost melodious voice of Father Simons snapped Theodore out of what could only be described as a trance.

"Thank you, Father, but we aren't what you would consider religious, far from it. I know you mean well and you are not to blame, so don't take this personally, but If your god or any god is real, I would want to..." Theodore stopped, he could feel anger, he wanted to tear god apart. But he didn't believe in god, so knew his anger was misdirected and felt ashamed. He continued

"Can I see my her? And my son?"

The doctor answered "Nurse Matthews will take you up to the neonatal family room, the team will take you to your son as soon as they are ready. You will be able to see your wife later, but now is not the time, I am sorry."

The chaplain, wanting to offer some comfort continued "While you may not believe in our Lord. I will share with you, that I have, lost faith many times, the comforting words of the Bible, well at one time, they felt meaningless, especially when I lost my daughter unexpectedly. But with the support and compassion of the church, my congregation, friends and family, the words of scripture once again had a place in my heart and it gave me a stronger love for our Lord and Saviour. So let me finish by saying. When you are ready, we are here, even if it's not our Lord's word that you want to hear."

Theodore just stared at Father Simons, thinking of how to respond. Millions of thoughts were firing in his head, on the one hand, this religious man was still a person, he had lost someone he loved, as much as he loved his Izzy, but then, this man believed in an invisible idea, an invisible idea that from Theodore's perspective had forsaken humanity, had not intervened over the millennia, allowing for wars, disease and suffering to continue. He had considered that religion, conveniently, allowed free will, but it was just that, a convenient get-out clause. If God was real then so must be the Devil, else God could not be all good. And then if the Devil was real, it was winning the war, so how could God be all-powerful? All Theodore could say in reply, was the most human and appropriate response.

"Thank you"

Father Simons left the room with Dr Kumar. Theodore stood placing the still-full paper cup of coffee on the table.

"The coffee doesn't agree with me either. I Never could go back to instant coffee once I tried fresh beans. Are you ready to follow me up to Neonatal?"

"Yes. I…" he was about to say that they should get Isabella, as she would want to see the baby, but then he achingly remembered that she couldn't, she wasn't here anymore. His heart raced, and he collapsed back into the chair, lifting his hands to his face he began to cry uncontrollably.

Nurse Matthews sat next to him and leaned in to give him comfort. After minutes of sobbing, Theodore started to calm down, he whispered, something unintelligible.

Nurse Matthews sensing Theodore was almost controlling his emotion spoke "I am so sorry. " She paused and looked towards the door before continuing in a quieter voice "I know I shouldn't do this, But do you want something a little stronger than coffee?"

Theodore looked at Nurse Matthews with a confused look, he wiped the tears from his eyes, and she continued "I don't mean, oh, I guess I should have just said whisky. Would you like a whisky?"

"Sorry! I don't drink, I haven't had a drink for a few years. Thank you, but no thanks. It's not the answer."

"Sorry, I shouldn't have offered, forgive me, I have a drink problem, I am trying to deal with it, but I relapse, this job can be so hard."

"Don't apologise. We all have our troubles and I won't tell. But if you want to stop, I do know a man who might be able to help you, if you are up for it?"

"I guess. Who is this man?"

"A friend. Actually, he is my godfather, he won't mind me saying, he had an alcohol problem after my father died, they were partners in the Police. The drink, for him, well it got so bad, his career suffered, he was offered a choice, he took the help and he has been sober ever since. He is a good man. He will help you"

"Thank you. I will give you my number to pass on. Do you want a few more minutes here?"

"No, I want to see my son now"

#

Theodore had been waiting for at least an hour before he was invited in to see his son. While he was waiting, he didn't think of anything, not Isabella or his son. He didn't want to show his weakness, his emotion.

He just sat and watched nursing staff frantically move between rooms, pulling bits of equipment from here to there. Then there were the sounds, an almost constant electric bleep or chirp and all too often, a rhythmic alarm of various medical equipment alerting the medics that a baby needed attention. And finally the crying, more than a dozen tiny souls all letting it be known, at unpredictable intervals, that they were not happy and needed attention.

A few other parents were milling around, some were attending to their babies, and others were quietly sitting next to their Children's cots gazing at them lovingly. One father was spread across three hard plastic chairs, their coat a makeshift pillow, trying to get some rest, as going home to their bed was not an option.

"Mr Newton? I am Nurse Sanna. I am the neonatal nurse looking after your son, if you would like to come this way, I will introduce you to your baby"

Theodore followed the nurse, a short walk down the corridor to a ward bay, there were six intensive care cots in the room, three on the left and three on the right. Every one of the cots had all manner of cables running between various medical equipment and the tiny infants. Some had oxygen tubes either to their nose or mouth. The pumps rhythmically offer comforting assurance.

"This is your baby boy. He was weighed at 4 pounds and 1 ounce. Which is a little low, but we aren't worried. His heart has a very healthy and strong beat. His airways are clear and he has passed his meconium, that's his first bowel motion. We have been feeding him via a small syringe, every couple of hours with a newborn formula, he seems to be tolerating it."

"Thank you. Is he well? Have you done any tests?"

"He certainly is doing well. We did take some small blood samples, just to make sure, you know, as a precaution. Do we have a name for him yet?"

Theodore misses the nurse's question, focusing more on his son's health "When will the results be back?"

"We expect them back quite soon. The Doctor will go over the results with you and if there are any indications, will discuss the course of action. No hurry if you don't have a name, but we can register the birth here if you do, saves you a trip to the Registrars office"

"Thank you, nurse. We do. Isabella chose a name for him before she passed. A name for either sex. We didn't discuss a middle name, but I wanted something for him to remember Isabella, his mam in his name, so we are calling him Theo Isidore Newton"

"Oh that's beautiful, is Theo short for Theodore or"

Theodore interrupted "No, It's just Theo, I think Theodore is a bit too formal, I never really liked my name, I got Ted a lot growing up and Izzy used to call me Teddy"

"It's still lovely. Where did Isidore come from? It's unusual and a lovely way to remember his mam?"

"I don't know if it's a real name, while we were thinking of names, I was thinking of boy's names that were similar sounding to Isabella or Izzy and somewhere in the back of my mind Isidore popped up, It was unusual, he doesn't need to use it if he doesn't like it, I was going to mention it to Isabella, but in the end, I never got the chance and decided to forget about it, until today"

"I am sure she would have loved it. Theo is so peaceful. Other than a short time after arriving up here, he hasn't cried once."

Theodore slowly started to find he was developing an attachment to the tiny child. His heart had made a connection to Theo as if he knew him and loved him already "What are the wires on him?"

"So we have a vital signs monitor, they use little pads which are attached to Theo's chest" She pointed out as she explained "That is recording his heart and respiration rate. Then we have an oxygen saturation probe on his toe to read his blood oxygen levels, it also does his pulse rate. As a precaution, we also have apnoea pads on his body, as a secondary way of measuring his breathing. Finally, there is a little temperature probe to keep an eye on his body temp, he is a little higher than normal, but nothing to worry about. The cot he is in is a neonatal incubator, it tries to replicate the temperature and humidity of the womb, just to keep him comfortable for the first few days."

He couldn't explain it. He was looking at his son. Instinct taking over, he knew he needed to protect Theo, watch over and guide him. Something deep within him had been switched on

'Thank You, nurse. Can I hold him?"

"For the moment, we do ask that in the first 24 to 48 hours parents just observe. Then you can help with basic baby care and when the doctor says it's okay, you can have your first cuddle. Sorry for being strict, but it's for the baby. He is about 10 days premature, so It won't be too long. I am sorry"

"That's ok. Theo, Daddy can't wait to give you cuddles. Thanks, Nurse. Sorry, I am quite clueless. What do I do now?"

"Well.." She glances at the wall clock "It's 5:27 a.m., I guess you haven't slept. You can try and get some sleep in the parent's room, but it's not the most comfortable and people will be in and out. Or you could go home for a few hours. The Doctor's round will be after 10 a.m., but they are on the ward for the rest of the day, so you could come back when you are ready. It's up to you"

"Thank you. I want to see Izzy. Can you sort that?"

Nurse Sanna "I will need to ring the hospital team responsible for her now, take a seat in the parent's room and I will find out."

"Thank you, nurse"

Theodore made his way to the parent sitting room. It was sparsely furnished. On the wall opposite the door, was a fridge freezer sporting a large laminated sign asking for all food items to be labelled with the Child's name and date it was put in the fridge.

In front of the fridge, was a small table with a biro taped with a bit of string to the tabletop, next to that was a plastic wallet with tiny sticker labels.

Along the wall to the left as you enter was a sink with a couple of cupboards and a single drawer. Next to the sink, a large catering kettle was attached to the wall, it intermittently started to boil the water it held, before going silent, except for a steady drip of water from the tap onto the countertop below.

In the sink were a couple of used teabags and a single teaspoon. A cracked mug with a missing handle was the only item on the countertop, besides the pool of water that was steadily increasing in volume.

In the centre of the room, was a metal-legged table, which wouldn't have been out of place in a school dining hall, on the table were to be found a stack of old and tatty magazines. Four plastic chairs circled the table.

To the other side of the fridge was a low-backed blue vinyl sofa with enough space to seat at least four people, except it was occupied by an unidentifiable individual with their back to the room, wearing a black hoody with the hood up and over their head. A pale green hospital blanket covered their body.

The final side of the room was composed of windows looking onto the main hospital car park. Theodore thought to himself, that he couldn't think of a more depressing and uncomfortable room, nevertheless functional. He could visualise parents spending endless days in this room while worried about whether their child was going to pull through.

Theodore opened the cupboard next to the sink, to find a jar of supermarket-brand instant coffee, a bowl of white sugar sachets and a box of branded tea bags. Clearly whoever replenished the cupboard was a tea drinker. However, other than the chipped mug with no handle, there were no other mugs to be found.

Pulling one of the plastic seats away and sitting down at the table, it dawned on him, that time in hospital as a visitor, involved sitting on uncomfortable plastic seats and waiting for an indeterminate length of time.

'Best make sure I bring supplies with me' he thought to himself.

He pulled a couple of magazines from the stack, '*New Mother*' from June 1996, '*Practical Parenting*' from January 1993, '*Autotrader*' the cover featuring the launch of a new Super mini that Isabella had considered, the

'Randall Strutter', speaking out loud to himself "Ahh, March 1997", he put the magazines back down disappointed at the choice, he couldn't bring himself to look at what else was in the stack.

He took another look at what the room had to offer, there was a noticeboard on the wall above the table with the *'secure'* pen, and most of the information provided was dos and don'ts for parents using the room. There was a clock above the door, made by a brand called *'Agamemnon'* it was 5:42 a.m., he stared at it, something was amiss, standing up to get a closer look, he realised that the second hand wasn't moving. He continued to stare, *'anything to pass the time'* he joked to himself, the hands were not moving. Reaching into his pocket he pulled out his mobile phone, clicking a button revealing it was indeed 5:42 a.m., "strange coincidence" he muttered to himself. Turning around to scan the remainder of the room he noticed the person lying briefly fidget, otherwise, they didn't change their position.

He let out a long sigh and walked over to the windows. He must have been standing watching the occasional car enter and then leave the car park for at least fifteen minutes before Nurse Sanna entered, she indicated for him to come with her.

Exiting the parents' room, she stopped in the corridor.

"It took a while before I was able to speak with someone, your wife is still being prepared, erm, I'm sorry that didn't come out how it should. She is being made presentable, to give you a memory of how you expect her to look. Unfortunately, you will have to wait until 10 a.m. before you can see her. I can let you have the details of where to go at that time if you wish?"

"Please it's ok. I understand how these things work."

The nurse proceeded to write the details on a notepad before tearing the page and handing it to Theodore. She recommended that he go home and get sorted if he needed. He could come back and see his wife, and then by the time he was back up to see Theo, the doctors would be doing their ward rounds.

“Thank you, nurse. I may see you later.”

Nodding she escorted Theodore to the ward exit where she pushed a button to release the door, Theodore turned and thanked her again before leaving the hospital for home.

CHAPTER 5 CHILD

EVENTS TO MARCH 11 2001

Lo, children are a heritage of Jehovah; [And] the fruit of the womb is [his] reward.
Psalms 127:3 ASV

Theo was discharged from the hospital seven days after he was born. He was making remarkable developmental progress and gaining weight at an above-average rate. The medical team at Darling Memorial Hospital called him a miracle.

Adjusting to life with a baby and having sole responsibility for caring for him, was daunting to Theodore. It was made easier than it could have been, as months before Theo was born and her illness became more severe, Isabella saw to it that the nursery was ready, it was a massive help and one less thing Theodore had to consider.

While there weren't too many practical changes the couple had made to their life and their home, besides the nursery being ready months in advance, the other change they had made, was buying a car. Theodore had insisted that they get one for Isabella's safety, he didn't need one himself, walking to the office or sometimes running being his preferred way to commute. They did what many new parents, who didn't need to worry about money would do and went with a safe and practical choice, purchasing a one-year-old Volvo V70 Estate, the idea of a supermini a distant memory.

After initially trying and struggling to manage working from home whilst caring for Theo, Theodore eventually opted to take a three-month break from work. His home office sufficed for most of his Director duties, but, he still had occasions where he needed to be at head office, usually to attend board meetings and there were occasions he had to visit the gyms the company operated.

While Theo was a calm and quiet child, Theodore found the regimented routine of feed time, sleep or lack thereof and nappy changes too difficult, his self-care was down on the list of priorities and he was close to burnout. Being Director and co-owner, the decision to prioritise his life was his decision and no one could tell him no, however, he did still want to attend the occasional board meeting.

Theodore was enjoying being a parent and watching Theo grow, but his heart was heavy, every day when he woke, he would roll over to Isabella's side of the bed and whisper good morning, but she wasn't there, he would lie there imagining her staring back and he would cry. He missed her so very much, that he had taken to spraying some of the perfume she loved onto her pillow at night, somehow, it gave him peace and day by day helped him grieve.

In early February, Isabella was cremated at Dunthorpe Crematorium and Remembrance Gardens, it should have been in January, but unusually, a stop was agreed by the Coroner, until a further autopsy could be completed. Isabella had her first post-mortem a couple of days after she passed, however, after some tissue samples were sent for analysis and her body signed off for release, some unexpected results came back, and a further request for additional samples was submitted.

The post-mortem and follow-up examinations did not detect cancer in any part of her body, furthermore, her blood was 100% group X, and her natural blood group O could no longer be detected. Her cause of death by the coroner was noted as 'Death due to complications of leukaemia'. Analysis of the placenta did not show any signs of it breaking down or failing, despite ultra-sound and imaging results to the contrary.

Following the release of her autopsy, Theodore was confused and angry, he was considering legal advice for medical negligence. He wanted answers and an explanation, in his mind Isabella was made to suffer needlessly with a misdiagnosis and treatment that could have resulted in Theo not surviving and possibly her eventual death.

But before being able to progress for any substantial legal resolution, The hospital together with Dunthorpe University Hospital Research Centre presented a united front and prepared a thorough evidential-based account of Isabella's condition together with signed agreements for a course of treatments. They acknowledged that Isabella's post-mortem results were highly unusual, but requested that at the earliest convenience, Theo be available for a medical study, focusing on his unusual blood group with a specific study on how he appeared to have antibodies for diseases that did not come from Isabella.

On reading the letter from the hospital, Theodore froze, and a cold chill ran down his spine, dropping the letter on the floor, he remembered Dr. Williams who mysteriously resigned after initially seeing Isabella, where was she? How did she know Isabella was pregnant? Did she have a part to play? What about the mysterious object that was injected into Isabella, what was it? Why was it absorbed into the foetus? What will it do to Theo?

Theodore refused to sign the form, he would not agree to any unnecessary tests on his son. It was after this, that, perhaps coincidently, home visits by the midwifery team became more frequent. Checking on Theo, ensuring he was getting the correct support, ensuring Theodore was adhering to their prescribed feeding regime and that the child was appropriately cared for.

On one occasion, unexpectedly, a social worker was in attendance with the visiting midwife, citing, normal procedure as they were looking out for the welfare of recently bereaved single parents and the child. Theodore while finding the manner of the social worker suspicious, let it go and considered that he didn't know if it was a genuine welfare call or not.

Theodore, without realising it, was very slowly beginning to distrust officials. He began to feel that they wanted to take Theo from him. He could not rest, none of the answers made any sense to him, he felt there was a missing piece to the puzzle which began the morning Isabella had collapsed.

The police investigation the morning Isabella went missing drew a blank, no CCTV cameras were providing any useful footage, and no witnesses or suspicious activity in the vicinity of Broadacre Park in the hours leading up to, or after whatever had happened to Isabella. D.I. John Richardson had kept Theodore updated at every turn of the investigation. He even requested a forensic investigation after Theodore informed him of the incision Isabella had sustained, something that his superior did not take too well when they found out, citing a waste of police resources and cronyism for his ill-considered decision to help a friend.

The forensic search turned up nothing, not even hair or clothes fibres, if anything the site was too sterile, as if something in the intervening moments between Isabella being taken away by ambulance and the forensic team arriving had cleaned the site with unbelievable precision.

Unreported by the local groundkeepers at Broadacre Park, it was discovered that all plant life in a two-meter radius of the bench Isabella was found at were dying, nothing would grow. They thought it unusual and had initial concerns, but considered that it was still winter and made a note to check back again in the springtime. This was something that DI John Richardson had personally observed when he revisited the park a day after Isabella's funeral. It was only after inquiring with the ground maintenance team at the park that their observations were corroborated. To John, there were enough signs indicating something had taken place. However his superior, Chief Superintendent Hess disagreed, and John was under pressure to close the case.

It was at this time, that D.I. John Richardson began to notice Theodore's paranoid behaviour, he was concerned for his friend. John knew that sharing what he was beginning to discover about the case could push Theodore too far. But, he didn't not want to tell him. He knew he had a right to know the details, he knew that if the information was exposed by anyone other than himself, it could damage their friendship and the trust Theodore had.

It weighed heavy on John's mind, only when he found himself holding a bottle of whisky while shopping for groceries, did John realise the investigation was taking a mental toll on himself. Once he had finished his shopping, he headed to Joanne Matthews's home.

John had started to build a close relationship with Nurse Joanne Matthews, sharing a connection following conversations the pair had about alcohol abuse. John's experience in the rehabilitation centre had taught him some mindfulness techniques which he shared with Joanne. He coached her on how to recognise triggers, such as stressful situations, emotions or even people and how not to act on them. Breathing techniques and focusing the mind to step away from a moment that was a trigger, to listen to the body and concentrate on the five senses, to be calm and to exercise. Techniques that John continued to employ.

The couple often went for walks along the River Brent or enjoyed having a coffee together in some quiet tearoom tucked away from the hustle of life. So on arriving at her home, Joanne was overjoyed to see John.

He discussed with her in confidence, the difficult choice he had to make regarding Theodore and the new information. She agreed it was a difficult choice, but shared a pearl of wisdom.

'that truth is always a critical pillar of friendship, even if sharing it could cause pain, as a friend, the pain is not yours to withhold, neither is the truth'

John agreed, that he should tell Theodore what he knew, also coming to the realisation that he was, from a personal point of view, too close to the case and that he would need to hand the investigation over to another DI at the earliest opportunity if indeed there was a case to investigate.

Joanne revealed to John, that she had information to share from the hospital and wanted to explain to Theodore what she knew, but John suspected she wanted an excuse to see baby Theo.

The pair arrived at Theodore's house, noticing the Volvo parked outside, John took a deep breath.

He stopped the car on the opposite side of the street, leaving the engine running "I have known Theodore since he was almost a baby, I have been there, seen everything he has experienced, every step of him growing, to being the successful man he is today. Yet, I am anxious, I do not know how he will react to the news I have for him. He can be rational and considerate, thoughtful but calculated, angry and vicious, which Theodore will I see today"

"Don't second guess him, be there for him, be supportive, be the friend he needs. Explain it as you explained it to me" Joanne leaned over and kissed John on the cheek.

Shutting the car engine off, the pair climbed out of the vehicle. Before they were able to reach the front door of Theodore's home, it opened to be greeted by him holding a smiling Theo.

"I was wondering if you were ever going to get out of the car, Theo's nappies aren't that bad you need to avoid visiting" He winked at the pair, waving a hand to invite them in. He continued "Please go into the sitting room. Can I get you a drink?"

Joanne seeing Theo "I will take this handsome boy off you. If you have a fizzy soft drink, I would love one, thank you" Carefully passing Theo to Joanne, Theodore replies "Lemonade or cola? And for you John?"

"Either is fine, non-fat if you have them"

"Americano with.." Theodore interrupted

"Two cubes of demerara sugar but no milk! And I have a sugar-free lemonade"

John was taken aback "How did you know I switched from white sugar and no longer take milk? Wait! Don't tell me. You have expanded your card trick from being limited to just cards?"

"Card trick?" Theodore shrugged his shoulders at Joanne's query

"He has this card trick, I haven't worked out how he does it, but he shares the same talent his dad had. He can tell you what the top card in a shuffled deck is, although the last time he performed for me, he was also able to tell me what the bottom card of the deck was. Quite clever."

Joanne was excited at the prospect of some magic "Oh I must see this trick" Theodore hearing the conversation forced an uproarious laugh.

After a couple of minutes, Theodore entered the room with a tray of drinks and a selection of biscuits. Joanne was cradling a now sleeping Theo.

Joanne whispered "Do you want me to put him in his pram? He seems to have put weight on well"

"Please" Theodore replied

"How is he?" John asks

"He is doing very well, he is already making sounds and is at 85% of the weight percentile for his age, which is incredible given the start he had. He is such a settled baby. I was prepared for bad nights, crying, burping, being sick, everything this book told me to expect" Theodore held up a book '*Parenting for Beginners*' "But it's only really the advice around feeding and caring that I need. You know, I have not needed to give him any baby paracetamol or gripe water. The kid is amazing"

Joanne having worked on a children's ward, drew on her experience "It does happen, but it is very unusual. Let's just see when he hits the terrible twos" she chucked

John, lowering his voice "And how about you? How are you holding up?"

"I have started working from home again, Theo isn't any bother. We have a creche at the head office now, there are enough parents to justify one. And since it's attached to the gym, we have a customer demand also. It's proving very successful." John interrupted

"That's great." He paused and changed the tone of his voice to a more caring and sincere tone "What about **YOU**? How is Theodore?"

"I am ok I suppose. While having Theo has filled some of the void in my life and given me purpose, I am deeply lonely, but I have a routine, and I try not to dwell on it. I go to a bad place when I do. I so so miss my Izzy, I feel I have lost a large part of me which I will never get back. I'm incomplete"

Joanne reached out to take Theodore's hand "I am so sorry. It will take time and we are here for you. Gradually, day by day, you will heal. And you do have your beautiful boy, he has Isabella's eyes"

"Thank You. He does. And her nose"

"Your hair though. Poor kid, there is no hope for him with hair like that"

"Watch it, John. I can take you, remember" laughing

John laughed "You do seem in good spirits. It is good to see"

"If you had come yesterday, I probably wouldn't have answered the door. It comes and goes, today is a good day."

John stopped laughing, bringing the conversation back to a more serious one "Have you had much more hassle from the hospital since we last spoke?"

Joanne wanting to share her information jumped in before Theodore could respond "Actually, on that point, I overheard a conversation between Mr Jenkinson and one of the senior hospital managers. It seems there is some interest in Theo from some U.S. department or a U.S. Organisation, I can't be certain what. I heard them say that the Americans have requested some organisation be involved and to cooperate"

"Why do they want to test on Theo so badly? None of it makes any sense…" he paused "But, maybe.." He paused again "I don't know. I need to protect him. But if there are some answers as to what happened to my Izzy, answers that can only be revealed by some tests on my boy, then, don't I owe it to ourselves, to Izzy to let them find out"

"While I understand your protective nature, I also understand the need to find answers, to find the missing jigsaw pieces and complete the picture. But as your friend, I will support you. That leads me onto what I came here to tell you." John stood looked at Joanne and continued "There are two things, let me get them out before you interrupt."

"Go on"

"You remember I asked for a forensic examination of the park bench and surrounding ground. And I told you the tests came back completely negative. What I didn't tell you, was the tests displayed that the site had been sterilised. So much so, that no fibres, no prints, no evidence of any human presence at the scene. Not even from Isabella herself. It was as if the site had been deep cleaned to a level of precision that is baffling to the forensic team. It was reported on the morning she was found, that she had vomited. We expected to find evidence of this, but there was nothing…" He paused and gauged Theodore's reaction, but his friend was listening intently, showing no signs of interrupting, John continued "We can only conclude that someone or a group, took a meticulous effort to clean the site after Isabella was discovered, sometime in the period roughly 24 hours after she was found. We can't explain it, we have no CCTV, no eyewitnesses, no additional leads. However, I went back to the park recently and noticed that in a couple of meters circumference around the bench, no plants were growing, not even a weed, everything was dead. I spoke to the grounds staff and they say they had noticed the same thing, but didn't think too much of it, they made a note to check back around spring when they would expect new growth to have appeared…" He paused again and took a sip of his coffee before continuing "And the last thing, I am too close to this case, personally, I shouldn't be on this case, to be honest, from a police enquiry point of view, there is no case, it's only because you and Isabella are my friends, that I began to investigate it, but I need to pass this over to someone else, I can't say if the case will stay open or be closed. But what I do know is this is beyond my expertise. With no disrespect to anyone, this is more of a case for Mulder and Scully than a Police matter"

"Thank you for your honesty. I have.." Pausing "I have played the story around in my head millions of times. I've been to the park, sat at the bench, and observed the plants starting to bud across the way, but not by the bench. I have thought about the incision that Izzy had, the bizarre tube which was inserted into her, and her subsequent cancer. And none of it makes sense. You know I am not a godly man and I try to rationalise things, but this. This feels unearthly. If I want the truth, to find the answers, I need to agree to Theo being tested. If I don't agree then I need to forget all of it and move on. So I understand you handing the case or lack of case to someone else."

John was relieved at his friend's reaction "I am amazed you have managed to rationalise this decision so."

"Oh well. I had but, now I am wondering. Why the Americans are involved? Is this bigger than we can understand?"

"You know it could just be an American research clinic associated with Professor Madhani, it could be nothing" Joanne suggested.

"Maybe or it could be something. You know, I need closure, this could consume me. I am going to agree to tests on Theo. But under my terms"

"I'm surprised, you were so strongly against this last we spoke." Theodore shrugged his shoulders with a defeated look on his face. John continued “OK. We will support you, we will be there for you. So you are OK with me handing the case over?”

“Yes, as long as you can keep track of any developments and keep me informed. I trust you, John, just you.”

“OK. That shouldn’t be a problem, but you assume the new investigating detective won’t keep you informed?”

“I trust you. I know you, you have a personal connection to what happened to Izzy. And you know how important it is to me, I can not assume others would risk their career or care as much to try and find answers, to what is, as you have said before, a case with lots of unusual events, it could be dismissed as nothing to investigate”

“I know what you mean. It does, without evidence of a murder, constitute a cold case, but the nature of the criminal activity is very grey. It is more a medical investigation than a Police matter”

Joanne getting up, walks over to look at the sleeping child “Which I suppose is what you have come to realise, do you think Theo holds some answers?”

“I do. He is special, in more ways than being my son. I can’t explain it. It’s not something necessarily tangible. I don’t know what I am trying to say. It is a feeling I have. Going back to the card trick and the sugar guess earlier…” Theodore paused and laughed, he stood up and walked over to where Theo was sleeping and gazed at him before continuing “It’s almost as if being around Theo has strengthened my third eye, if I can call it that”

“Oh come on. You aren’t telling me you can predict things like cards. This I need to see” Joanne begged.

The group of friends continued to chat, laugh and be baffled as Theodore demonstrated his card trick for Joanne’s benefit.

CHAPTER 6 WISDOM

MARCH 22 2001 3:21 P.M.

..and how long will they not believe in me, for all the signs which I have wrought among them?
Numbers 14:11 ASV

Theodore had been waiting for at least 20 minutes past his appointment time, the corridors of Dunthorpe University Hospital Research Centre were buzzing with activity, yet no one seemed to pay any attention to him, as if, it were an everyday occurrence for someone to be squatted down and leaning against a corridor wall.

He pulled his phone from his jacket pocket and reread the SMS message-

'Mr. Newton, we would like to invite you to attend a meeting to discuss the preliminary results of Theo Newton's tests. We apologise for the short notice. If you could attend at 15:00 on 22/03/2001 Building C, Brentside Court Campus, DUHRC? Please reply or ring to confirm.'

The date, time and location were all correct. He stood, stretching his legs and arms in an attempt to hurry the cramp away, just then, the door across the corridor opened and Professor Madhani greeted him.

Prof. Madhani "Apologies for the delay Mr. Newton. We have just been reviewing some additional results that have, in the last few minutes been passed over to me. Come on in and take a seat."

The professor extended his hand to greet Theodore. They briefly shook before the professor raised his hand onto Theodore's shoulder to usher him through the door.

In the room was a rectangular table with three other people waiting, a variety of folders set out in front of them. To the far side of the room was a desk with a computer and printer that was noisily printing something. Behind the desk was a cluttered wall of shelves brimming with all manner of books, files and models of human organs.

Prof. Madhani "Let me introduce my associates" Stretching out his arm the professor proceeded to gracefully indicate in the direction of each of the seated group "First we have Mr Jenkinson, who you know, to his left, we have Dr Mikhail Mashkov, he is the most eminent specialist in human evolution and lead of one of the teams mapping the human genome and seated to his left we have Professor Andrea Ramirez, she is research lead of Hematology at the American National Institutes of Health, the NIH"

The group stood and one by one shook hands with Theodore.

Prof. Madhani "Please Mr. Newton, be seated. Where is young Theo today? My colleagues were eager to meet him."

Theodore took a seat "Thanks. He is being cared for by a couple of friends. I didn't want to unduly interrupt his routine."

The professor continued "Of course, of course. I understand. Children are creatures of routine. But let us begin." Briefly pausing, he opened a folder which was placed in front of him, he continued "During your late wife's pregnancy, as you will be all too aware, we took several blood samples and of course some tissue samples. While initially, the results were counter indicative, that is, there was a suggestion of blood cancer, there was also lack of those indications, leading to uncertainty."

Dr Ramirez "If I may" Prof. Madhani nodded and gestured with his hand, she continued "Mr Newton, thank you for being here. We know this is an incredibly difficult time. Your wife sounded like she was a remarkable woman."

Theodore "Thank you, She was. Please continue."

Dr Ramirez "Let's discuss the enigma we face. Initially, Isabella's blood results seemed counter-indicative, as the Professor suggested. With No signs of Leukaemia in her post-mortem. But the laboratory team dug deeper." She paused and looked at Dr. Mashkov "Your child's, sorry, Theo's blood type for a time, appeared to mirror Isabella's, it was identified as Group O. However, further examination showed that it had changed to this mysterious blood group X. It's unprecedented. We've ruled out lab errors, contamination, and chimerism. The same was true for confirmation of cancer. The samples being tested fluctuated."

Mr Jenkinson "Mr. Newton, during Isabella's pregnancy, we noticed something extraordinary. The foetal blood type matched Isabella's, it was, for a period Group O. But then it changed to this mysterious Group O. Such things... that does not happen."

Theodore "Sorry, you are losing me! What does this mean?"

Dr Mashkov "We suspect a genetic mutation. One that defies Mendelian inheritance. Your child's blood group X holds the key."

Theodore "Sorry, what is Mendelian Inheritance? In layman's terms"

Dr Mashkov "What colour were your wife's eyes?"

Theodore "Blue"

Dr Mashkov "And your son?"

Theodore "Blue"

Dr Mashkov "And your eyes are Brown. Your wife carried a gene for blue eyes and a recessive gene for an alternate colour but that was more than likely also blue. You have a dominant gene for brown eyes and a recessive gene for an alternate colour but from what we know it is doubtful that it was brown and more than likely blue. Theodore inherited his mother's eye colour, but it would appear you also supplied a blue gene, however, it could have been a different recessive colour. Understand this is layman's terms, so simplified."

Theodore "I understand. So Theo received my recessive eye colour gene, from me, the blue eye gene. And Isabella also supplied a blue gene, meaning Theo's eyes would be blue. But If I had supplied my brown eye gene, he more than likely would have been brown-eyed?"

Dr Mashkov "Correct. However, when we look at the blood groups, your wife is type O and you are type A. We would expect Theo to be either type O or type A, however, he is neither. In fact, his group type is unknown. Hence why we are referring to it as group X. To understand this process further we would need to do a more thorough test on each of the three blood samples from yourselves, to investigate the dominant and recessive blood groups."

Theodore "I understand, so if Isabella was OO and I was AO, then Theo could have been blood groups O or A. If I had supplied an O he would have been group O, but if I supplied an A, he would have been group A, as if I am correct, A is dominant over O."

Dr Ramirez "Yes, that is what we would expect. Your understanding of blood groups and dominance is excellent. This is Mendelian Inheritance"

Theodore "But you are saying that either my wife or myself have this X group, so my wife could be OX or I am AX and the X is dominant over O but not A.." He paused "No, wait? Only one of us was the X carrier. It must be me?"

Dr Ramirez "We think so. You are right in your understanding. We suspected your wife's blood genotype was OO, as that is why she is blood group O. It should not work if she had a different genotype, because of the dominance of A or B over O. However, Theo is not O nor is he A or B. You are A, but if our theory stands you must be AX and A is dominant over X. However, our very first result from the placenta, of the foetal blood, indicated Theo was initially blood group O. Later tests revealed it changed to this group X. This does not make sense to us."

Dr Mashkov "But either blood allele could have been passed from yourself to Theo, either way, he should only have ever been Group A or this Group X. So some, as yet unidentified process appeared to have occurred in the foetus"

Theodore "So.. I am partly responsible for Isabella dying?"

Mr Jenkinson "Isabella's immune system waged war against itself. The X cells from Theo became part of her. They triggered an auto-immune response which led to leukaemia. But here's the paradox, They're both friend and foe. While they were killing her, we also suspect they were keeping her alive, enough for the baby to grow"

Theodore "This is heavy." A tear rolled down his cheek, it was obvious to the room that Theodore was emotional with the weight of guilt, remembering his now departed wife. Prof. Ramirez grabbed a tissue and handed it to Theodore. He paused and composed himself before continuing "What does this mean for Theo?"

Mr Jenkinson "We will discuss Theo next. But Isabella fought bravely, there is nothing in our current medical knowledge that would have saved her. We had no way of knowing what we were dealing with. From a human evolutionary perspective, it's never been observed before."

Prof. Madhani "Dr. Mashkov may explain further, but his team's research is very close to completing the sequencing of the entire Human Genome. Dr. Mashkov"

Dr Mashkov "Thank you. When The Professor contacted my team, we were intrigued and wanted to assist. We sequenced the part of the child's genome relevant to this investigation. The X cells defy logic. They're not merely blood cells; they're messengers. The DNA whispers ancient tales, encrypted in base pairs."

Theodore "Ancient tales? Sorry, Doc! I don't understand. Are you telling me Neanderthal or Cro-Magnon or something?"

Dr Mashkov "Your knowledge is impressive. This is very early days in our understanding of the Human Genome, we haven't got enough sequenced data for different races of humanity. Our sequencing has been primarily based on European volunteers. However, we have been running sequences in tandem with other research centres that are part of this project. Now imagine a symphony of genes. Their harmonies were lost to time. The X cells carry fragments from extinct lineages. Genes that we suspect predate humanity. We've named it the '*Ancestral Code*.' Of course, we need to do lots more research. Lots more coding across many species. But this is very exciting."

Theodore "Shouldn't we all carry a little bit of, what did you call it?"

Dr Mashkov "Ancestral Code. This is the exciting premise. We expected to find it at some point in most of us, but we are certain we have found it in your son. He carries genetic code that doesn't match what we have sequenced so far in our research."

Theodore "And therefore in me?"

Prof. Ramirez "Yes. But, that's also the enigma. The Ancestral Code we suspect, influences the child's immune system. It shields against infections we, that is, Homo sapiens have never encountered. It's as if evolution rewound, then fast-forwarded."

Theodore "Sorry. You have lost me now?"

Mr Jenkinson "If you can recall. We sampled some blood from the Foetus and ran tests in triplicate, that is when we identified blood X, but we also found antibodies for Chicken Pox. Isabella never had chicken pox and never had vaccines for it. Her blood did not initially show antibodies for the disease. So how do we explain how Theo, in the womb, had antibodies for chicken pox? And still has antibodies. He has antibodies for diseases that we have never encountered and for diseases that have long since been eradicated. However, at post-mortem, we discovered in your late wife, some anti-bodies for chicken pox as well as other diseases, our overriding belief is, that these anti-bodies came from your son"

Theodore "So essentially, what you are saying is, my son, is some kind of Jesus" Theodore laughed "Are you seriously trying to say, Theo has some ancient genetic code that has instructions to write antibodies for diseases? That he has for of natural immunity? And therefore, his blood is what triggered an immune response in my wife, which resulted in her death?"

Prof. Madhani "All our investigations thus far suggest yes. That is indeed the case"

Prof. Ramirez "Mr. Newton, Theo's blood, its viscosity fluctuates. It's not just plasma and cells. There's something else.." She paused and looked at Prof. Madhani who gave her a reassuring nod, she continued "We've isolated multiple proteins in Theo's blood, but there is one, we have called it Xenozyme-170301. It catalyzes reactions we can't explain. It repairs damaged DNA and rejuvenates cells, we believe it is part of the mechanism that decodes a set of genes which hold instructions for producing an antibody. It's like Prometheus's gift."

Theodore "Prometheus?"

Dr Mashov "In Greek mythology, Prometheus stole fire from the gods to empower humanity. Xenozyme-170301 is our fire. A genetic Prometheus. But it's also a double-edged sword."

Prof. Madhani "The child's immune system is hyperactive, yet precise. It eradicates pathogens, but it also targets normal cells. It's a paradox."

Prof. Ramirez "If we have understood it correctly and each of us here, well.." She paused glancing at each of her colleagues who nodded in unison "We can't stress this enough. More work and more research needs to be done. But Theo's blood is a cure for the diseases of the world, but as it is right now, there is no other way of saying this. It could kill everyone."

Theodore "Great Scott, I beg your pardon but Holy SHIT!"

Dr Mashkov "Shit indeed. Mr. Newton, we have alluded to this, but let me speak plainly. We believe that carriers of these genetic markers, this blood group X, over the millennia, every time they encountered a new infection, pathogen, or immune response. Their bodies were able to quickly and efficiently create a defence, but as part of the defence, recorded in DNA the genetic code of the infection. And the child's blood group. We feel that calling it group X is not enough as Prof. Ramirez explained, Theo's blood is more. We have named it XΩ. A fusion of the mysterious X allele blood group and the omega symbol. Omega—the end and the beginning. As that is what it represents for humanity"

Mr Jenkinson "I'm not religious are you?, Mr. Newton, Isabella's courage lives on. Your child's blood, it's a bridge between epochs. It carries wisdom and vulnerability. We'll continue testing. Perhaps the Ancestral Code holds answers waiting to reveal themselves. But remember, science bows to wonder. Your child, their existence defies textbooks."

Theodore "I am not a believer. And I don't for a second believe that anything of what you have told me is godly, that my son is the second coming or the anti-Christ. There is more chance that this is alien intervention than from a god. Have you any idea what the mystery object was that Isabella had injected inside of her, that was absorbed by Theo?"

Dr. Mashkov "Just consider this. What does Theo mean?"

Theodore "He is just a child. I don't understand!"

Prof. Ramirez "I think, what my colleague is trying to ask is, do you know the meaning of the word Theo, the name you have chosen to give your son?"

Theodore "My wife chose it, she liked my name, but we British don't go for your American naming conventions, Theodore the 2nd, doesn't work." He winked at her "Actually I don't know, but If I was to have a guess or read your mind, I would probably say it's something to do with religion or god maybe?"

Dr. Mashkov "Yes. The literal translation of Theo is God's Gift. Derived from the Greek word 'Theodoros'. Theos being 'god' and Doron being 'gift'. Ironic do you not think?"

Theodore "Co-incidence. Look, I don't believe, I don't believe in creationism. Keep me updated as to the progress of your research"

Prof. Madhani stood "Thank you, Mr Newton. And please, if you don't mind. Do not go spreading any stories of this. I would advise discretion on this matter. If we are all done here?" The group stood and nodded. They each in turn shook Theodore's hand and thanked him. He left the room. As the door closed behind him he had but one thought in his head "Holy Shit"

Theodore proceeded to walk down the corridor and then stopped. He turned and walked back to the room he had just left. He hesitated before knocking on the door.

"Mr. Newton. Was there something else?"

"Yes. I never did get an answer about the object injected into my wife"

"Yes. Come in."

Theodore made his way back into the room and asked if he should sit again.

Prof. Madhani responded "That won't be necessary. Mr Jenkinson, if you can answer this one. Mr Newton has an inquiry about the object that Mrs Newton had injected into her womb."

"Well, this has been the most mysterious of events. We did send the MRI and ultrasound imaging to a forensic investigation unit which was able to do some analysis. Unfortunately, the results were, in the main, inconclusive. What they were able to determine, was that the object was a carbon-based tube enclosing elemental metal."

"And this was absorbed into Theo. What have his scans revealed?"

"No trace. Nothing. Whatever it was, we assume it either broke down naturally. His XΩ immune response obliterated it or he excreted it. We may never know. Suffice it to say, whatever it was, has not had any impact on his development or health. It is yet another mystery to add to the list."

Prof. Madhani appeared unsettled, as if he had somewhere else to be "Quite a mystery. Is there anything else Mr. Newton?"

"Yes. If it is, that is to say, if I am a carrier of this X gene. Or whatever it is. Should I not have some of the immune ability that Theo appears to have? When I was a child I had Measles, should I not have had a natural immunity?"

Dr Mashkov answered "We still have a lot to learn about the human Genome. We believe that only 1% of human DNA provides the instructions that define our uniqueness, that is, defines our hair colour, our eye colour, how tall we will be if we are likely to have a congenital defect such as a cleft palate or a hereditary condition later in life. As we have discussed there are dominant and recessive pairs in our genes. In your case, if you are indeed a carrier of this X gene, it is recessive and as such, the mechanism which we still do not fully understand, has not been activated in you as the X gene is not the dominant one. It is like a light switch it can either be on or off, it's essentially binary. However, all of these unique instructions, that Theo appears to have within his genetic code, should also appear within you. They may well appear within all of us. After all 99% of all our DNA is the same. It is therefore safe to assume, that these instructions are more likely to appear in the 99% that is the same, than the 1% which defines our uniqueness. We will not be able to confirm this without mapping your and Theo's entire genome. There is also a very slim possibility, that the instructions only appear in the 0.5% of Theo's DNA which characterises his uniqueness. Remember you provided Theo with 50% of his DNA and Isabella the other 50%, of which approximately 49.5% for each of you would be if we have our sequencing correct, almost identical."

Prof. Madhani all the while was tapping his pen on the table the frustration of not being able to bring an end to the proceedings painted across his expression "What Mikhail is saying is, you provided half of a per cent of what makes Theo unique, and within that, half a per cent is the coding for Theo's blood group and the mysterious omega or rather Xenozyme-170301 protein, which we suspect activates something in the remaining 99% of the DNA that Theo potentially shares with the rest of Humanity. But I must stress, we do not have the evidence at this time."

"Further research?" Theodore asks

"Correct. Further research. Does this answer your question?" Professor Madhani directs his question to Theodore, who just nods. "We could talk all day, Theo is an enigma which will have many specialists in all areas of medical science, theology, genetics, and human history, discussing and debating the known understanding of their respective fields. We do require your ongoing cooperation in this matter and discretion. I will be in touch. Thank You, Mr Newton"

"My mind is blown! Thanks again."

#

Theodore arrived home exhausted, Joanne was sitting on the living room floor with Theo, who was lying on his play mat beneath the colourful mobiles suspended from the frame.

John was sitting on the sofa reading a newspaper.

Joanne on seeing Theodore enter announced "Theo. Daddy is home"

"Has he been good? Where is my little tinker"

Theodore bent down and carefully picked up his son from beneath the frame and proceeded to cuddle him.

"He has been wonderful. He is so alert and bright. I asked him to look at the giraffe. He reached out and grabbed it. He knew what I was talking about. Didn't he John." John looked at Theodore and nodded.

"Your kid is advanced for his age. Joanne suggests it's not normal, what do you say? 9 months would be considered the earliest age for the start of recognition and association?"

“Yes about that.”

“After what I have just been told. You could have told me Theo was walking and I would believe it.”

John glanced up from his newspaper “Sounds interesting. What did they say?”

“Interesting doesn’t start to cover it. Where to begin? I can only really give you a layman’s account of what they told me. Most of it went way over my head, I tried to keep up. I have been told to use discretion when discussing this and not to divulge it, so this stays within the confines of this room.”

Theodore proceeded to explain the basics of what was revealed at the meeting earlier in the day. John and Joanne sitting together on the sofa were in disbelief. Joanne having a medical background was more incredulous.

“Just run that by me again. I need to make sure I understood you” … Theodore laughed.

CHAPTER 7 ACTS

EVENTS UP TO JULY 16 2009 1:37 P.M.

..With men it is impossible, but not with God: for all things are possible with God.
Mark 10:27 ASV

The continued investigations into the XΩ within Theo's blood yielded no additional confirmation or discovery. Quite the opposite, the Xenozyme-170301 protein did not show in further blood tests, yet the indications were that his blood group was indeed X, the initial supposition presented to Theodore remained unconfirmed.

Dr Mashkov and his team sequenced Theo's entire genome, while there were initial indications of unique base pairs and genes, potentially responsible for the differences Theo was displaying, upon further analysis, the results appeared to vary. It was concluded that, as Theo grew older, an unknown mechanism began to obfuscate his DNA from being accurately decoded. Indications suggested that the substrate used in the process of DNA mapping was no longer reliable in instances of reading Theo's code, as if, there were some defence process taking place outside of Theo's body. The investigations stalled and no further research was carried out concerning his DNA.

Analysis of Theodore's DNA confirmed that he was indeed a carrier of the X blood group, in his case a dominant allele. Attempts to isolate the exact gene and therefore identify the base pair within Theodore's genome proved impossible.

When the geneticists compared the genomes of Theo, Isabella and Theodore, they found it impossible to isolate the specific genes which explained the results which they originally arrived at. There was no doubt that both Isabella and Theodore were Theo's parents, but when attempts were made to dig deeper into an understanding of Theo's unique individuality, the results were garbage. Again, some mechanism, similar to the reading of a quantum state, was destroying the data being read.

The Police investigation into the events surrounding Isabella's collapsing and receiving the mystery injection was closed, not long after John relinquished investigative control of the case. No investigating officer was assigned to the case.

Theo's attendance at clinical appointments gradually became less frequent, until on his second birthday, he was discharged as an outpatient. However, he smashed all of his childhood milestones, bringing incredulity from each of the respective professionals he encountered.

When he was 5 months old, he had almost complete recognition and association skills. He attended a child development clinic, the paediatrician Dr. Hong, placed a series of paired colourful cards each featuring a different picture in front of Theo. They asked him to point to or pick up the named card. He successfully demonstrated a skill that a child usually develops between 12 to 18 months old.

At 6 months, Theo began to crawl, this lasted a couple of days. He would crawl over to the sofa and pull himself onto his feet. Initially stumbling and falling for lack of balance. It did not take him long to walk unaided.

Theo gained weight and growth at an unusually fast rate, at 12 months old, he was already at the development level of a child twice his age.

By 9 months Theo began to utter his first words, by 12 months old he was able to make basic requests and speak a simple sentence. By 18 months old he had mastered the art of speaking. At 24 months old he was running around, talking and able to meaningfully operate the television remote control.

The staff at the nursery he attended considered him *'the golden child'*. Each day they would argue over which member of staff would spend time with Theo, each devising a new test for him. While he hadn't fully grasped a more complex understanding, he was able to count beyond a level with which they maintained patience or an interest.

Theo was able to read simple children's books by 30 months and by the time he reached 4 years old was able to read books beyond the level of an average 8-year-old.

He started primary school at the age of 4 year old. Commencing in September of 2005. He attended Dunthorpe Primary Mixed Junior School. A non-sectarian school administered by Dunthorpe Town Council, catering for children between the ages of 4 and 11 years of age.

Theo excelled. At the end of the first week at the school, Theodore was invited in for a meeting with the school head, Mrs Schofield. She explained that children in the first year at school generally have a very basic if any, understanding of reading, writing or numeracy.

But, Theo was already displaying the ability and comprehension of a child at the very least, two years older. While Mrs Schofield was happy to keep Theo in her school, she had concerns, it was understandable that Theo required schooling at a level which meant he was challenged and able to learn. Staying with his peer group, those in the same 1st-year class as himself, would not provide this challenge, it would, however, let him develop social interactions at the correct pace. The option was presented to Theodore, to move Theo into a class of children older than himself, but of a similar ability, this presented an alternate problem, that of potential bullying, more advanced levels of social play and potentially challenging peer interaction.

Theodore opted to place Theo into the year group above him, after all, he would be 5 in December, and the children in this class would be 5 turning 6. Mrs Schofield agreed. Theo was quick to demonstrate that he was the brightest in the class, his class teacher challenging him with a level of learning at a higher level than his classmates. With the social and peer interaction of play, Theo was able to fit in well. This solution appeared to offer the best compromise for his first full year at school.

Shortly before Theo was due to recommence school, beginning his second year of education, but moving into the third year class of pupils, a letter was delivered addressed to Theodore. Dunthorpe and Brent Local Council had received numerous objections from concerned parents, citing, that having Theo in their children's class was presenting various educational challenges, interfering with the pace of learning for the rest of the class.

Theodore knew that his son was eager to raise his hand and answer class questions presented by the teacher. He had been made aware on several occasions, that Theo was often considered for school student of the month, even when he wasn't selected as the winner, the parents believing, the emotional, often jealous outbursts by their children, were due to the impact Theo was having, often hearing *'Theo was chosen again, it's not fair'*

Rather than invite Theodore to discuss the situation, the local council ruled that Theo's placement at the school be withdrawn with immediate effect. The letter closes with the words.

'No alternate placement can be provided at this time'

The primary argument cementing their decision is, that the needs of an individual cannot overrule the needs of the many, in this case, Theo's advanced ability was making other parents parenting more challenging, the parents now actually having to 'parent' and the school was ill-equipped to handle the fallout.

Enraged, Theodore contacted the education department at the local council and demanded at the very least, home schooling. To his surprise, this was granted for only the next academic year. To ensure Theo still had interaction with children close to his age, the Catholic School, a street away from where they lived allowed Theo to play during school breaks and at lunchtime. As a thank you, Theodore arranged for his company to be a sponsor for the school, assisting with much-needed fundraising.

On occasion, the local Catholic Priest, Father Michael O'Connor, would visit Theodore at his home, to thank him for his company's continued support and donations to the school and by extension his church '*Our Lady of the Apostles*'.

It came as a surprise to Father O'Connor when he discovered that Theodore was not Catholic or indeed religious. He explained that, while not unheard of, he has, in his experience found it rare, that a man *without god in his heart*, would do something, in his opinion, *Christian*, as donating significant amounts of money and support, which exceeded the value that Theo was benefiting from in the arrangement.

Theodore explained, that while he did not have god in his heart, being human, having humanity or humanist morals, was not exclusive to religion, to Christianity or any other religion. That caring for strangers, for supporting a cause, for giving back, paying it forward, were the signs of a good person and that there were far too many selfish people in the world already.

When asked by Father O'Connor, if he believed in '*Karma', 'the soul', a 'higher purpose', 'destiny', 'voodoo' or 'shamanic'* based beliefs, Theodore's response was that did not know, he hadn't given those beliefs much thought. He did however have a response for '*karma*', He didn't believe in it.

Theodore did not think, that a person's actions be they positive or negative, good or bad, or '*what comes around goes around*', were judged by the universe and appropriate punishment or re-action dealt out, such as coming back as a '*two-faced banana slug*', no, he suggested that it was more likely a view from an observer or victim's perspective, suggesting that karma was dealt out, when in fact, given any lapse of time, an unconnected event would happen to a person irrespective of a good or bad deed. That karma was implied after the event.

Such as, if a person were to win the lottery and give the entire winnings to a charity or worthy cause, what would be the karmic response? Or is karma just a one-way deal, is it the person doing the bad act that has a response considered karma and is the victim or their loved ones tormented until karma gets its man and that their reward is justice? In which case, if a teenager steals a car, knocks down and kills a serving police officer, at what point would a person say that karma got them? Would it take for that teenager to be struck down with cancer? Die in a drug overdose or be knocked down and killed, what frame of reference in time should such a response occur? Does karma expire after a year? A decade? A generation? A lifetime? Their next lifetime.

Eventually, bad things happen to all of us, irrespective of good or bad actions. Although Theodore confessed that he did not know much about ancient Indian religions and the origin meaning of karma. He also confirmed that he did not believe in an afterlife so by extension a soul.

The Father believed Theodore to be a considered man and while he did not have god in his heart, he could see he was striving to be a good man, to be kind, considerate, and caring. He exuded the best qualities of Christianity. Father O'Connor could see, that one day, Theodore may carry out the ultimate sacrifice to help a stranger.

The evening of Father O'Connor's visit, Theodore found it difficult to sleep. He tossed and turned in his bed. His mind wandered back to the conversation he had that day with the priest.

How could he dismiss all of these religious beliefs, that had existed for millennia, countless generations before him, have lived their life dedicated to a god or gods, or something more than a human existence?

Yet, Theodore found himself seeking theological inquiry. Lying eyes wide open staring at vague shadows blurred against an almost black ceiling, he considered,

'how can I read minds or predict the face of cards before I see them with my own eyes? If I can do these things, if my father could do these things, without teaching or study, how can that be explained? What does that mean? Can Theo do these things?... But you don't believe. If.. if there is a higher being, why do they punish me? I lost my mother when I was two, my father, when I was sixteen, my wife when I was twenty-four.'

Theodore began to cry, he lay there, his heart was breaking, He ached to hold his love, his Izzy, to smell her hair once again, to kiss her, to laugh with her.

He found his feelings drifting, now he desperately wanted to speak to his dad again, to ask him about all the things he never had the chance to do when he was alive, to learn more about his mother, who she was. But they were gone, they were all gone.

It was now just Theo and himself. In that moment he made a promise. He would talk more about Isabella, about Theo's Grandfather Levi and the man he was. He wouldn't let his son grow up not knowing who these important people were. It would start in the morning.

As Theodore started to drift off, the door to his room slowly opened, and the slightest crack of light flowed into the room, lifting his head, Theodore looked towards the door, Theo was slowly pushing the door open all the while peering through the ever-expanding crack.

"Daddy, why were you crying? Were you also thinking of Mommy" Theodore shot bolt upright, *'did I hear him right?'* He thought to himself, *'No, but..'*

"Come here son" Theo made his way over to the bed and climbed onto the mattress, Theodore continued "Theo, what made you think of Mommy?"

"I heard you talking to me, in my head, you were wishing you could cuddle Mommy, and then you were talking about Grandpa. You were crying, it made me upset, I wanted to come and cuddle you, to make you feel better"

A single tear rolled down Theodore's cheek. Surely his son was dreaming, just a coincidence, maybe Theo heard him cry, maybe he was talking in his sleep, about Isabella, perhaps Theo heard him.

"What do you mean I was talking to you?"

"I heard you. What is carmel? You were talking to me about carmel, you didn't think it was real, you were telling me that it was made up." Theodore had a sudden chill run down his spine

"Do you mean Karma? You heard me talk about Karma?"

"Yes Daddy, Karma. Why isn't it real?"

Theodore had been thinking about Karma, but only thinking about it. Stopping him from sleeping. Or was he asleep, talking out loud, it was all so vivid, he was sure he was awake, sleep evading him? But Theo was with John and Joanne at the park when Father O'Connell visited, so he had no awareness of what was discussed.

Glancing at the alarm clock, it was 5:52 a.m.

"Theo, would you like to get some breakfast and I will tell you all about Mommy?"

Theodore spent the day with Theo, showing him photos of his mother, sharing stories of how they met, and the holidays they had together. They visited her memorial plaque in the crematorium gardens. Had ice cream and walked through Broadacre Park. Then Theo again gives his father a chill.

"Daddy, this is where mommy was poorly"

Sure enough, they were walking towards the bench where Isabella was found.

"Theo, how do you know that?"

"You were just telling me. But you weren't telling me with your lips"

Finally, it was making sense to Theodore, that his son had a much stronger version of the gift he had, one that he suspects his father also had. While Levi and he, could see the faces of playing cards and more recently Theodore could read the simple thoughts of people he knew, Theo appeared to have a more advanced telepathic ability. Could his son read his mind? He considered testing this theory, then and there. He thought about asking Theo if he wanted to go to see some dinosaurs.

"I would love to see the dinosaurs"

"Ok. Let's go and see the dinosaurs at the Natural History Museum" Theodore was taken aback, his son had an unbelievable ability. While it required massive self-control and discipline, Theodore knew he had to start, ironically, being mindful of the thoughts he had whilst around Theo.

#

Theodore was extremely careful what he said to people after the day at the Natural History Museum regarding Theo, he was so tight-lipped. He encouraged Theo to keep it a secret, between just them, no one else was to know but the paranoia started to build, he wouldn't be able to rest until he had Theo promise that if he was able to control it, he shouldn't try to read people's mind. Theo agreed but his response was unexpected *'I know the bad people will come for me'*.

Everything after that day appeared plain sailing, Theo realised that he wanted to be at school with other children, so by himself, with no influence from Theodore, just decided to act like a normal child of his age, this meant he would deliberately make mistakes at school, just to fit in.

From then on, Theo hadn't put a foot or thought wrong. Except for being a little taller and a little more developed than his peers, he hadn't given anyone any reason to suspect he had an advanced mind or indeed any telepathic abilities. Theodore did allow the occasional game at home where his abilities were tested, fun night Friday as it came to be known.

But this all changed on the afternoon of Thursday the 16th July 2009. It was the School sports day, and parents were invited to take part in events, should they wish, or they could just watch their children. Theodore, who maintained his fitness and still had time for the occasional boxing spar, knew he would likely win the 100-yard dash, however, he was happy to watch.

The children followed the parents. There were three separate events for those children who wanted to race, Theo was in the 3rd race, to keep things fair, they would race against those of equal height and Theo was a tall 8-year-old.

"Don't you worry if you come last, you are up against some 10-year-olds? Good luck son."

"Thanks, Dad, but I won't be coming last"

"**THEO**.. what do you.." Before he could finish the sentence Theo was already ducking through the crowd of eager parents at the start line. Theodore positioned himself midway down the sprint route.

There were 12 children including Theo lined up, even from 40 or so yards away, it became even more evident how tall his boy was for his age, he could easily pass off at 10 or 11 years old.

The teacher at the start, instructed the children to stand on the line, telling them not to push or pull any of the competitors, no tripping was allowed. Parents were shouting their child's name, yelling supportive comments, and pushing their child to kick arse and destroy their opposition. For any neutral watching, the entertainment was observing the parents and not a dozen innocent children taking part in a fun activity, which would be replicated up and down the country.

The '***Go***' command squealed out of the megaphone, and all 12 children, 5 girls and 7 boys lurched forward, one boy immediately tripped and fell flat on their face, in their desperation to get back onto their feet, stumbled again and tumbled to the ground.

The was a group of 6 children all neck and neck by the halfway point, Theo was one of them, he glanced back towards his dad, before dipping his shoulders slightly, and started to drive harder with his arms while increasing his leg turnover rate, as if out of nowhere, Theo surged past the girl, who, until that point, was leading, he kept driving with his arms, extending his stride slightly, landing perfectly on his forefoot giving him the perfect elastic bounce to propel forward, he was extending his lead with every foot strike.

Theodore stood in amazement as he finished a clear 10 yards ahead of second place. Jogging towards Theo, Theodore tried to avoid the children, dramatically flopping themselves on the floor and lying on their back, panting away trying to recover their breath, as if replicating what they may have seen in a 'Games' track race. Theo just stood there shrugging his shoulders as if to wonder what the fuss was about.

"Theo! I had better say well done, but, did you know you were going to win?"

"I didn't, you know read anything, I just knew I could beat them all. I am stronger now."

"Stronger? What do you mean stronger?"

Before Theo could answer, the father and son were interrupted by another parent who introduced themself as James Harvey.

"Hi, that was some win, is it Theo?" Theo nodded. He continued "I am Sofie's dad, she came second. I haven't seen you at Dunthorpe Running Club, I am one of the coaches there, Sofie is one of our junior sprinters, not to brag, but she is one of the best juniors in the region. She hasn't mentioned you in her class"

"I'm not in Sofie's class"

"Theo is eight years old. A couple of classes below your Sofie." James had a look of disbelief on his face

"Theo is eight? He looks ten. And he can run like that?"

"I can see you are surprised. Believe me when I say I am just as surprised as you. I honestly had no clue" Theo was just grinning.

"Can I interest you in bringing Theo down to our next training session? No pressure. Theo has an amazing talent, It would be great to see how far he could go."

"Please, Dad. Can I?" Theo begged.

"Let me think about it. Theo, I am not saying no. It needs to fit in with our other activities. If that is ok James?"

"Of course. As I said, no pressure. We meet every Tuesday and Thursday and then every first and third Sunday of the month at Dunthorpe Athletics Stadium. 6:30 p.m. for children. Thanks and Well done Theo."

For the next 3 days, Theo did all he could to persuade his father to let him go to the running club. He cleaned his room without being asked, he vacuumed the house, and he even went as far as starting to wash the car, before Theodore had to ask, "What are you doing Theo? Or do you want me to guess?" Theo's response was a huge cheesy grin, he knew his father had already suspected the motive behind his helpful streak and that he had decided he could go.

"If I am going to play mind games on you, Theo, with success I may add. Then you are going to have to learn intent and motive, then decide if I am bluffing. If word ever got out, if others out there knew of your ability, it could be used against you. Just like I have"

"Dad. You were thinking 'If Theo did more around the house, then I may let him go to the running club' and I could hear you saying that with my mind and so I did, but you were tricking me?"

"Yes" he was now grinning back at Theo

"DAD!!!"

"I have to confess something. I have a limited version of your ability. I can read minds too. I think your Grandad Levi could also"

Theo being a very inquisitive 8-year-old bombarded his father with question after question trying to uncover all he knew about his mind-reading ability. Theodore however, had learned to compartmentalise his thoughts, to hide certain memories, more to protect Theo from learning too much too soon, after all, he was still a child.

But Theodore knew, one day, he would need to teach Theo this technique, maybe there were others like them. They needed to be prepared, just in case. At this time, Theodore had not revealed the full details of his mysterious blood group or the full events surrounding his mother's death. He wished to keep it this way until Theo was mature enough to understand and while he had the intelligence of a child much older, Theodore had to give him as normal an upbringing as possible.

CHAPTER 8 NUMBERS

EVENTS TO NOVEMBER 15 2014

but I buffet my body, and bring it into bondage: lest by any means, after that I have preached to others, I myself should be rejected.
Corinthians 9:27 ASV

Over the next few years, Theo appeared to explode out of childhood into adolescence akin to a sprinter launching out of the blocks. He was always tall for his age, but at 14 years old, he had grown into a towering 6 ft 4 teenager. His physique, honed by years of sprinting, was lean and powerful, a testament to his dedication and discipline.

Gone were the days of childish antics. Theo now possessed a critical mind, brimming with scientific curiosity. His intellect, always several levels ahead of his peers, had blossomed into an unparalleled ability to retain, comprehend, and articulate complex information. With each passing day, Theo's thirst for knowledge grew, leaving behind the innocence of childhood and embracing the profound depths of intellectual exploration.

In the days leading up to Theo's 10th birthday, his father asked him how he would like to celebrate, Theodore made some suggestions, such as a party or spending the day at an amusement park inviting his friends. It took all of five seconds for Theo to choose.

"I would like to visit the Natural History Museum and see the exhibit of prehistoric man." Theo requested

"Prehistoric man? Just that exhibit?"

“No, of course not, I would like to see the other sections of the museum, but I am fascinated with pre-history”

Theodore wanted to know more about this new interest his son was showing “In what way? What fascinates you? I don’t know a lot about pre-history”

“I have been having dreams, actually, for a while now Dad.” Theodore interrupted “What kind of dreams?”

“I am in them or at least I think it is me. I am experiencing the dreams in the first person. Do you know what that is Dad?”

“The first person? Yes, it’s like a story where you are the narrator describing what is happening, what you are seeing or experiencing. Like in some computer games. So you are, in these dreams, observing what is happening through the eyes of the person who is there witnessing it”

“Yes. So in one of the dreams, the person whose eyes I am viewing through, is squatting down at the base of a tree, with a wooden spear in their right hand and a rock, maybe a kilo in size in the other hand. They are in a woodland, the sun is behind them, low in the sky, it’s dawn. In front, there is a herd of deer. I move to a crouched position and start to slowly move closer, I raise my spear into a javelin throw position then when the time is right, I hurl the spear into a buck. It hits them in the lower third of their neck. I start sprinting towards the fallen animal and use the kilo rock to..” Theodore interrupts again “I get the picture. So are you a hunter-gatherer? Do you know where you were?”

“I am not sure, I think I was in Northern Europe, way off in the distance was an Ocean, maybe to the west and a short distance off to the north, I could see some glaciers. It was cold, I was wearing animal skins. I guess I was a hunter-gatherer, except I remember, in other dreams going back to a village, we had wood and earth homes”

“How many of these dreams have you had?”

“Lots, they aren’t all the same. It’s like I am living their life, I may have two or three different dreams a night”

Theodore's eyes were wide listening to his son “This is amazing. How did you know you were looking to the West?”

“The position of the sun in the sky, but..” He paused “This is strange, I felt, like a small change in pressure in my ears, when I looked North, everyone I lived with could do this, we were born with the ability to know where North was.”

“This is amazing. Care to share another dream with me?”

“Sure. So the most bizarre of all the dreams happened a couple of nights ago. I was following a mammoth with several of my tribe. I must have been a leader of some kind as I instructed some of my group to go around and flank the animal.

Before I could attack, Einar, who was with me, was attacked by a wolf, I was spun around and knocked off my feet by the beast, as it launched itself at me. Einar had enough strength to bury his spear into the animal, this gave me enough time to escape. Several of the wolf pack came and began tearing at Einar.

But I was fast on my feet, leaping over fallen trees and bushes in my path. I made it to a rocky outcrop, which I climbed. At the top, I rested as I was exhausted.

I found I couldn’t move. I was rooted to the spot. Then everything went blinding white as I passed out. When I woke, I found myself in a round room, there were windows on all but the wall behind me.

The windows were all looking out onto a beautiful view of a city with mountains and forests in the distance. There were two suns in the sky. I felt confused, but I wasn’t scared. A woman came into the room, she looked human but she was also different, something didn’t quite look right about her.

She was clean, she wore clothes but not from skins, she was painted. She didn't speak to me, instead she spoke directly to my mind. I don't remember everything, but she said that some of my tribe and I had been given a gift. I then passed out and that's when I found myself back on the rocky outcrop. I felt a pain in my stomach, and when I looked I had a small cut there. I must have woken then as the dream ended"

Theodore thought for a moment, not able to conceal his mind from his son. He had realised that when a thought was attached to an emotion, the thought became stronger and seemed to spill out like an overflowing cup.

"My mam had the same cut? When she was pregnant with me. It was never explained was it?"

"No Theo, it wasn't. At one time I would have said that your dream made no sense, but since you now know about your mam, I think it's all part of a greater puzzle. I can't explain what your dreams mean. How do you know about what happened to your mam? How we can both read people's thoughts."

"I started to write down some of my dreams if you want to read them."

"If you don't mind, it might help us piece some of the puzzle together. But first, why don't we go to the museum, today and see if we can get more clues. We can arrange to do something else for your birthday. Deal?"

"Deal.." Theo paused for a moment before continuing "Dad, you don't seem too surprised by my dreams!"

"To be honest Theo, since before you were born, I have been told and I have experienced some bizarre stuff. When something new happens, I just add it as another clue in this mysterious puzzle. One day all the clues will tell us what it is all about"

His dreams put Theo on a course of curiosity and inquiry with pre-history and human evolution. His dreams stopped after that day, as if, he was being directed on a quest to investigate and uncover something.

#

At 10 years old and a year younger than he should have been, Theodore was enrolled at Dunthorpe Academy, a secondary school and college. He continued to soak up knowledge, developing an advanced understanding of all the subjects he studied.

He continued to enjoy his athletic pursuits. His physical education teacher wanted him on each of the inter-school sports teams, however Theo was only interested in running. The teacher had to settle for him on the cross country team during the autumn and winter and the athletics team during the spring and summer.

In the June of 2014, two years ahead, for his age, Theo was sitting his GCSE exams. At the request of Theodore, the school were told that there was to be no media attention drawn to Theo or his achievements, he wanted to keep Theo out of the spotlight for as long as possible.

That summer, Theo received the results of his GCSE exams, the letter confirming the high-achieving student he was;

*English Literature A**

*English Language A**

*Biology A**

*Chemistry A**

*Design and Technology A**

*French A**

*Geography A**

*History A**

*Information Technology A**

*Mathematics A**

*Physics A**

In September 2014, Theo began his A-levels studies. His love of science and history is reflected in the subject choices. He would continue to participate in physical education with his age group and represent the Academy in inter-school sports leagues.

It was disappointing to Theo that he was limited to the number of subjects he could study, the most that a student could normally take was four, he was permitted to take a fifth. But he felt like he could absorb any number of subjects.

#

The new school year started without a hitch. Theo embraced the challenge of studying a more advanced level of the subjects he enjoyed. His attitude had matured, any cockiness or ego that he may have once displayed was now tightly controlled. He was more thoughtful and considerate and displayed humility.

Theodore knew that Theo was special, bestowed with some unexplained gift, almost a rain man, but without the social awkwardness, he had seen the growth of social media and advancement of sophisticated mobile devices, changes that had occurred in the short few years since Theo was born, this made him uneasy. It was more important now than ever before that Theo be mindful of his actions. It meant that his behaviours and interactions could be recorded and shared in seconds.

Theo agreed to his father's request, that he needed to demonstrate that he had flaws and could make mistakes. That he could no longer, at least for the moment, be the perfect student, he railed in his brilliance, just enough, to allow for errors in school essays and exams. Theodore was proud of him, Theo displayed a level of maturity and understanding, but these were indeed uncertain times.

Autumn marked the start of the cross-country season, the first race in the calendar, Theo missed, as it clashed with the opening of an exhibit and lecture discussing some recent Stone Age discoveries.

The second of the five races in the series was to take place on Saturday 15th November 2014 at Parliament Hill Fields in Hampstead Heath. Theo was eager to take part, he did enjoy cross-country running almost as much as he enjoyed competing, but he preferred track and field more. He wanted to support his running club and represent them, after all, he knew, he could win every time. However, in his heart, he was all too aware that it wasn't right. Cross Country wasn't the event for him, at that point, he was stealing the glory from others in his club, who worked as hard as him and had a deeper passion for that particular event.

Theo arrived at his club's assembly zone, a tatty pop-up tent, dirty with mud and grime from countless years of repeated use greeted him. Inside there was a camping table where the club secretary Mr Babbitt registered him as attending and assigned him a number and a few safety pins.

"Johnny and Ethan can't make it today. So I am sorry to say, the pressure is on you to get the low points for the club. We are 3rd in the league. Take a look at the table if you want" Mr Babbitt pointed to a sheet of A4 paper sellotaped to the table. Hampstead Heath Harriers were in 1st place with 20 points, 2nd were Finsbury Park Striders with 23 points and 3rd Dunthorpe Athletic with 27 Points.

"Mr Babbitt, how many are on our team today?"

"We have a full team of 7 today. We may be lucky as Triple-H don't have their top boy running today by all accounts."

"I'll try my best"

His reply seemed to annoy Mr Babbitt "NO Try not! Do or don't bother taking part"

"Erm…OK"

Theo didn't particularly like Mr Babbitt, but he respected him, in his day, he was an extraordinarily talented runner having once been the British Marathon Record Holder and even more extraordinary, was that this was back in the 1960s when the sport didn't have the sort of materials in equipment and shoes that the runners of today could benefit from. But he was a cantankerous old man, who spoke his mind, the mind of a different generation.

Theo made his way towards the start line, it was about 3 Celsius, a grey overcast day with a constant drizzle and then an occasional heavy downfall of rain and hail. Unlike the other 13 to 15-year-old boys who were being corralled into the starting pen, Theo wasn't cold, even though, like the others, he was wearing a thin running vest and shorts.

Theo joined his team. His school friend, Graham Barnes draped his arm over Theo's shoulder.

"Theo you made it. Did you hear we don't have Johnny or Ethan today, they claim they are sick. But I think they just wanted to go to the match. So you going to win it for us today?"

"I heard, Mr Babbitt told me, he also told me to win it! Do you mind not doing that"

"Oooh, tetchy! You probably don't want me to do this either" Graham began to massage Theo's shoulders "Go on Newts you got this, stick it to them"

"Funny. How did you finish last time? What place?"

"I came Ninth, Johnny came seventh and Ethan came fifth. The rest of the squad didn't help much with the scoring"

Theo looked at the other boys on the team, they were all shivering. Glancing around the rest of the competitors he could see that most of them were the same, their jaws were chattering away, arms crossed rubbing their arms and shoulders trying to keep warm.

It was then that he made eye contact with Richard Tenui.

"I thought Tenui wasn't running today?"

"That's what I was told. But there he is!"

Richard ran for Hampstead, of Kenyan background, he was tipped to be Britain's next thing, having won the individual national cross country league trophy the previous year. An incredible talent, he also held the under-15 boys record for the 4-kilometre Hampstead course in a time of 15 minutes 54 Seconds.

Richard glared back with a smug grin of arrogant self-confidence, Theo just nodded back at him, as if to indicate his acceptance of superiority. Theo didn't want any conflict, he was aware that his rival was a member of a gang and while exceptionally talented was deeply troubled, often being detained for anti-social behaviour and carrying a knife.

Theo was improving his ability to control his mind and not invade the thoughts of others around him, however, at this moment, he wanted to know what Richard was thinking, and what his tactics were.

Theo considered whether this was cheating, the ability to *actually* get into the mind of an opponent, what a powerful tool. *'I'm not harming him'* Theo thought *'Focus on Richard'*, he was in, *'Newton, I am better than you but if you come close on the backstretch, I'll trip you, you'll never see it coming, no one will see it happen. You can't you won't beat me.'*

Theo wasn't surprised at what he learned, the pair had competed against each other numerous times, often with a confrontation, always initiated by Richard, but Theo was gaining confidence and strength each time, but did he need to win? Was coming second to Richard so bad? There wasn't too much time to decide on tactics as the starter was calling for the boys to line up.

Richard positioned himself as he always does at the very front of the pack, left or right-hand side depending on the position of the first bend. On this occasion he was on the right, a long uphill climb was awaiting them before taking a sharp turn towards Highgate No 1 Pond.

Theo positioned himself a couple of places to Richards's left on the second row of starters, close enough to keep him in sight. The starter once again comes over the tannoy,

"Runners, this is a 2-lap race, follow the Marshall's instructions. The course is marked and taped. A reminder that at the top of this bank is where the second lap will intersect with the course. There you will loop back around following the same route, you do not return down this starting bank. Again, the Marshalls will direct you that you are at the end of your second lap, guiding you to the final 400-metre finish stretch, which is for the most, downhill and which will take you along a parallel route to the running track. The course is partially paved, but in places it is boggy. Good luck"

Theo had studied the route before making his way to the starting pen, it was very routine, nothing too surprising. The tannoy boomed again "Runners. Set..." There was a couple of seconds pause before the air horn was blasted.

They were off. Richard, predictably with his trademark start, went off hard, accelerating away from the pack as if he had mistaken the event for a four-hundred-metre sprint. A couple of boys tried to stay with him, but he was going too fast, the climb was about 500 metres, gradual, but enough to punish those unprepared. Theo allowed Richard to pull, away, but he was working hard enough to keep within about 20 metres of his rival.

At the first bend, Richard had slowed slightly, he glanced back over his right shoulder as he took the turn towards the pond, seeing the tall stature of Theo, closer than he liked, he was maybe in 10th place. He felt confident that he had enough of a lead and plenty of energy still in the tank to maintain a commanding lead. However, what he did next was unexpected by the chasing group.

Rather than settle into a rhythm with a comfortable yet hard pace, he dug in and pushed harder. It was on a slight downhill towards the pond and he wanted to take advantage and gain more of a lead before the left turn and a flat section. Theo considered his options, he knew he could easily catch Richard, but he didn't want to leave it too late in the race, after all, he didn't want to reveal too much of his actual ability to everyone. If he wanted to win he needed to make it look natural, not supernatural.

Theo began to increase his pace, his long legs providing a stride length which dwarfed his competitors. By the flat section parallel to the pond, he was 10 metres behind Richard and into 4th place, the leader wasn't pulling away now, he hadn't glanced back at the left turn, so was unaware of how close Theo was now.

At the next left turn was a long 500-metre climb bending up towards a point called *'Boadicea's Grave',* Richard looked back over his left shoulder but did not see Theo, unaware that he had gained places on the leader, he assumed Theo must have fallen back.

The climb was uneventful, except the 3rd place boy started to struggle with the combination of pace and climb, his breathing became more laboured and his pace started to slow, Theo nipped passed him, as the boy shouted "Go get him" He looked back Theo realising it was one of his team.

At the top of the hill, the route passed through a wooded area before breaking through the tree line, Parliament Hill viewpoint, the highest part of the course was just ahead and so was Richard. Theo could see the 2nd place boy was right on the leader's shoulder. Richard swung his left arm back, catching the 2nd place boy on his jaw, the boy stumbled, narrowly tripping. Theo sidestepped out of the boy's way, avoiding a coming together. Unbelievably Richard had lashed out at one of his own teammates, fortunately for the leader, there were no other witnesses at this point on the course.

The route followed the contour of Parliament Hill and was heading back towards the ponds, from this vantage point, the London skyline was just about visible through the bleak grey view. Theo was feeling good it was like he was taking an easy run. With each birthday, he was feeling stronger and faster, his father had drilled it into him to not be a show-off, not to bring too much attention to himself. But, there was always that gnawing thought in his mind, what was he capable of if he removed his father's restraints?

He had already decided, he didn't want to do cross country any more, this would be his last season. So what harm would there be if he happened to win one of the races and even sweeter, beating the course record holder on their home turf?

Theo wasn't wearing a watch so he could only guess how much time had elapsed, his mind was made up, he would wait in second place until the final stretch then breeze past for the win.

The second lap was uneventful, Richard was aware his opponent was right on his shoulder, matching stride for stride. The 3rd place boy was nowhere to be seen, looking backwards at the opportune moments on the course, would indicate the nearest runner was at least 100 metres behind. The pair had a commanding lead as they rounded Parliament Hill for the final time.

The Marshall indicated they were to go straight on in a generally southeast direction towards the stadium. One Marshall shouted that there were 400 metres to go. Richard was starting to breathe harder as he began to dig in, running harder and faster.

Theo kept with him, dwarfing his opponent by at least a foot in height as he drew level. Richard was lean, with long and powerful legs, Theo was more muscular with his tall frame, it was all going to come down to a sprint finish. The pair had to cut through one more tree line before joining a path which would indicate a straight line 200 metre finish.

Richard had the inside line as they cut through the trees, briefly turning his head to look right expecting to see Theo on his shoulder, but he wasn't there. He twisted further looking back to the direction he had come, but could see no sign of the second-place runner.

Theo stopped. The view in front of him had changed, he could no longer see the stadium nor the houses which bordered the Heath. He turned around and looked back towards the direction of the hill which he had just descended, it too had changed. Instead of paths and trees, it was a lush dense forest as far as he could see. Off to the right, about 50 metres away were several wooden huts, smoke gently billowing near the structures.

He observed several figures emerge from the forest, two of the individuals were carrying what appeared to be a deer lashed to a pole. It was raining quite heavily. He held his hand out to feel the rain then ran his other hand down his face, both hands were coated in a fine wet dust. The ground was saturated underfoot, he was no longer wearing running spikes, instead, he had some simple leather or perhaps a hide strapped to his foot.

'What am I looking at? when am I?' He thought.

He turned back towards the direction he was travelling. Again he was looking towards London, Richard was only a few meters away from him racing towards the path. Theo gave chase, but his legs were heavy and tired. He felt lethargic and disoriented, no matter how much tried to catch the leader, his body, didn't want to respond. He looked back towards the hill, but he couldn't see any other runners.

Richard was too far ahead now, gaining distance with every stride. Theo pushed on with a jog, reaching the finish line a minute behind Richard.

Richard boastfully "What happened to you? Did you fall? Better luck next time Newton" Theo couldn't talk, he was exhausted, all he could manage was to put his hand out to shake the winners, but Richard just slapped it away.

Theo slowly walked in the direction of his team tent, his breathing coming in ragged gasps. The world around him blurs as he stumbles forward, and Theo's vision narrows to a tunnel. The roar of the crowd welcoming the stream of finishers, fades into a distant hum, and the vibrant colours of the banners and flags dulls.

Theo's heart pounds in his chest like he had never experienced before, each beat echoing in his ears. Sweat pours down his face, making it hard to see. He tries to take a step, but Theo's legs buckle, and he falls to his knees.

Disoriented, Theo tries to look around, but everything seems to spin. Trying to stand, his muscles refused to cooperate. A wave of nausea washed over him. He blacks out and falls on his face, his cheek pressing into the wet muddy ground.

Voices shout around Theo, 'Get St. Johns here, we have a boy down' Theo is unaware of anything, he is out cold. A medic hurriedly arrives and performs a limb check, content that nothing appears to be broken, they check his breathing and take a pulse count. His heart is still racing. Not long passes before Theo is loaded onto an awaiting Ambulance before being whisked away.

CHAPTER 9 FATHER & SON

NOVEMBER 15 2014 13:07 A.M.

What is man, that thou art mindful of him? And the son of man, that thou visitest him?
Psalms 8:4 ASV

Theodore arrived at the hospital in a panic. As Theo's next of kin contact, he received a phone call from a Marshall at the race informing him that his son had collapsed in the finish zone and had been taken to Accident and Emergency at Hampstead General Hospital via Ambulance. No other information was provided.

The anxious father approached the reception desk

"Hi my son has been brought in, his name is Theo Newton"

The receptionist, an older lady, barely glanced at the man making the statement "What is his Date of Birth?"

"26th December 2000" Theodore answered.

"Your name please and are you his parent or registered guardian?"

"Yes, I'm his father, Theodore Newton" The receptionist slowly inputted the details into the computer, occasionally letting out a '*tut*' or other auditory sound, her keyboard proficiency seemed in doubt as she continued to thump the delete key. Eventually, she continued her questioning. Theodore thought he was keeping his cool, considering.

"Mobile number ending 112"

"That is correct"

"And can you con.." Theodore cut off the receptionist "Is this going to take long, I may appear calm, but I am not, I would just like to see my son"

"I understand sir, but I do need to verify that our details are up to date" That was it, Theodore could tell she was a jobsworth, at least that was his perception.

"He is registered at Dunthorpe Central GPs, our postcode is NW9 8PQ, number 23, Hill Crescent" the receptionist, spent the next 5 minutes in silence, switching from entering information into the computer, picking up the phone dialling a number, waiting a few seconds, putting the phone down, moving the mouse around a tatty 'North London HS Trust' mousemat, then more keyboard entry. She didn't look up once or acknowledge Theodore any further during that time. All things considered, he thought he was doing well not to **COMPLETELY** blow his top. As he was about to say something, the receptionist looked up, "Can you take a seat, Mr Newton? A nurse will be out to greet you in a few minutes."

"Thank you for your assistance" was his reply.

'She was a charmer, doesn't appear things have improved much since last I had the misfortune of being in a hospital' Theodore thought to himself. He walked over to the rows of hard plastic chairs. *'Great, my old uncomfortable friends, it feels all too soon that we should meet again'*

He cast his gaze around the waiting area, there were all manner of ages, ethnicities and ailments present, from dislocated or broken bones to one elderly gentleman who was coughing and hacking as if he was trying to eject a lung from his body. *'Perhaps he should quit smoking.'*

Upon closer inspection, he could see the old man's hands, calloused and stained, could tell the story of a life spent toiling in the depths of the earth, perhaps as a miner, where the air was thick and the darkness enveloping. Each cough that escaped him, rattling with the dust of years spent chipping away at the underground, was a testament to the perilous dance between man and the bowels of the earth.

His face, etched with lines of hardship, bears the marks of a man, who sought solace in the ephemeral haze of cigarette smoke and the warm burn of a drink after long hours of labour. The smoke clings to him like a familiar friend, a companion through the years of sweat and toil.

It's a scene that whispers tales of sacrifice, of a life poured into the foundations of progress, each cough punctuation in the narrative of a worker's journey through the age of industry. *'Maybe I was too quick to judge, this poor man deserves more than to have to sit here and wait, he should be compensated for the unknown hazards that he now suffers'* Theodore, shuffled a couple of seats over to speak to the man.

"Excuse me, I couldn't help hear you and your coughing but.."

"I am sorry young man…" he stopped himself as he began coughing again.

Theodore continued "Let me get you some water."

Getting up from his seat, he walked over to the water fountain, but there were no plastic cups, instead a sign above the water dispenser provided instructions;

Hampstead General Hospital

NOTICE

Plastic cups are available from the reception desk.

Please note only one cup will be provided per person.

Your name must be given before a cup is provided.

Please dispose of used cups in the waste bins located around the reception area.

Abuse of North London HS Trust employees will not be tolerated and will be reported to security and the Police.

Thank You

Theodore considered the sign '*Wow, now that is a friendly notice. And what is with the police state? Names must be given?*' Theodore approached the reception desk and stood in the queue. Meanwhile, the gentleman continued to violently cough.

'*Why does no one else offer to help? Is this what we have come to as a people? unwilling to stand up and help a stranger?*' Theodore unwilling to wait any longer, interrupted the balance of the queue, apologising, skipped around the waiting line and moved up to the reception glass, it was the same receptionist as before

"Hi again, could you be so kind as to provide me with a plastic cup for that gentleman.." Theodore indicated in the direction of the elderly man

"Can I have his name please?"

“Sorry, I don’t know his name, but as you can see and hear, it may help him to drink some water.”

“I am sorry sir, if the cup is not for you, then I can not provide a cup unless I have his name”

“Hang on..” Theodore let out a forced cough “It appears I need a cup of water for myself, could you let me have a cup, my name is Theodore Newton”

“I am sorry, we are all out of cups at the moment”

Theodore glared at the receptionist, there were various names he wanted to give to the jobsworth, but he remembered the sign.

‘Was this lady being deliberately awkward to provoke a response that could be construed as abuse? Would it be their word against mine?’

He wanted to tell her what he thought of her service, but thought better of it “Your service is so refreshing - it’s like a Monday morning, every single day!” He turned and glanced around the waiting area, noticing a vending machine, he proceeded to purchase a bottle of water and returned to his seat.

He unscrewed the cap and handed the bottle to the gentleman “Here, drink this. I am Theodore” The gentleman took a long drink of the liquid, then handed the bottle back.

“No, you keep it, I expect you need it more than I do”

“Thank you, son, it’s a rare thing these days, to find the kindness of strangers, that you have displayed. I am Bernard Chapshaw”

“Pleased to meet you Bernard, and I do hope not, maybe it’s naivety, but I think there is kindness out there”

Bernard “Oh, there is, but, it is a lot less common than it once was. A lot less common. Everyone is in a hurry..” He stopped to cough again, Theodore indicating that maybe another sip of water would help “.. sorry son, as I was saying, everyone is in such a hurry, impatiently going from here to there, other people just get in their way and it leads to frustration and unkindness.

I remember London many many years ago, it was buzzing with people, people of all types, it was busy, but people were still friendly, folk would say hello to you as you passed on the street, and random strangers would engage with you in conversation. You could even talk to children without having to consider what people may think you are doing. That's all gone now. It's a different time. So thank you for the water, I appreciate it. Restoring a little bit of faith in people"

Theodore was quite surprised "It has changed that much? London is still busy, you could argue that it has even more people of different types as you put it, more diversity and beliefs"

Bernard continued "That is true. But there are more people, much more people than there should be, it's overcrowded, there are too many people, too many people with their own beliefs and they are scared and so their fear makes them keep to themselves, or keep to their group."

"I agree, London is vastly overcrowded. It is interesting what you say about fear, I suppose I agree. I guess, people don't know how someone else is going to respond, whether they have a deceptive motive. When perhaps, they don't have a motive beyond just wanting to have human contact, maybe they are lonely"

"You hit the nail there, Theodore is it? People are not trusting anymore. You know what I think is to blame?"

"Yes, it's Theodore. What is to blame?"

"Television and those god-awful mobile things everyone seems to be carrying. People have got too much interest in things, in information, they are addicted to it as much as I am to cigarettes and a good drink. But whereas the cigarettes rot my lungs and the alcohol rots my liver. This modern world is rotting everyone's brains. And it's going to get worse."

"I suppose I have never given it much thought."

"I bet you haven't. You have had to embrace this modern world as you have grown up with new technology. What you must be mid 30's?"

"I am 38"

"When I was 38, I had just finished working at a Pit in the north, Durham way, 15 years in all, I was mining for the stones. I had to stop as my chest couldn't take it anymore, breathing in the black-gold dust. Before that, I was in the army. I didn't get a TV until 1962, I was the talk of my terrace when it were delivered, I remember local boys would peer through my sitting room window, mind back then we only had three channels, not long after, most folk had a television set. There were no internet, I was late getting a phone, I held out until 1973. I would have my paper delivered every day, that, the TV and a healthy conversation at my local was the way I got my news about the world."

"What did you do after mining?"

"I was medically retired, so got my mining pension straight away, mind they fought that, didn't make it easy. I didn't work for a year or two after, I was told that I probably had 5 years left. It was in 1970 that I started working at a steelworks in Sheffield. Did that for 10 years, then I moved to London, worked on the buses and the Tube. I retired in 1987."

Theodore was genuinely surprised, more so at how frank Bernard was "Wow, so you were told when you were 38 that you only had about 5 years, due to coal dust inhalation? But here you are now."

"Here I am, for the moment. They think they know everything, and have all the answers. But they don't consider the human factor, our spirit, our resolve. We are more than just flesh and blood, much more.." The conversation was interrupted by a Nurse calling out *'Theodore Newton'*, Theodore stood, acknowledged the nurse and shook Bernard's hand

"I wish I could stay and talk some more, but I have to go see what's up with my son. Take care, Bernard"

Theodore headed over to the Nurse

"Were you talking to Mr Chapshaw?"

"Yes, very interesting fella"

"He is here most days. He just sits coughing, occasionally having conversations, but mostly alone, then he leaves."

"That's sad. Why? What is his story?"

"His wife passed away last year, he has no children or other family that we know of. Since then, he has come in around the time she was brought in and then departs around the time she passed on. We try to help, but he keeps coming back"

"That is so sad, he never mentioned her. He never gave any indication that he was grieving." Theodore held back mentioning that the receptionist was quite clearly being obstructive, as she clearly knew the name of who the cup he requested was for.

"No, I know. Anyway. If you would follow me I will take you to your son"

Theodore "Thanks Nurse, how is he? What happened to him?"

The nurse pressed her lanyard against a panel on the wall which released the magnetic locks on the doors, Theodore grabbed a handle pulled the door open and indicated to the nurse to go through first.

"He is awake, from what we can assume he fainted, perhaps with low blood pressure or over-exertion. In here, room 4"

She pushed the door open for Theodore to enter before continuing "I'll inform the Doctor that you are here. They will want to speak with you before Theo can go home"

"Thank you, Nurse"

Theodore turned to look at Theo. He was sitting on a chair with a mylar thermal blanket loosely wrapped around his middle, he had been on the bed as it was stained with mud.

Looking at his son, he was relieved to see him up and alert "How are you feeling? What happened"

"Where do I begin? I feel fine, at least now I do. It was the most extraordinary thing. I was right on the shoulder of Richard Tenui, in second place. We must have been around 300 metres from finishing, we were getting faster, ready for the sprint finish. It was when we passed through the last set of trees down from Parliament Hill, that... well... erm... I don't know how to put this. Well, Richard was no longer near me. No one was. I appeared to have briefly travelled back in time. Remember my last dream, I was a hunter-gatherer. I think I was the same person. I looked back towards Parliament Hill, but it was covered in forest. Next to the tree line were some buildings. Then I noticed a group emerge from the forest carrying a deer. It was pouring down, and the sky was dark and ominous, I have never seen it so dark, but it was daytime. I looked back towards where I was heading and Richard reappeared, and so did London."

"Are you sure you didn't faint? Pass out and dream. The nurse said you had fainted?"

"I did but that was after. When I spotted Richard, I realised I had returned to now and tried to chase after him, but I couldn't, my body was weak, weaker than I had ever felt before, I felt exhausted and unbelievably light-headed. I could only manage to jog, but that was still difficult. I remember getting to the finish line and that's when I must have blacked out. I really wanted to beat Tenui"

"Are you completely sure you didn't momentarily faint?"

"I am Positive Dad. The whole time hop thing took no more than five seconds. It was strange, It felt so real, It was Parliament Hill, Hampstead Heath, It was London, but thousands of years ago. I caught enough of a view of the scene before returning to the now, to have clarity, that what I was looking at, was in the past. It was tangible, I could even taste the rain, but it was dirty."

"I believe you son. It sounds like a, what do they call it.... A time slip. Did you tell anyone else any of this?"

"No, just that I felt unwell, slipped, got up and felt dizzy on the final part of the run and collapsed."

"Good. Don't tell anyone else. Stay with the story of feeling unwell. You, my son, are very much a deepening mystery. Can I get you anything?"

"Can I have an Orange Lucozade and a chocolate bar please Dad?"

"You got it. I am very proud of you son. Just remember that. I really can't tell you how much I love you. I won't be long." Theodore kissed his son on the forehead and then left the room.

Theodore had been gone a couple of minutes when Dr Schofield entered Theo's room.

"Hello Theo, I was told your father was here?"

"He is, he popped out to get me a drink. He will be a moment. Here he comes now." The doctor turns and looks at the door, he stares at the closed door for a moment and turns back to Theo

"Appears not" Just at that moment Theodore enters, and he continues "Mr Newton?" Theodore nods and puts his hand out to shake before continuing "That is some party piece you have there, although you may want to work on your timing"

"Sorry? Party piece.." Theo connected with his father and explained, "Ah yeah, he is getting better, my walking style is the giveaway, sorry to ruin the mystery"

"Still a good trick. Sorry I should introduce myself, I am Dr. Schofield. I feel like I know your names. Did you happen to go to school at Dunthorpe Primary?" Directing his question to Theo

"Yes, when I was 4 or 5"

"That may be it, my wife was the head teacher there. I remember her telling me about a gifted young boy. I am sorry about what happened to you, she was quite upset when she was informed you wouldn't be returning to her class."

"I am sorry. I was of the understanding that she decided that Theo wasn't to return."

“Not at all. She was in favour of Theo continuing, however, the education department at the council received too many letters and complaints from parents that they made the decision. My wife was going to contact you, to make sure that you knew the full story, but she became unwell. Anyhow, that unfortunate affair is in the past. But on behalf of my wife can I say we are very sorry.”

“Thanks. I hope your wife recovered and is well.”

“Thank you, I will pass on your regards. As for young Theo here. We monitored him on arrival, he is in excellent health. His blood pressure is slightly low, but not enough for concern. His heart rate, well, we would normally have concern that a lad of your age has a resting rate of 45 beats per minute, however, given your fitness levels, and your athletic ability, we can, with some certainty rule out bradycardia. We took a blood sugar test and your levels are normal.”

“Was there any reason then why he blacked out?”

“Quite possibly a case of over-exertion. He just pushed himself harder than he should have.” Looking at Theo, he continued “However, if you experience any more blackouts after intense exercise you need to see your registered GP or if the circumstances dictate, return to A&E.”

“Thank you Dr I do tell him he gets too involved, you know what these young uns are like, they want to win at all cost”

“Yes, all too true. You are free to go, Theo. Oh, I’m sure Linda, sorry, My wife would like to know. How are you doing at school, looking forward to your GCSEs next year or so?”

“I took them last June, I passed all of my subjects, and I have just started studying my A-Levels subjects”

“Quite incredible. If you haven’t decided on what career you want. Please consider a future in medicine. We really could do with someone with your brain.”

“Thank you again Dr. I’ll ensure he considers it”

“Thanks, Doc. Bye”

The father and son exit the hospital in silence and don’t speak until they are sitting in their car, parked in the Hospital's multi-storey car park.

“Show me” Theodore requests. Theo lifted the running vest, he was still wearing the same running gear from earlier, on his stomach, an inch below his belly button was a small cut. Theodore stared at it, then turned and banged his head onto the headrest, turned and looked out of the car’s side window before turning back to look at Theo “Do you have any recollection of when or where that happened?”

“No. None. The race was pretty uneventful. No one caught me with their spikes. I didn’t catch myself on a branch, it’s not from a safety pin. It wasn’t there when I put my vest back on after taking it off to attach the race number.”

“And when you had your time slip, do you remember any other detail? Did it appear real rather than an illusion?”

“It was real. I said I felt the dirty rain on my face. I could sense the thoughts of the people when they came out of the forest. They were real, the rain was real. Whatever this cut is, it’s real.”

“OK. Let’s try and figure out what is going on here. This is all connected. What happened to your mam, her collapsing and having the incision? Your Grandad Levi being able to predict cards, my ability to predict cards, then being able to read your mind. Your ability to read the minds of others, your strange dreams, which take you back to a point in early human history. Today you say you had a time slip into the past, then come back with this cut, the same cut that your mam had..” Theodore felt he was missing something

“You are forgetting that in one of my dreams, I or the person whose eyes I am looking through also has the same cut”

“That right, you said that you or the person appeared in a room looking out over another world”

"Yes. And also the X Blood group. Do you think it's all linked?"

"What does your mind tell you? When you have eliminated the impossible, whatever remains, however improbable must be the truth."

"Dad. First of all. Sherlock Holmes you are quoting, was fictional. According to Einstein and his General Theory of Relativity, he proposed that Space and Time are malleable, that they could warp and curve, matter and energy could cause that. He proposes that if a person could surpass the speed of light, it may be possible to travel backwards in time. However, he also says that the closer you are to the speed of light, the more energy would be needed and at the speed of light the object's mass would be infinite. So surpassing the speed of light would be unsupported by our current understanding of physics as per GToR. I am certain that I don't possess the power to time travel."

Theodore was impressed with his son's knowledge "Keep going."

"Ruling out time travel. We can rule out a simulation. Unless we, here and now are living in a simulation, but the fact that I could feel the rain on my face is physical evidence that it wasn't a simulation."

"Was it raining at that exact moment during the race?" Theo starred at his dad, he then closed his eyes and thought

"No. And I time slipped the moment I passed into the tree line, the trees would have sheltered me at that moment if it were raining."

"I think we need to pay a visit to those trees."

"Agreed Dad"

"So if it isn't actual time travel and if it isn't a simulation. Then maybe some form of projected thought?."

"Or a planted memory?"

"Perhaps. You might be right. You had been experiencing very real dreams, and then what you experienced today, from what you describe, could be a continuation of someone else's experience. I don't believe in reincarnation. But this does sound a lot like that."

“Why didn’t I think of that? Sounds improbable enough, there is the mystery of the scratch on my stomach.”

“We will have to think some more. It’s too dark now. Too dark to search the scene now, tomorrow is Sunday, if we get up close to sunrise, we can take a look tomorrow if you are up for it?”

“Yeah, why not. Good thinking Batman.”

“I prefer Batdad”

#

The next day they were up and out of the house just after 7 a.m. It would be sunrise at 7:40 a.m. The father and son team chose to cycle to Hampstead Heath, a distance of just under 6 miles. They didn’t need to hurry as they wanted some light to work with.

It took a little over 35 minutes with a gentle cycle to arrive at Parliament Hill lookout. They chained their bikes together using a tree trunk as an anchor, just as the first light of dawn crept across the sky, the pair stood with the expanse of Hampstead Heath before them, shrouded in the misty air of a cold, damp November morning.

The grass, wet with dew, glistens under the faint glow of the rising sun to the East, which paints the sky in hues of pale orange and soft pink.

London is already awake, the distant sounds muffled by the fog that clings to the ground. The air is crisp and carries the promise of winter, biting at their cheeks and noses, however, they don’t feel the cold.

They turn and look southwest towards the trees, their attention drawn to a faint blue glow emanating close to the ground. The ethereal light shimmers softly, appearing as some otherworldly beacon, perhaps providing some clues to help unravel their mystery

Theo pointed to the trees “That is where I was when I had my time slip. The blue glow, it’s almost like an argon electrical excitation, it’s beautiful but kind of creepy”

Theodore pulls out his phone and starts video recording "Let's get closer, but with caution." As they move closer, they see a very feint, circular shaft of blue haze, almost completely opaque. As the sun continues its rise into the sky the blue column quickly begins to fade from view.

"Dad. It's gone!"

"Or we just can't see it. Let's just keep back. What the hell was that? I couldn't make out how high it went."

"I couldn't tell either, it kind of just stopped at the upper branches of the trees. Do you think this is what happened with mam? I mean, in the park, afterwards?"

"Theo, I think, Yes. I don't know what that was, how to explain it, where it came from, what it does and why, but I am pretty sure, that if we check the soil, that area will be sterile. If we were just a couple of minutes later, we would have missed it."

"Or was it the intention, of whatever is behind all of this, for us to see it?"

"That suggests that you think there is someone or persons behind all of this? To what end?"

"I don't know dad. But while it's kind of exciting, it is also creeping the life out of me!"

As they began to cycle away, the pair were unaware of a black helicopter which was steadily coming closer, descending on its final approach to Parliament Hill. By the time it had landed, the father and son had long since vacated the parkland.

Three people exited the aircraft, they were paying particular interest to the site where the blue glow had been observed.

CHAPTER 10 CHRONICLES

NOVEMBER 16 2014 10:00 A.M.

He that maketh many friends [doeth it] to his own destruction; But there is a friend that sticketh closer than a brother
Proverbs 18:24 ASV

The father and son didn't stay too long at Parliament Hill, they agreed that while they could not see the mysterious blue glow, it could still be there. If it was indeed the same phenomenon that caused the soil sterility at Broadacre Park, then they best stay clear, at least for a while.

Theo presented concerns that potentially some innocent person could pass through the area and be affected. However, the ground had been churned up by all of the runners over countless hours, only a fool would choose that route. Additionally, as far as they were aware, there hadn't been any reports of people falling ill at the other sites.

Theodore had decided that it was time to confide with his friend, whatever was happening to Theo was too big, too mysterious to keep a secret any longer. Once home they changed clothes and headed back out in the car to a fast food drive-through.

Theodore parked the car after receiving their order. He pulled his phone out and dialled.

"John, are you free?"

"Just a moment Theodore" his friend opened the calendar on his laptop computer and quickly scanned through his day's events "I can be. What's up?"

"Meet me at 1992"

"Got it, I will be about five or so." Theodore hung up the call and looked at Theo.

"I trust him. It is time we had his thoughts on all of this"

"I agree, I trust him too"

"You haven't asked what 1992 is, but then you don't need to, do you?"

"Over there" he pointed to the road intersection "That's where Grandpa Levi was knocked down in 1992. John was parked up on the side of the road. Grandpa had picked up some lunch and was starting to cross the road. He didn't see the car fly through the red light. He died not long after"

"I remember the day so vividly, the look on Johns's face when he told me, the first time my world ended, was that day, but he pulled me through, secretly, he wasn't coping, he did so well to hide it from me until the drink took hold. He is a good man. I haven't been back here since it happened, always avoiding coming this way, but it was the first place that came to mind when I thought of where to meet"

"I am sorry Dad. He is here" The silver Volkswagen estate car pulled up next on the left-hand side of their car.

"Theo, do you mind jumping in the back?"

"Sure Dad" he opened the door and climbed out, pushing the door shut, John climbed out of his car.

"How are you, Theo? I heard about what happened yesterday. I trust everything is ok?"

"I am ok. Thanks. You?"

"I am great. Never better" John climbed into the front passenger seat and Theo got into the back of the car. "Theodore, everything OK?"

"Can you turn off your phone, you too Theo" Theodore plucked his phone from the cradle on the dash and powered his phone off. John pulled his phone from his jacket pocket and did the same.

"Theodore, what is this about, are you in trouble?"

"No. Sorry for the mystery. As of right now, what we are about to tell you, stays between us three. Don't even tell Joanne. You are still with Joanne?"

"Yes. I was going to swing by your place tonight. We got engaged." Theodore extended his hand out to shake John's.

"Look at you, congratulations, it took the pair of you long enough. I am so pleased for both of you. I suppose it makes it a little more awkward. But for the time being, just keep this to yourself."

"Congratulations Uncle John"

"Thanks, Theo. OK, What am I keeping to myself?"

"The events, have taken a bizarre turn"

Theodore proceeded to chronicle in detail everything, from the reported blood group X, the mysterious healing capability of Theo's blood to the results being mysteriously retracted. The mind-reading ability that went beyond card reveal. Theo's exceptional mind, his athletic ability. The dreams, the time slip, the mysterious incision that Theo shares with his mother and the ethereal blue light.

"And only the pair of you know all of this?"

Theo jumped in to answer before his father could "Thats right, except you, oh and Aunty Joanne knows a little"

"Obviously. Some of this I already knew. Well. If you were strangers and you came to me with any of this, I would think you needed some psychological help. But.. Some weird shit happened that day with Isabella. We haven't been able to find anything to progress that case. As you know, it was closed."

"Which it will remain?"

“Which it will remain. So if I had to try and explain, to answer what any of this means, who is behind it, what is the motive, the purpose, I can only come to three, perhaps four explanations”

Theodore provided the first “God moves in mysterious ways being number one. Not that”

John was all too aware of his godson’s belief system “Still not a believer? OK, how about this is some foreign agency, Russia or China? Or number three, the US or hell, even ourselves!”

“If it is Russia, China, USA, Belize or god damn Montserrat. How? What technology? What purpose?”

“So that leaves number four”

Theo couldn’t help adding a touch of humour to the discussion “ET phone home” John and Theodore, turned and looked back at Theo who was grinning from ear to ear. He continues

“The pair of you were taking too long to get to the obvious. Of course, it’s Aliens.”

“It is a big ass sky out there” John begins to laugh, Theodore looks at his friend and starts to laugh with him. In moments, there is a cacophony of uproarous laughter. To the casual observer, they would see the car they were sitting in, bounce and rock as if someone was being interactive to the tune of ‘*Bohemian Rhapsody*’

John composes himself and wipes the tears from his cheeks, “I've not laughed that hard for some time. There has to be another answer than Aliens. Surely”

“Don’t call me Shirley” the comment sets off the friends once again. However, Theo didn’t get the relevance of the comment.

“The boy needs to watch Airplane”

“John, I think the radio in your car is requesting you” John lowers the car window, sure enough, his police radio is requesting that Detective Chief Inspector Richardson respond.

"Good ears, thanks Theo" he climbs out of the car and gets into his own, closing the door behind him. He responds to the radio, then proceeds to power on his mobile phone. A minute later he is talking to someone at the other end of the phone. Turning he looks at Theodore with an exasperated look on his face. Hanging up the call he once again switches cars. Before he can speak Theo vocalises "My god"

"I have just spoken to base, it seems an hour ago there was a fatal incident at the Shopping Centre. A boy has been injured in a gang attack. Sorry both, but I need to go. I will try and pop around"

"Thank John, see you soon."

John climbs back out of the car and into his own, starts up the engine, turns on the lights and sirens of his unmarked police car and races off. Meanwhile, Theo moves back to the front seat.

"It's Richard Tenui, dad. He was stabbed and killed"

"I know son, I got that also. John is getting pressure to try and tackle the knife and gang issue. Poor lad. He beat his course record yesterday, such a talent"

"I know I shouldn't speak ill of the dead, but he was a dick. But he didn't deserve what happened to him."

#

Theo and his father returned to the site of the blue glow near Parliament Hill a few days later, there were no further clues to be found. The path through the trees that Theo had taken, was still a churned mess of mud and leaves. The trees looked dead, but then it was late Autumn and almost all of the trees in the park had lost their green canopies. Everything around them looked lifeless.

Theodore suggested that they would probably have to wait until spring to see if anything had changed. But Theo had an alternate plan. He had for a while, been interested in taking part in Park Runs, while there were two other closer events to their home the extra distance to reach Hampstead

Heath didn't make much difference and the run route would come within eyesight of the area they needed to observe. Theodore's only request was that Theo switch each week between the Gladstone, Sunny Hill and Hampstead Heath Park Runs. Citing safety as his primary concern.

Theo looked forward to each Saturday at 9 a.m. for the start of the Park Run. He would get up at 6 a.m. Spend 45 minutes in the home gym doing strength work with his dad. He then had a light breakfast while Theodore continued in the gym. Theo would shower, then do some studying until 8:15 a.m. when he would change and cycle to that day's Park Run. Even with this new regime, He remained a member of Dunthorpe Athletic Club, training every Tuesday and Thursday with the squad.

Every other Saturday or so, he would take part in the Hampstead Heath Park Run, he wouldn't race it, instead treated it as a gentle trail run. Each time glancing over to the trees to see if there were any changes. By late winter when the trees were starting to show signs of a fresh layer of foliage, he could see no issues, plain to see, the trees were developing their leaves. Then in spring blossom. Whatever the blue light was, that he and his father had witnessed, did not seem to have had the same impact as what had occurred with the scene of his mother's incident.

Theodore took some comfort that what had happened to Theo was not the same as what had happened to his beloved Izzy, even still, he had concerns. He persuaded Theo to see his doctor and have some blood tests, faking some symptoms which could be an indication of cancer. Theodore felt ashamed of this, his guilt weighed heavily in his thoughts. When his company issued their annual bonus in May, he donated the lot to several cancer-based charities.

The blood tests came back showing no sign of any cancer and as expected, revealed Theo to be an extremely healthy teenager.

#

By mid-June 2016, Theo had completed his final A-Level exam. He knew he had done well. His mid-term coursework was of an outstanding level. His results were announced in August of that year, and once again he aced the exams achieving the top grades available.

Theodore expressed concerns with his son, that he seemed to be spending too much time studying and training, more so in the latter. Theo had quit doing cross country and park runs. He was completely focused on being a multi-disciplinary track and field athlete.

He had repeatedly won 100m to 400m sprint events for the club. Since he could sprint, it was the inevitable next step that he would be asked to take part in the long jump.

Then at one athletics meeting, he was asked to step in and cover the javelin event. His raw talent and quick learning saw him take the second spot. The club coach asked Theo if he wanted to up the ante and become a decathlete. Theo returned home that evening to inform his father.

"Coach wants me to try out for the decathlon."

"Wait. That's quite a move from sprinting and the occasional jump. What have I missed?"

"One of our throwers didn't make it to the meet today. I won the 100m and 400m by the way. Anyhow, I was asked if I could do javelin, it clashed with the 200m, so I figured what the hell. I came second."

"Well done. But doesn't that take practice? It's not an easy sport, the technique, takes a while to master. I was no good when I tried it."

"Seems I am a natural. It's not as much about strength as it is about the angle and release vector. Put enough momentum with balance and that thing can launch"

"So decathlon aye? Can I ask? When are you going to make time and get a girlfriend? Or a boyfriend. I won't judge"

"Dad! Hang on. It's been 16 years since Mam died. I don't remember you making any effort to move on. You have never, to my knowledge been on a date. So how about you?"

"This is not about me. You have your life ahead of you, I'm just worried you won't stop and enjoy life. I rarely ever see you with any friends. What social life do you have? It's not normal. I am concerned?"

"Again. Let's look at you. Other than Uncle John. Who are your friends? Come on, where are they? When do you go out and have a social life? You are 40 years old Dad. You need to have a life too. It's not normal. You never go on holiday. You never enjoy yourself. You spend your time at work, or the gym, which is **ALSO** your work by the way. The only other place you occasionally go is to the sparring mats. Why did you give up your boxing? Why don't you compete? Let's talk about that"

"Let's back this up a minute. You are 16 years old. You are still a child. You are still my responsibility. **MY RESPONSIBILITY**. I will spend the rest of my life the way I see fit. But you my son, you will listen to my guidance, my instruction. I am saying I have concerns that you are too focused on avoiding human and social contact, that you don't seem to be enjoying the part of your life when you should be enjoying your life."

"Again look at you. You expect me to make friends, you expect me to have a social life to have a girlfriend when **YOU** have not shown me how to do those things? You haven't been a role model for those things. You expect me to know how to talk to a girl? To tell a girl that I like them, that I want to take them on a date? Or should I just instinctively know?"

"I suppose or I assumed, that with your great intellect, your physical presence and handsome looks, the girls would be queuing up at the door?"

"**DAD**, That is not how it works, this isn't the 1980s or '90s anymore. Life is far more complicated than it was when you grew up. There are so many differences between us, I am not you."

"Theo. Let me understand."

"You first Dad. Why haven't you dated?"

"We are just going around in circles"

The father and son continued to argue, their first-ever argument. Theodore had a strong resolve he would not back down, he was the adult, the father. Theo was just like his dad, stubborn, opinionated, expecting equality, expecting to be treated like an adult. In all but age, he was an adult, he could easily pass for eighteen or nineteen years old, and he had the maturity and intellect of someone much older.

By 1 a.m., they had not reached any agreement or rational point of concession. Theodore ended the conversation and went to bed, still hot-tempered and frustrated with his son. He knew his son was right, he also knew he was right. He had known for a while, since 2000 in fact, that his world ended for a second time when his beloved Izzy was lost. His only motivation, the **ONLY** reason he had to continue was to see his son grow and become a man. He was also acutely aware that his son was the same age he was when he lost his father. He felt out of his depth. He didn't know how to father his son from this point on.

The next morning, Theodore was up early. He went down to the kitchen and made an americano coffee. Mug in hand he walked through to the conservatory at the back of the house and sat looking at the early morning sun. It was going to be another glorious summer day.

Not long after, Theo comes in and sits across from his dad.

"I am sorry son. I have some explaining to do."

"You don't dad."

"Please. More so for me, than for you. I need to say this." His son nodded "Your mam was the love of my life. No one compares to her, no one ever could compare to her. I have thought a few times about moving on, but, I don't think I could, whoever I meet, could never live up to your mam. I would always be comparing them to her. If it wasn't for you, if you hadn't survived, I would have ended my life. You were the only reason I didn't. I made a promise, more to myself or your mam's memory, that you my son, would be all I needed."

"Dad. I wish you would have said something."

"I thought maybe you would have figured it out. But recently, I came to realise that you" He hesitated "Well, you are the same age I was when my dad died. I was 16 with no father. I had no mother. John became my guardian, but, bless him, he wasn't my father. I panicked. I realised that I had run out of skill. I had no one to show me how I should be a father when I was your age. Here we are, in uncharted territory. I kept thinking back to what I was doing at your age. I was going to nightclubs, to pubs, getting into bother with my friends. Meeting girls and living a normal teenage life."

"It is OK Dad. I realise this."

"You are an amazing man. Let's be truthful here, you are a man. You look like a man. You are responsible, intelligent and talented beyond your years. I want you to be happy."

"Come here" the father and son embraced, shedding a few tears.

"I love you son. It's still Summer. Why don't we get away for a week? We can go anywhere. What say you?"

"Anywhere?"

"I know that look. We aren't going to Egypt or what is it now Turkey?" Theo winked at his dad

"I love you too Dad. Egypt would be great. I would love to see the pyramids, and visit the Cairo Museum. Turkey, again would be amazing, what they have unearthed at Gobekli Tepe, Boncuklu Tarla and Mohenjo-Daro. But they aren't holidays are they?"

"We could always go one day. Turkey would be a bit more complicated. Where else? I was thinking more on the lines of Jamaica, The Canaries, Balearics, Corfu or some other warm island break."

"Any of those would be good. You do know I have never flown? I've never needed to use my passport."

"Well let's correct that. We will see what offers are available. Even then, if the location and dates are right, it doesn't even need to be an offer"

After breakfast, they headed to the high street. Where they booked a last-minute all-inclusive holiday to Tenerife for a week.

Theodore promised a hike up Mount Teide, some jet ski lessons, lots of swimming and relaxing in the sun.

Returning home the postman had been. A large envelope sat on the mat addressed to Theodore. He walked through to the kitchen tearing open the mail. Pulling out the paperwork held together with a paperclip.

It was from a legal firm 'Burgess, Hoyt and Mann' representing the estate of the late Bernard Chapshaw.

"Theo, listen to this." Reading the letter.

Dear Mr. Newton,

We hope this letter finds you well. We are writing to you on behalf of the estate of the late Mr Bernard Chapshaw, whom you may remember from a brief encounter in November 2014.

As the executors of Mr. Chapshaw's will, it is our duty to inform you that Mr. Chapshaw passed away in March 2015. In accordance with his wishes, his assets were liquidated, and the proceeds were to be distributed among ten beneficiaries who, in his eyes, had shown exemplary human kindness.

It is with great pleasure that we announce you have been named as one of these beneficiaries. Mr Chapshaw was deeply moved by the generosity you displayed during your fleeting interaction in the hospital waiting area. He believed that such acts of goodwill should not go unrecognised.

Therefore, you are the recipient of a 10% share of the net proceeds, amounting to a total of £215,000. This sum is a testament to the principle that even the smallest gestures of compassion can resonate beyond the moment and touch lives in ways we cannot foresee.

Please find enclosed the necessary documentation to proceed with the transfer of funds. We request that you review and return the signed documents at your earliest convenience.

Should you have any questions or require further assistance, please do not hesitate to contact our office.

Yours sincerely,

Mrs. J. Christaller LLB LLM

Burgess, Hoyt & Mann

"Who was Mr Chapshaw?"

"I can't believe he remembered me, let alone trace me. He was an elderly gentleman I met at Hampstead General, the day you had your cross-country incident. He was coughing, I remember trying to get some water for him, but there was a rather rude and unhelpful receptionist, so I bought a bottle of water from the vending machine to give to him. We conversed for a while before I was called in to see you. I really can't believe it. What I did for him was so small, but it must have had quite an impact on him. It shows you, that everything we do has a consequence. Huh!" Theodore started to laugh.

"What? What's funny Dad?"

"Oh years ago, I had a conversation with Father O'Connor, the local Catholic Priest, we got talking about Karma. I said I didn't believe it. I may have to reconsider my belief system."

"Or you did a nice thing for an elderly man, he appreciated it and wanted to thank you. So what are you going to do with the money? You **ARE** accepting the money? Dad?"

"I will have to think about it."

"What is there to think about?"

"Ah Theo, you are very intelligent, but maybe you need to work on your wisdom?"

"Ah, I see. I have already considered, what it is, that you are thinking about.."

Theodore interrupts his son "Go on then"

"You are trying to decide if you think this is an act of Karma. So you are thinking, You did a nice thing, and now karma has rewarded you with a gift which you perceive, significantly outweighs the value of your perceived value of the gift you gave. Remember this is your perception. Now if you accept the gift, you are trying to decide, whether you are accepting a contract, not only with the law firm in acceptance of the gift but with whatever or whoever is the administrator of karma. In accepting the contract, you are wondering, is that the cycle and the contract being fulfilled or put it another way, is karma fulfilled, or by accepting the gift is there now a new cycle of karma which has been established, thereby placing the onus on you, to ensure the continuity of karma is fulfilled in some reciprocal act of kindness, perhaps by paying it forward.

To summarise. If you accept the money, do you now need to do another, but bigger, good deed? If you don't will you be judged by karma as greedy?" Theo smirked at his dad "Gotcha"

"Son. I do sometimes underestimate you. So I guess you think I should accept the money"

"Yes, you should. Else you will be turning down a generous gift put in place by a dying man. What does karma say about that?"

"We could have a philosophical debate about this for the rest of the day. I will read the enclosed papers first. But yes, I think I will accept."

"Awesome. So what are you going to spend it on" Theo walked off, repeating the same question as he went.

CHAPTER 11 CHAMPION

AUGUST 4 2021 5:30 A.M.

To them that by patience in well-doing seek for glory and honor and incorruption, eternal life
Romans 2:7 ASV

The past five years marked a period of success for the Newtons. Theodore remarried. It took almost a year for the final administration of the will of Mr Chapshaw to be completed and for Theodore to receive his share. Due to various complications, taxes and errors in the estate, he was still in receipt of £145,000.

Theodore was already quite wealthy, the gym company he co-owned, went through a period of rapid expansion, making it a lucrative proposition for investors. It was acquired by an international competitor wanting to enhance its portfolio. Theodore could now count himself as a multi-millionaire.

He used the money from Mr Chapshaw and some of his own wealth, to establish a charity working to tackle the gang culture in London. By providing free hang-out venues across London for those up to 25 years of age. The community hubs, known as DexBox London, provided a safe, non-partisan and inclusive place for the learning of life skills, traditional crafts, music, computing, boxing and self-defence.

It welcomed everyone, from any background, religion or nationality. The name was a mash-up of the two interests that Theodore had after losing his dad, he believes they saved him from going in the wrong direction.

It was while appointing staff to work at DexBox, that Theodore met Dr. Louise Nash, whom he had originally appointed as a consultant for her expertise in youth engagement programs. The couple instantly had an attraction. Professional quickly turned to romantic, they were engaged in 2019 and married in early 2020 before the pandemic restrictions came into effect.

The new Mrs Newton was appointed CEO of the charity, while Theodore was hands-on with interacting with the teenagers, particularly with boxing and music. Theo gave his father's new marriage his complete blessing.

Theo was granted early entrance to the University of Central London at the age of just 16 years where he studied a Bachelor of Science in Archaeology attaining a first-class degree. In the following September, he returned to UoCL to study for a 1 year Master of Science in Paleoanthropology and Palaeolithic Archaeology.

In October of 2021, Theo is to commence a three-year research degree in Archaeology once again at UoCL, in which he could gain a PhD and the title of Dr.

As incredible as his academic success appeared, it was just the tip of his achievements. Not long after returning from the week with his father in Tenerife, Theo committed his athletic focus to the multi-disciplinary skill of the decathlon.

He had already proven himself to be a very talented sprinter, this naturally meant he was predisposed to being a very capable jumper. But he was also strong and demonstrated a fantastic understanding of the techniques involved in mastering the throwing disciplines. He was the epitome of an all-round athlete.

From 2016 to the present day he focussed most of his efforts on honing his technical skills, he already had the speed and power required, which he maintained through a well-crafted timetable of study, rest and training.

Theo recalled his vivid dreams. He couldn't help making a connection, between what he could do and the survival skills of palaeolithic hunter-gatherers, their need to be able to run hard, over long and difficult distances, chasing down a pray and striking it with a lethal blow.

He was more certain than ever, that something WAS influencing his destiny. He remembered what his dad told him, about *'Ancestral Code'* when he recounted the meeting at 'Dunthorpe University Hospital Research Centre'. He couldn't help thinking there **COULD** be something in his DNA.

In 2018 he won the *'English Athletics Age Group Individual Championships'* for the under 17 category in the decathlon. Then in 2019 at 18 years old and competing as a senior, placed second in the *'English National Championships'*. The following year he won those same championships at 19 years old. He was an unstoppable force.

His success continued, winning his event at every attempt. In 2021 he was selected to represent Great Britain in the Tokyo Games. He was about to make his presence known on the world stage.

While extremely proud of his son, Theodore had concerns. He knew he couldn't wrap his son in cotton wool all his life, he had to allow Theo to make his own decisions and therefore mistakes, but he couldn't help thinking, here we have a young adult, with a beautiful mind, achieving incredible academic success while also at the precipice of becoming a world-class athlete.

His life WILL be scrutinised, not only by the media wanting to sensationalise even the smallest aspect of his life, but potentially, also by foreign powers or agencies. Once on the biggest stage of all, there would be no turning back for Theo Newton. In the end, Theodore had to let Theo go free into the world.

Upon receiving the call-up to represent Great Britain in the Tokyo Games, Theo was elated, he felt his hard work and his dreams had finally paid off. But on the evening before he was due to fly out with some of the team, he lay on his bed, again thinking about his life and how it had taken him to this point. For the first time that he can remember, he felt unsure that this was his true destiny.

He knew as a child, that he was more eager than most and that he had an insatiable desire to learn. His brain was a sponge, soaking up as much as it could, but it seemed endless, capable of absorbing more and more information.

When he was older, he would often try to resolve why he wanted to learn so much. It wasn't that he needed to know how things worked, why the world was the way it was, or to reach an explanation for everything. It was more, why did he want to know these things? While he couldn't explain it, deep inside, he felt he already knew everything that he was being taught. This made him consider his purpose.

While it's human to want to know what the meaning of life is and what purpose an individual has in their short life. Theo felt that his question was stronger than that of other people. Everything that had occurred in the weeks following being conceived, then born and then as a growing child, it was, to Theo, as if it was deliberate. Sure he still suspected his DNA played its part, but there was something else.

He was starting to believe that he was the result of some grand plan. As if he had less control over his future than he would believe and instead, he was being controlled as if a puppet, his every action coordinated and manipulated. He considered the meaning of his existence, did he have a god complex? After all, he was a genius, intelligent beyond the standard and athletically, world-class. And while this wasn't unique amongst humanity, he wondered, did others of a similar level, have strange encounters in their lives which he had experienced?

Ultimately, Theo could only resolve three possible outcomes to answer his question. The first would be in a demonstration of free will, that he would take himself somewhere and not return. The second was that he stopped everything he currently did to try and have, would most people would consider, a normal life and the third, was to keep going down the same path and see if more definition for his purpose be revealed.

He enjoyed his life, he was certain he had a purpose, even if he didn't know what that was, he knew he wanted to find out. In the end, he decided the third option was the only acceptable choice. And yet, he still wondered, was this whole thought process pre-defined in destiny?

Theo left Great Britain on the 16th of July with some of his fellow Team GB representatives, their destination Tokyo, Japan. It was only the third time in his life he had been on an aircraft. The first was the holiday with his father to Tenerife, and the second was a week-long field trip, as part of his University Degree to Rome, to experience first-hand the mastery of the Roman Empire and its impact on Archaeology.

Due to commence on the 23rd of July, the 32nd Games was originally to have been held the year earlier in 2020, however, due to a fortunate twist of fate and the onset of the Covid pandemic, Theo made the team, an achievement that would not have occurred if the games were to have taken place on their original date.

Theo had time to settle and adjust to life in Japan, his Decathlon event, a two-day affair comprising 10 events scheduled for the 4th and 5th of August. This allowed him to visit several archaeological sites close to Tokyo including; Noge Otsuka Ancient Tomb, Musashi-Fuchu Kumano Jinja Kofun and Shimura Ichirizuka. But his focus there wasn't on his academic pursuits, so decided to cut short his plans to visit further afield sites such as Chino City Togariishi Jomon Archaeological Museum to the West.

Returning to the Athletes Village, Theo concentrated his preparations on the technical elements of his sport. In his off time, he wanted to socialise with other athletes, remembering what his father had said to him 5 years prior. However, the Games playbook for Tokyo stressed basic precautions for infection control, which included rules on socialising, handshakes and hugs, COVID was most definitely still impacting people's lives.

The days were repetitive and could be broken down to eat-train-eat-sleep-train-lift-eat-sleep or variations thereof, occasionally Theo would spend time in the health spa circling a semi-rigid routine of swimming, steam room, swimming, sauna, physio and stretching, swimming and ice plunge pool or cryotherapy.

Until the day of his event, he didn't experience much live viewing of the many sports taking place across the city, instead watching on the various big screens or televisions dotted around.

He spoke to his father by video chat. Theodore had hoped to get out to see his son, however, he had commitments that prevented him. He wished his son all the best of luck and would speak to him again after his first day of events.

The 4th of August eventually arrived. Theo woke at 5:30 a.m., as he always did. Against the team coach's instructions, Theo went for an easy six-mile run, before showering and grabbing some breakfast. Reluctantly he headed back to bed for an hour.

At 8 a.m. he was back up and waiting for the team transport to take the Athletes to the Olympic Stadium, he was the only representative for his home country.

The first event's arrival came all too soon, at 9 a.m., Theo was warmed up following a brief period of stretching. Waiting eagerly on the start line for the 100m sprint. The first of 3 races. Eight competitors lined up, his main rival in this race was an athlete from the USA and a favourite for '*The Games*' title, however, while they would be racing each other, the aim was to achieve the best possible performance to gain points. The athlete with the highest cumulative total over the ten events, being the gold medal winner and '*The Games*' champion.

The official ordered the athletes to get into their starting position, the sound of the stadium deafening with cheering fans, drums and air horns. The athletes positioned themselves in the blocks, making slight adjustments to their hand and foot positions to give the maximum amount of kinetic potential off the line.

Theo glanced left to right, quickly assessing each athlete's state of readiness, he would not mind read, he had learned how to switch off that ability, deeming it an unfair advantage and a form of cheating. The Jamaican athlete in lane one was composed and steady, tunnel vision already directing his thoughts to the job at hand. Polar to this was the American Clyde Rogers, who had been drawn next to Theo in lane three, he had his necklace in his mouth, playing with it using his tongue, he glanced at Theo and winked. Followed by a self-assured grin of unbinding confidence.

The stadium at that moment fell almost silent, the anticipation of the go command from the starter palpable. While not carrying the sensational buildup and grandeur of the individual 100-metre race, the sprint events in whatever form, always delivered a tense spectacle of pure human power.

Theo was poised, his fingers gripping the track, preventing the slightest slip. His legs staggered, one foot forward, the rear back pushing against the block, his gluteus maximus tensing ready to unleash its potential energy. His arms were extended forward, his powerful shoulders squared, and his muscles defined as they provided balance.

'**GO**', the starter gun fired. The sound of the bang began its voyage around the stadium, taking less than 0.02 seconds to reach Theo, he reacted, springing forward out of the blocks in an almost inhuman 0.1 seconds, a fraction over the legally allowed limit. His legs were bound with energy like a coiled spring, pushing him forward and up in one fluid motion. His quadriceps, hamstrings and calf muscles engage in a symphony of human power, tendons stretching, storing more elastic energy. He was almost completely upright before any of the other competitors had responded. He had the perfect start out of the blocks.

The American was the second to respond, by the time he was upright, Theo had already gained a five-meter advantage. Theo's tall and powerful stature explodes away. Standing tall, providing a vertical power line from the stance foot through the hip to the head, his legs driving like pistons, the ground blurring beneath his feet. His arms pump vigorously, elbows driving back and forth, rhythmically in balance with his legs.

The crowd finally catch up with the action, as it goes from deathly silence to a thunderous roar, caught up in the raw power of the sprinter's explosion.

By the third second, a quarter of the track had been devoured. Theo was still pulling away from the second-placed American, the rest of the field over ten metres off the pace. The leader demonstrating a different class of athlete, surges yet further ahead. His stride lengthens as he maintains a slight forward lean. His short, quick step catapulted him onto the next foot strike.

The crowd seem to increase their roar further, witnessing the gap widen. From 30m to 70m, Theo kept accelerating, each 10-metre segment faster than the prior, 0.83, 0.81, 0.79, and 0.74 seconds. By the final third of the distance, Theo was more than 10 metres clear of the second-place American, himself, well clear of the rest of the field.

At the 80-metre mark, the speed display had registered Theo's maximum speed at 28 mph, a new human record. He glanced back over his shoulder to see the rest of the field, nowhere near, except for the American who was too far back to challenge his lead.

If this were an individual sprint, Theo would have eased off, allowing his forward momentum to carry him over the line, except this was a decathlon sprint, every fraction of a second was a point.

He kept driving, crossing the line, and his timer stopped.

A sudden silence befalls the stadium. The crowd points with occasional gasps and as quickly as the silence begins, it ends, an earth-shattering roar erupts the stadium. The realisation of what had just been witnessed hit them. The track timer reads 8.97 seconds. Theo had not only obliterated the previous world record of 9.58 seconds, but he had defied what was considered possible for a human, he had broken the 9-second barrier for 100m.

Before he was able to react to his world record, a track steward was ushering him off the track, Theo voiced his displeasure, he wanted to circle the track and acknowledge his appreciation of the crowd, but the official insisted that he accompany him for a routine doping check. The crowd witnessing what was happening began to jeer and holler, protesting at what was happening to their champion sprinter. Theo however, conceded that it was inevitable, he would need to be tested for illegal substances, after all, he had just smashed several human records.

The testing was very routine. Theo had experienced the process several times over the past couple of years. Often suggested to him, by other athletes, that it was more to do with his skin colour than his performance. However, Theo considered himself more fortunate than others, he had personally experienced little racism in his life. He believed the games committee were indiscriminate in their approach to testing, this being obvious when a further 4 athletes entered the testing area after him, he was the only one of obvious colour.

It was over quite quickly, a blood sample was taken, then he had to supply a urine sample and on this occasion, saliva was also taken. The results would be made available later in the day.

The three sprint races had concluded and the long jump event had started before Theo made it back onto the track. He was leading the

Decathlon, his record-breaking 1365 points for the sprint event put him 237 clear of second place, the American Clyde Rogers. Rogers had just completed his 2nd of three attempts, setting a new games decathlon best of 8m 24cm and 1123 points.

Theo was unfazed, he was due to compete in the second phase of the event and he was on a high after the sprint.

Before he was able to go through to the warm-up area, a swarm of reporters surrounded him. The questions varied between asking him to '*describe how it felt to break the world record*', '*would you consider taking on the Brightwell Islands Games champion*' whose record he just smashed, to, did he '*feel confident the drug's test will come back negative*'. Theo briefly answered about being a clean athlete and that any future events to be considered, once he was able to finish the decathlon. He politely excused himself, drawing more of a frenzy from the reporters, who were eager to get a more expansive and exclusive comment.

The rest of day one of the tournament went to plan. Theo was mindful now that, while he knew he was capable of winning every event and confident he could do so with the same level of incredulous success as he demonstrated in the sprint race earlier, he did need to restrain himself. He finished second in the long jump, third in the shot put, first in the high jump and first in the 400 metres with a decathlon record time of 43.18, which was once the individual world record. Finishing the day on 5165 points, over 1,377 points ahead of Clyde Rogers.

Theo was preparing to head back to the Athlete's village when he was stopped by a group of officials.

"I am Mr Bassein, I am the lead athlete engagement official for '*The Games*' committee. Mr Newton, if you don't mind, for your safety and because we have questions to ask, if you wouldn't mind accompanying us"

"I don't mind, is this about my doping results?"

The French official responded "Not at all, I can tell you that those results were clear of any known banned substances. We have to say, your performance today was, well, not short of being super-heroic. It has created quite a stir amongst the media delegation here. They are demanding to speak with you, to get answers."

"Theo" he turned to look at the man now addressing him

"Mr Newman, we met on the flight over here, good to see you again"

"That's right, good to see you again. I have to say, that all of us at Team GB are overjoyed with your performance today. However, we need to discuss with you, how you should handle the media, you need to represent all that is great about Team GB, so we need to brief you, and give you a crash course so to speak on media engagement."

"I understand. I guess I have caused a media headache for you all." He winked.

The French official had a stern look about him "That and a whole lot more young Theo. You need to brief us as much as we need to brief you."

Theo was escorted down a ramp way under the main stadium concourse, to a secure garage where a fleet of Mercedes people carriers were waiting. He was guided to get into the third vehicle. Mr Bassein and Mr Newman joined him. The van quickly departed via a series of tunnels that exited at a security gate well outside the boundaries of the Games stadium.

Theo seeing the elaborate system of tunnels looked confused.

Seeing his expression, Mr Bassein began to explain "The tunnels we have just taken, are a standard requirement now at all '*The Games*' sites where we have dignitaries and high profile guests such as the President of the United States or your Royal Family. We will arrive at the Athlete village, quite soon"

Sure enough, through the privacy glass, Theo could make out the village in the distance. After a short drive on some public roads, once again, the van passed through a security gate and down a ramp, entering another tunnel, eventually exiting inside the perimeter of the village.

The Frenchman continued "We take all the necessary precautions. Please Mr Newton, if you would follow me"

The driver opened the boot compartment and grabbed an item before moving around and opening the passenger door. Mr Bassein stepped out, followed by Theo who was handed his holdall by the driver, "Thanks" Theo said, taking the bag, he placed the longer strap on his shoulder before unzipping a side compartment and pulling out his mobile phone. The display showed 5 missed calls from his father and multiple text messages.

"I will follow you up to the conference area, I will be five minutes" The Team GB official disappeared leaving Theo with Mr Bassein.

Glancing around, he could see they were behind the main conference building in the athlete village, no one else was around.

Theo followed Mr. Bassein through a rear door to the building. The short corridor had a door to the right marked as '*Stairwell D*' leading to the upper levels. Opposite the stairwell door was a lift.

Mr. Bassein called the lift, the doors slid open and the pair entered.

"We will go to a debriefing room, so we can discuss further your remarkable achievements today, we will cover some media training with you. So you will know how to present yourself and which questions to answer and which ones you should not answer, we will provide you with some standard responses for those questions."

Theo only nodded in reply, he hid the fact he was feeling anxious and very unsure, he just wanted to speak to his dad, besides, this felt too forced.

Arriving at the 4th floor, the lift exited directly into a room containing a conference table with enough chairs to seat 12 people. To the left a window, straight in front double doors of frosted glass embossed with the '*The Games*' logo, and to the right a large projector screen. The room is adorned with framed *'The Games'* memorabilia, photos of legendary athletes frozen in time and medals glinting under spotlights.

"Please take a seat" the Frenchman indicated to a specific spot at the table.

Theo pulled the seat from under the table and sat down. Presented in front of him was a bag of jelly baby sweets, a bottle of chilled water and a bottle of isotonic energy drink. He grabbed the water and downed half the contents before replacing the sports cap and placing the bottle back down. Mr. Bassein opened a locked cupboard, retrieving a laptop, he placed it down on the table and proceeded to wirelessly connect it to the projector.

While Mr. Bassein was preparing his notes, Theo took the opportunity to check the messages on his phone.

Three were from his father;

'Best of luck today son. Whatever happens, remember, I am so very proud of you. Love you. Dad xx'

'OMG THEO!! HOLY SHIT! 8.97 SECONDS! HOW? WHAT! CALL ME WHEN YOU CAN. Dad xx'

'This is going to be too much to handle. Do you want me to fly out? I still can't believe it. Call me. Dad xx'

Theo replied

'Thanks, Dad, no need to come out, the committee & T GB have it sorted. Will call later, too busy right now. Love T x'

Theo chuckled to himself, he considered the pandemonium that he had caused, simply because he did something extraordinary.

Mr Newman entered the room accompanied by three other people. The group sat at the conference table ensuring there was an empty seat to each side of them.

Mr. Newman "Sorry for the delay. Theo, if my call back home is anything to go by, Theo, you have just become the most famous person in '*The Games*' history, if not the history of the world. You are trending. Everyone wants to know who this 20-year-old British athlete is."

Mr. Bassein "If we are ready. Could we each introduce ourselves for the benefit of Mr. Newton here."

"I'll start, I am Chris Newman, I am Athlete and Media liaison for Team Great Britain"

"I am Mei Lin Song, I am the Japanese Director of Communications for the Tokyo Games"

"I am Dr Demitrikov, I am the Athlete performance director for '*The Games*' committee"

"I am Dr Silvia Demarco, I am an advisor to the '*The Games*' committee, and my specialism is the study of performance-enhancing chemicals"

"I am Mr. Bassein, I am the lead Athlete engagement officer for '*The Games*' Committee, and I am also media liaison."

"I am Theo Newton. I am a decathlete representing Team GB, who happened to do a thing today"

Mr Bassein "Thank you. Please, Mr Newton, don't sell yourself short. The thing you have done today. We were not prepared for it. Dr Demitrikov if you would be so kind"

Dr Demitrikov "Theo Newton, '*The Games*' Committee wasn't prepared for the events that unfolded today. We've spent years analysing human performance and predicting incremental improvements. Our model is highly tuned to athlete data. Every race meeting, every athlete, everywhere. We study the data and extrapolate, we have highly sophisticated, high-precision calculations. It tells us when to expect the next performance improvement and gives us a tolerance plus or minus, we can even tell who the athlete is likely to be. But today, your time. It defies our model."

Mr Newman "We don't want to take anything away from your performance. However, we do need some answers. The media are asking some very difficult questions. As Ivan has just said, we were not expecting a new world record in the 100m race this year. You see Theo, The fact that the record has been broken isn't the main issue. It's how it was broken and who broke it."

Dr Demitrikov "We expect records such as the 100m to be broken by established specialists, that is, we expect someone who trains specifically for the 100m, that same person we can see, when we analyse their performances over time, demonstrate a progression, reducing their personal best by fractions of a second, bringing them closer and closer, to the point where and when all the conditions are perfect, that they finally break the record. Mr Bassein if you could be so kind" He pulls up a slide on the screen displaying a graph of 100m world record times.

Dr Demitrikov "You've catapulted us into uncharted territory. Look here" Using a laser pointer he highlights the gradual curve of the 100m records, it progresses with a dotted line beyond the 9.58 seconds of the prior record. The vertical axis scale stops at 9.25 seconds. He continues "You have taken us off the chart. We are talking about a sub-9-second 100m. That's... superhuman"

Theo "I understand what you are saying. Perhaps your model doesn't consider all potential data points?"

Dr Demitrikov "Our model predicted the 9.58 world record down to a hundredth of a second, it predicted when it would happen and by whom. We have all data points covered"

Mr Bassein "What we need to know Theo, because the future of Athletics is at stake here, is, have you taken any performance-enhancing chemicals? Or have you ingested anything different? Anything. Your world record stands, we could not detect any known substances in your blood, urine or saliva. Dr. Demarco please"

Dr Demarco "We don't want to call you a cheat. The scientific evidence before us says you are not a cheat, that is we could not detect any known performance-enhancing substances and yet your record defies human explanation. We did detect some unusual blood chemistry however having looked at your medical history, we can see when you were a young child there was a note regarding some undocumented blood elements, specifically a new blood group. Can you elaborate on this?"

"You are right. When I was a baby, the doctors thought that I had a rare blood disorder or blood group, they were not certain, but in follow-up tests, they were not able to verify those results. I was discharged with no follow up"

Dr Demitrikov "Maybe there's a genetic outlier? A unique combination of fast-twitch fibres and lung capacity. Or perhaps it's something else entirely."

Theo "What if it is my hard work and dedication paying off"

Dr. Demarco "Hard work alone doesn't explain it. This performance does not reflect your personal best. If this record stands and it's my job to find reasons why it can't, we're entering a new era, Theo. An era where the impossible becomes possible. It's both exhilarating and terrifying. But based on everything we know, what you have done today, can only be explained by one fact and one fact alone. We will be keeping a close eye on you."

Theo "So you think I cheated?"

Mr. Newman "Theo, you are innocent until proven guilty. Please can I ask you to stop this discussion? Can we move on to the media awareness"

Theo remained in the conference room for another 30 minutes while briefed on how to respond to media questions, with specific emphasis on ensuring he remained true to the spirit of '*The Games*' and Team GB and not to be drawn into unnecessary debate or speculation. Which he found ironic given what he recently had to endure.

The media engagement, as predicted was complete madness. The frenzied display of the news reporters was akin to crowds of screaming fans during a Beatles performance, except the screaming was of questions directed to Theo, everyone wanted their question answered.

The barrage lasted an hour and varied greatly, from questions like

'*Do you believe you are the greatest athlete of all time*'

'*Do you think you should run in the 4 by 100m metre relay for Team GB*' to the ridiculous like

'*Are you an alien?*' Or '*Do you think you should run backwards next time to give other athletes a fair chance?*'

In the main the questions were fair and balanced, asking if Theo would repeat his amazing first-day performance tomorrow or will he consider participating in the individual sprint from now on, to the last question Theo had already considered his answer.

"I am a decathlete, I will always be a decathlete. Athletes who dedicate themselves to being the best they can possibly be, at their chosen event, deserve nothing less than my complete respect, I know what is involved, in training and with the complete commitment they, **WE** give. However, I am a multi-event athlete. I strive to be the best multi-event athlete, that is not to say, that individual event athletes, with the correct support from coaching, physio and medical couldn't move to multi-events, I am sure they could transition quite comfortably, it's about the mindset, focus, dedication. Once you have that. Anything is possible. It is up to the individual event athletes to bring their A-game. I have thrown down the gauntlet."

It was almost 11:30 p.m. by the time Theo was back in his room. It was approaching 7:30 am back home. He wanted to sleep but needed to speak with his dad more.

He tried to keep the call as short as possible, but it was past midnight by the time his dad hung up. Always full of sage advice, Theodore advised his son to do his best on the final day of the decathlon, as, after all, the cat was out of the bag and there was no way it was going back in. Theo had one goal now, regardless of what else transpired, he wanted to be the first person to break the 10,000-point barrier in the decathlon, he was less than 4,000 points away from the world record with 5 events to go.

Theo slept soundly, his alarm waking him at 6 a.m., giving himself an extra thirty minutes in bed, unusually, he didn't want to get up. He lay there, gazing at the ceiling, considering the events that he was to participate in. He **knew** he could break at least 3 more world records, the 110m hurdles were a surefire candidate. His tall frame could skip over the barriers as if they weren't there. The javelin was the event that he had previously come closer to the world record of, than any other event, another record surely. Finally, there was the decathlon points record.

Theo climbed out of bed, deciding to skip a gym workout, he instead showered then headed down for breakfast. On entering the cafeteria, there was deafly silence, everyones gaze was on Theo as he entered. A group of athletes from Greece stood and started to clap, this was soon followed by the contingent from Australia, then Canada, eventually, the whole room was abuzz with cheers and congratulations.

A Team GB coach came over to Theo, shook his hand and asked what he wanted for breakfast. He was eager to assist the newest superstar athlete, a completely polar experience to the previous day, where he was just another unknown athlete, representing the team, with little prospect of achieving anything.

Breakfast was an eye-opening experience, before today and during his time in Japan, he had probably encountered a dozen people who he thought had a genuine interest in him. Now everyone wanted to get to know '*The world's greatest athlete*'. He didn't pass judgment on any of them, although he did find it bizarre that other athletes, some of them gold medal winners, were asking for his autograph.

Day two went almost entirely as Theo expected. Starting with the 110-metre hurdles, his was the final race of the sprint. He had been drawn in lane 8 closest to the crowd. Once again, as if a repeat of the previous day, Theo was out of the blocks in 0.10 seconds and kept surging away from the rest of the field. He finished before the second-placed runner had cleared the final hurdle. A new world record time of 12.50 seconds, 1177 points bringing his running total to 6342.

Unlike the previous day, Theo was allowed to do a lap of honour. Running and clapping, thanking the crowds for their support. Whenever he spotted groups of children, he would head over and have his photo taken proudly draping the Union Flag over his shoulders. It became clear to him, that he was an icon, he was adored, but he had an impact on the children, and he wanted them to remember. Maybe give them the ambition to drive for their own success.

Next came the discus throw, finishing first with 1007 points. Pole Vault, he finished 3rd with 1004 points. Then came the event he had been waiting for, the javelin. A throw of 62.3 metres would put him equal on points to the world record with one event remaining.

Theo new he had a big throw in him. Ever since his first dreams, as a hunter-gatherer, carrying a spear, he knew he could throw, he had been practising most nights in his sleep. Sighting a deer or mammoth, gauging the wind direction and speed, accounting for gravity pulling the spear to earth. He had honed his skill. He knew he was about to do something superhuman.

Theo's first-round throw was good, some would say it was exceptional, with 62.4 metres, 774 points and a new decathlon world record sealed. He could have stopped there. No one else could catch him, the gold was his and he still had the 1500 metre race to go. But Theo, as if he hadn't proven enough already knew he hadn't finished writing the story.

Theo picks up his javelin from the cage and walks across to his starting point on lane 3. The crowd holds its collective breath, eyes fixed on the towering figure near the edge of the javelin runway. The sun dipped below the stadium roof, leaving only the stadium floodlights to fully illuminate the field. The air crackles with anticipation.

Theo whispers to himself "This is it"

He grips the javelin, its sleek form, an extension of his arm. The weight feels familiar, years of training and dreams etched into muscle memory. He stares ahead looking for the distance markers: 70m, 80m, 90m, 100m.

Raising both hands, he begins to clap, motioning the crowd to join in. The stadium begins to boom with clapping and foot stomping.

He steps back, the javelin poised behind him like a lethal arrow. His heart races, adrenaline surging. The crowd erupts to another level of noise. Theo charges forward, his legs pumping. At the last moment, he drives his right hip forward, uncoiling his right arm and unleashing the full force of his strength, the javelin is released at the perfect angle, slicing through the air in a blur of kinetic energy.

The javelin soars skyward, defying gravity as it clings to the air as if it were a comet streaking across the sky. It passes 98.48m, a new world record, but it isn't down yet, impossibly it passes the 100-metre mark.

The javelin lands, embedding itself deep in the turf. The measurement officials scramble, their laser rangefinders confirming what the crowd believe they have witnessed. The display illuminates 'One hundred and four metres NWR'

Theo kneels in front of the fowl line. He looks to the sky and thinks of his mother. The crowd begin to chant his name with thunderous celebration.

At that moment, Theo knew he was more than an athlete, he was a symbol, a testament to human potential, transcending boundaries. The world was now watching, wondering what other barriers might fall.

Theo had added a further 1418 points to his score, 229 points shy of the 10,000-point target. In the next event the 1500m, he could afford to leisurely jog around the almost 4 laps of the track in a sedate 6 minute 8 seconds and break hit target points. He considered it for a moment, he could continue his laps of honour, but thought it selfish and inconsiderate to other runners, if not also very arrogant. Besides, maybe he had another record to break.

Theo left the track area, to prepare for the final event. He considered his game plan. He was an exceptional mile runner, easily capable of breaking the once elusive 4-minute barrier. But this was a slightly shorter distance and he only had one target time in mind.

While he was stretching, Mei Lin Song, the Japanese director of communication for the games whom he had met the previous day came over.

"Theo, that was an incredible performance. Congratulations on your four new world records. Yet I feel you are not finished?"

"Oh, how so?"

"Your current 1500 metre personal best is 3 min 35 seconds, No?"

Theo smiled. Thinking to himself, here is a beautiful girl, that has researched his performances, more than for professional reasons "You are correct."

Mei Lin Song "So if I have you correct, you will be close to obliterating a decathlon milestone, I think you know what I mean"

Theo "Very good Mei Lin. But I would need to knock over 10 seconds off my PB. I think four world records are enough, don't you think?" Theo gave her one of his cheeky winks.

Mei Lin "Good luck Theo. Here is my card, if you are ever back in Tokyo, give me a call"

Theo "Thanks. I will do." Theo placed the card in the side pocket of his bag.

An announcement came over the speakers for all decathlon athletes to make their way back into the stadium for the 1500m. Theo placed his bag on the luggage trolley. As he made his way out of the warm-up area, athletes from all nationalities congratulated him, wishing him the best of luck for his final event. Several stopped him requesting selfies. He obliged, although inside, it irritated him, he wanted to be accommodating, but he also wanted his space, as athletes, surely they also got that. *'Perhaps not'* he thought to himself.

The time seemed to fly by and before they knew it, the athletes were lined up ready for the final event in their discipline. Theo was positioned in lane one. He had his game plan figured out, it involved shock and awe.

As soon as the '**go**' command was fired, Theo took off at almost a sprint, some commentators would suggest too fast a start. By the end of the first bend he was already 20 metres clear of the rest of the pack. He slowed his pace slightly and settled into a 58-second lap pace. For Theo, it was a comfortable pace, but none of the other decathletes were 1500 track specialists. He continued to pull away. By the time he reached the bell indicating 1 lap remaining, he had already lapped several runners and was bearing down on the remainder. The timer indicated 2 minutes and 36 seconds for 1100m.

Theo began to wind up the pace, faster and faster, he surged past the 4th place runner on the penultimate bend. Down the back straight he could see the 2nd and 3rd placed runners, they were no more than 30 metres ahead.

The track stretched out before him, every stride pounding against the rubber surface rewarded him with positive forward motion. His lungs were burning, and his legs, after two days of competition were aching. But seeing how close the runners were, gave him a boost of adrenaline. He was closing the gap.

He visualised it. The moment he would speed past, then, tunnel vision in full effect. His heart was racing, not only from the exertion but from the thrill of the competition. The crowd's roar amplified, they could see what was unfolding before their eyes. The impossible. Theo seemed to use the energy of the crowd as his own, his posture seemed to relax, and his stride lengthened and became more controlled.

The crowd were desperate, willing Theo to close on the two runners ahead, who were actually behind him in the race. He had studied their form, their weaknesses. He knew their rhythm and their breaking point.

Theo's vision narrowed further, the world compressed into a point, the track, the crowds, all fading. It's just them and him. He was 5 meters away from them going into the final bend of the track.

Their shoulders were now inches away, he could smell their sweat, and hear their laboured breaths. His legs screamed, but he dug deeper, his body following the commands he imposed upon it. Completely fuelled by adrenaline, the lactic acid coursing through his veins, burning his muscles, a primal force of 'fight or flight'.

Then it happened, his muscles drawing much-needed energy from deep within, unlocking another gear. He seemed to accelerate as if they were standing still, past the pair of runners, on the exit of the final bend and into the home straight. Theo was eating up every metre of the track as if he enjoyed it.

The gap between 1st place and 2nd grew even larger, as Theo moved into a full sprint, the timer blurred by a sweat-covered gaze. His final surge is to be etched into the memory of everyone watching forever. He crossed the line, 450m ahead of 2nd place. He hadn't just beaten his competition. He had destroyed every athlete that had come before him.

The track timer was reading 3 minutes 22.5 seconds, shaving three and a half seconds off the previous 1500m world record, giving him 1247 points towards his final total.

With a final score of 11018, Theo Newton hadn't just broken the 10,000-point decathlon ceiling, he smashed through it and kept going. Finishing more than 2,000 points ahead of second place, the records kept falling.

He collapsed onto the track, lying on his back his chest was heaving, gasping for air, his vision blurred with sweat and disorientation. At one point he felt so faint that he thought he was going to pass out, but he clung to consciousness as if a tangible object he could grip and hold tight.

Slowly, his breathing settled as the air rhythmically filled and emptied his lungs at a controlled pace. His heart slowed. He wiped his eyes with a towel that had been handed to him. Returning to his feet the crowd applauded. Reverberating, **'Theo Newton'** chants filled the arena. He raised his hands above his head and clapped. Turning to the crowd nearest him, he bowed as he waved in thanks for their support.

It was over, he was the 2021 Tokyo Games Champion, with 4 individual track and field event word records and the decathlon world record to his name. The fastest-ever legal reaction time to the go command, twice. The largest ever margin of victory in the 1500m and points difference between 1st and 2nd place in the decathlon.

Even if he didn't want to admit it, he was now the greatest athlete of all time. But there would be questions. Fall out, because of one man who pushed the boundaries of human achievement.

Theo completed a slow walk of the track thanking the crowd, getting selfies with children and being hugged by random people, who just wanted to touch the fastest man on earth. The cheering never seemed to cease by the time he arrived at the Athlete tunnel. Walking towards the warmup zone, countless other athletes congratulated him, several athletes took the opportunity to kiss him on the cheek.

Before he could get to his bag, Mr Newman intercepted him,

"Sorry Theo, the committee would like to carry out additional tests. If you would like to come with me. While I have you, the team selection committee were wondering if you would consider taking a spot in one of the relay events. The 100m heats are tomorrow and the 400m heats the following day."

"I am honoured, but I am going to decline. Both our relay teams are fantastic and it would be quite poor form, to drop one of the lads who have put the work in to make it this far, potentially denying them a medal chance. Sorry it's a no"

"It's ok. I had to ask. But expect someone else to ask the same question before the final"

They walked in silence to the testing area at which point Mr Newman apologised and excused himself. After a few minutes, the tests were performed and Theo was excused. Heading back to the athlete area he bumped into Mei Lin Song,

"Theo, we should stop meeting like this. Congratulations. I knew I was right about you." She brushed his shoulder, wearing a congratulatory smile.

"If I didn't know any better, I would have said you were flirting with me."

"Sorry, was I that obvious?"

"Are you free now? Maybe we can go grab something to eat! I don't know about you but I feel like I haven't stopped all day." Mei Lin giggled as she shyly nodded.

"Great. I do need to shower and change."

"Meet me on level 3, the dignitary suit, in say 30 minutes?"

"OK. See you soon." Mei Lin leaned in and kissed Theo on the cheek, before coyly walking off, she looked back over her shoulder, her eyes wide open with a beaming smile.

CHAPTER 12 HOME

AUGUST 8 2021 9:03 P.M.

Hatred stirreth up strifes; But love covereth all transgressions
Proverbs 10:12 ASV

Theo spent the remaining time he had in Tokyo, between being interviewed by what seemed to be the entire media circus attending '*The Games*' and enjoying Mei Lin Song's company. They had become quite enamoured with each other.

At first, some of the questions from the media caught him off guard, but he remembered the briefing training and was able to brush them off with some quick wit or an official statement such as '*No Comment*' or '*No decision has been made*'.

Many of the questions were quite brutal, especially those presented by the USA and Chinese media. Accusations of cheating, doping or other forms of foul play were directed towards Theo and Team GB. The delegation from Brightwell Islands submitted a formal complaint to '*The Games*' committee towards the end of the tournament.

However, thanks to Mei Lin Song's intervention, an official '*Games*' statement was released to the media unequivocally supporting Theo's innocence, stating that no known or suspicious substances were detected in his blood or urine specimens and that an independent 3rd party also confirm no fowl play.

But the jealousy continued, abroad, various media outlets were publishing lies and false allegations about Theo. In the end, the pressure was that intense, that Team GB rescinded the request for Theo to represent the nation in the relays. His attendance was presenting a media storm.

The public expected Theo to attend the closing ceremony, but for his own safety, he was quietly taken out of the country. His farewell to Mei Lin was hurried. She promised that once the tournament were wound down, she would fly to London.

Theo arrived back home a little after 9 p.m. on the 8th of August, his games were now officially over. He was relieved to be home, after unlocking the front door, he dropped his holdall in the passage and went through to the living room.

"**THEO**" Theodore on seeing the champion enter the room jumped to his feet and embraced his son, giving him the biggest of bear hugs, which continued for what seemed like an eternity. Louise got up from her seat and welcomed her stepson home.

"It feels like we haven't spoken much the last few days"

"Yeah. Sorry dad! Have you been keeping up with some of the stories? The team have been trying to shield me, coaching me on dealing with what is being said, but, to be honest none of it bothers me."

"But still, they are wondering, how were you able to accomplish what you did? They do have that right, even if, they have taken it too far and it becomes a witch hunt" Theodore tried to hide from his son what he was feeling. He knew the British press would continue to hound the 'Fastest man in history', never relenting. He wanted to protect his son, as his father he had that responsibility but he also wanted his son to take ownership of his battles.

"You know I don't keep secrets from you, so you understand that whatever this destiny is, I am getting stronger. Every time I had another test, I thought, what are they going to discover, what don't I know? I was both scared and excited."

"I get that son. You did amazing. Whatever the reason, I am here for you. I just wish I was out there with you. But you have grown, I see that, even though it's only been a few weeks, you **have** matured"

"And I met someone, I was going to tell you when we talked the other day, but I couldn't get a break. Her name is Mei Lin Song, she is Japanese-Korean, her mother is Japanese and her father is Korean. She works for the Japanese Games Committee. She is a few years older than me, 24 actually, she went to the University in Cambridge."

"About time you met someone. Congratulations"

Louise was beaming with the news "When will we meet her?"

"She will be coming over here soon. Once the games have fully wound down, reports submitted, that kind of thing"

"Have you eaten?"

"Flight meal, about 6 hours ago. So yeah, I could eat."

"Good. We have ordered food. Pizza ok?"

"Perfect. I'll take a shower. Won't be long" Just as Theo motioned for the door, his father, grabbed his shoulder

"Wait. Can I see it?" Theo went out into the hallway, routed around his bag and found the medal. He placed it around his neck and walked back to the living room.

Theodore upon seeing the large gold medal around his son's neck, began to well up and gently sobbed "I.. I.. knew you did it, but, seeing the medal, it makes it so much more real" Theo removed the medal and handed it to his dad, he leaned forward and kissed his forehead, before turning and heading upstairs for his shower.

Theo didn't take long in the shower. Returning to his room, he flicked on his TV, watching while drying himself. A sports channel was playing.

'Just in. We have been hearing reports that the Brightwell Islands appeal to the 'The Games' committee has been rejected. You may remember, that the Brightwell Islands team submitted a protest appeal to 'The Games' Committee on grounds that Theo Newton was illegitimate to represent Team GB. That appeal was overturned and it has been confirmed that Theo's representation for his country was indeed legal.'

"Like it was ever in doubt" Theo muttered out loud.

'Continuing with Theo Newton, we will shortly be speaking to a former American athletics timing official who suggests that Theo Newton twice jumped the gun, in his 100m and 110m Hurdle record-breaking runs. That coming up soon.'

Theo clicked the TV off, dressed and headed back downstairs.

"It seems there is an American who is claiming I had two false starts and that my records shouldn't stand."

"I wouldn't let it bother you. It's done now, if the committee deem your run legal, they can't reverse that now. Can they?" Louise looked to her husband, Theodore just shrugged his shoulders before looking towards Theo "I don't think they can. Unless, I suppose, if they were to do a more thorough analysis of the start, they would have done that before now.

The problem is son, there are lots of jealous people out there, they hate you for what you have achieved. They are angry and fearful, they are lashing out because they feel weak and powerless. It will blow over. But it may be a while yet" Just then there was a knock at the door.

"That will be the pizza"

"I'll get it" Theo grabbed the money that had been placed on the mantle and went to the door. Opening it he was confronted by a cameraman and a reporter with a microphone, he spoke in an American accent.

"Mr Newton, Karl Bleeker live with East Coast Hard Hitting Headlines. There is increasing unrest from the world after your superhuman performance in this year's Tokyo Games. More nations are uniting to demand answers. Can you tell us, Did you cheat? If so how did you get past the doping tests?"

"**NO**, but I am more than happy to answer all of your questions in full at a more convenient time. It is late. I have just returned home from a very long flight and am looking forward to a relaxing evening with my family who I haven't spent time with for several weeks"

"I am sorry Mr Newton, but that will not do, the world demands answers from you. We do not believe that you did not cheat. How did you do it?"

"Listen to me, I am only going to say this one time. I did not cheat. I train, I get fast, I get strong, I am dedicated. I break records. **END OF**. Now please take yourself and your camera and get off our property" The reporter ignored the request and continued.

"Many athletes before you and after you will have trained with more dedication than you and yet will amount to nothing. Tell us your secret. You owe it to the world to tell us how you did it?" At that moment Theodore came to the door

"**LISTEN**. Why don't you do some real journalism and investigate why so many athletes have died due to cardiac-related events? My son has told you he has not cheated. He has requested you leave our property now. Now this is me telling you, **LEAVE**!"

Carl Bleeker instead persisted "And joining us we have Theodore Newton, the father of the cheat Theo Newton. Tell us Mr..." Theodore ripped the microphone out of the hand of the reporter, flicked the off switch, dropping the device. He proceeded to pull a can of spray paint from his back pocket and began coating the lens with the black chemical.

"You can't do that. We have a right" the reporter protesting

Theo stepped back from the doorway as his father shut the door in the reporter's face.

"Can you believe the front of that guy?"

"That was tame compared to some of what I had to endure. But thanks, Dad."

"That felt good. Do you think the spray paint was too much?"

"Possibly, they will probably come after you for damages. But I appreciate it."

'They can try. But it is water soluble. I will come right off. Do you think they have gone?"

"I can't sense them" The doorbell rang. Theodore glared at his son "You sure?'

"That's the pizza" Sure enough at the doorway was the pizza delivery. Returning to the living room, the steaming boxes in hand he continued "Is what you said correct?"

"About?"

"The cardiac deaths of athletes"

"Afraid so son. Jim Birch, do you remember him from the gym? he passed away a couple of weeks ago, from a sudden heart attack, he was only 42, fit with no prior health issues. His passing shocked us all. But then it was reported that some athletes in Tokyo had sudden cardiac arrest and didn't make it. I have been looking into it and there is a very worrying trend which goes against the normal background rate."

"I am so sorry Dad. Do you think it's Covid related?"

"Possibly, could be vaccine related, could be something else environmental, we may never know... But, this intrusion into your life from the media, has to stop. I don't know what we can do."

"They know where I live, they won't stop coming here. Probably know where you work too. They will know where I train." Theos usually composed demeanour was showing cracks, no amount of media preparedness could coach the overwhelming stress and emotional load away.

"Nothing we can do right now. Forgot about it for this evening. Let us eat our pizza."

The rest of the evening was a peaceful one. The TV was shut off, except for Theo sharing some photos of Tokyo and Mei Lin on his phone. After that, everyone turned their phones off, keeping all external intrusions to a minimum.

Theo enjoyed sharing his experience of the greatest show on earth. Talked about how amazing Japan was and how friendly everyone was, until the last few days when things started to get heated.

"You think you would want to do another '*Games*' then? You are only 20, the next one is in 3 years, and you could potentially take part in another three or four '*Games*'."

"If I remain good enough and if other things don't take over my life. I will be concentrating on my PhD. Who knows. I have already been approached by various companies wanting me to represent their brand. I am not going to." Theodore was surprised by his son's revelation

"Why? I mean, I agree with you. Given what you are going through, I don't blame you."

"I don't want to lie. I don't want to solicit myself, prostitute myself so to speak, representing a brand or product that I don't use, like or support, no matter how much money they pay me. I have higher values than that. I am not an influencer. Right now I wear a pair of training shoes made by a German company, next time, I might buy something from America or even the UK. I don't have brand loyalty. And for me to represent a brand, well it will be seen as me endorsing them, their products, their policies and behaviour, good or bad."

"Spoken like the Newton you are. But let me ask you this. You represented Team GB. You represented our nation. How is that any different? When you think about it, Who do you think you are representing when you Run for Great Britain or England? Is it an honest reflection of your heritage? Your identity? Your beliefs? You could have represented Jamaica, I was born there or Brightwell Island, your grandmother was born there. You could have represented Ireland, your Mam was born there, and we found out that her parents were Italian and French, technically, you could have represented either of those countries. But you were born and raised in England." Theo considered his dad's question for a moment before responding.

"That is a fair point. I don't believe in the political party running our government. So, I don't necessarily believe in a lot of what our current government stands for or its policies. I do feel multi-cultural, I embrace the Jamaican in me and it saddened me when Brightwell Islands, a nation so close to my Jamaican heritage, tried to make my representation illegitimate. We live in London, a metropolis of cultures, religions and beliefs, while I don't follow or even understand most of them, It enriches our culture beyond measure, but, it also taints and dilutes it, especially when you consider some of the more intolerant or orthodox behaviours, of which a large portion does come from people who believe they have a fundamental right to be British, because their ancestors going back generations lived here. I was born here because of a chance of luck, someone who is living day to day, struggling for food, water and shelter may curse their life and look at me with envious eyes. But because they don't live here, does that give us the right to deny them a more prosperous future?"

"You kind of moved away from my original question a bit there. But I do know what you mean. It's all driven by politics, by greed, by self-preservation, by racism, by xenophobia, by bigotry, by survival. Nothing will change until it is confronted globally under a united front. You may or may not agree with me on this, but my belief is that it all stems from religion. Remove religion and what happens?"

"Now Dad, that is very much a philosophical question. And one you propose far too late at night for me to answer. I am off to bed."

"Night son, think on your answer."

The next morning Theo was unusually late to rise. Not wanting to disturb his son, he left a note on the kitchen bench and headed out with Louise to one of their latest community hub projects in the South of London.

It was 7:30 a.m. by the time Theo woke. He climbed out of bed and pulled open the curtains. The view sent a chill down his normally calm demeanour. Outside the house were several TV news vans, and dozens of reporters were waiting. Fortunately, they appeared to have not noticed him opening the curtains, they were all too busy laying cables and adjusting camera rigs.

'This should be amusing he thought to himself'

The car wasn't on the driveway, so he assumed that either his dad or Louise or both had left the house early. After visiting the bathroom and brushing his teeth, he went downstairs. There were no signs of anyone up and about. Going into the kitchen he discovered the note from his dad.

'Got up early, busy day in Streatham with the new hub. You weren't awake and I didn't want to disturb you. We have headed out, taking the car and will be parking at the station, getting the train from there. Will be late home. If you are at a loose end, come join us. Otherwise maybe best to stay low for now. Love dad x'

Theo considered what his dad was saying about staying low

'I don't think I'm going to hide away from the world. Can't go out the front of the house. How far is Streatham anyway?'

He went back to his room, switching his mobile on. Within a few moments, it started to buzz and ping with messages and notifications.

The first message he read was from Mei Lin.

'Theo. Hope you are well, seeing some craziness on TV. Lots of complaints are being lodged with the committee. Nothing of any credibility or substance. Love Mei Lin'

He considered the message, however, it was the sign-off that caught his attention *'Love Mei Lin'* first time anyone other than his dad had used love. Did she consider herself his girlfriend? They hadn't discussed where their relationship was going.

The next message he read was from a contact at Team GB, Gemma Stonehouse.

'Hi Theo. We are bringing in consultation with our chief council, Lord Blenkinsop KC. He will draft a legal response which we will issue to the media, effectively a cease and desist to stop the invasion of your privacy. We will arrange a date to meet and discuss. Gemma Stonehouse'

Theo didn't consider the message other than it was about time the ante was upped.

Next were notifications from his installed news apps, he stopped on one, he stared at the screen in disbelief, not believing what the headline was stating.

'Dr from Theo Newton's past has revelations about the record-breaking athlete's past ***'Theo may be an alien'*** *read more'*

Theo couldn't believe the headline, clicking the notification brought up the full article, however, he could only read the first paragraph, trying to continue he hit a paywall requiring a subscription. The newspaper in question was from a sleazy organisation that prides itself on trash and sensational headlines. He wouldn't dwell on it further.

He brought up the maps app and calculated how far Streatham was from home, 14 miles.

'That's OK, a gentle run, a couple of hours tops with traffic.'

Theo went back down to the kitchen and made a protein shake which he drank without stopping. Showered and changed he put on some running gear but, although it was hot outside, chose a long-sleeved hooded top which while designed as an outer layer was more for winter training. It was a strange choice for a summer run, except it was hooded and provided a built-in face mask. In these COVID times, no one would think twice, it would provide a degree of anonymity, essential as almost everyone he would encounter would almost certainly recognise him without it.

The only thing Theo needed to consider now, was how to get out of the house, without the press, who were camped outside his front door seeing him.

He went through to his father's room and looked out of the window, the view looked over the conservatory roof and out to the garden. There was maybe a 30-metre stretch of grass and plants before a mature tree sat at the boundary between his garden and the garden behind. A 6-foot fence lay in between. He didn't know the neighbours who owned that house. Looking to the left and right of his garden were his other neighbours, each with perfectly manicured lawns, there was not enough cover.

He considered his only option was to go over the fence at the bottom of his garden into the one opposite and exit onto the parallel street. He sent his dad a message explaining he was on his way and that he would run to Streatham.

It was a little after 8:25 a.m., wearing a small backpack, Theo could see no activity in the house opposite. It was now or never. He jumped beneath the tree, caught a branch and swung himself up like a gymnast working the asymmetrical bars. Balanced on the limb of the tree, he had a clear view of the garden in front of him, to the left of the house was a passage leading to an open garden gate.

He leapt from the tree, landing on the top of one of the fence's upright supports, the fence swayed, before settling. Theo remained balanced. He could see the run to the gate was unimpeded. He vaulted from the fence and charged down the lawn to the passage, through the gate, down the driveway and onto the street, he didn't slow until he was on the next street.

'Made it. Don't think I was seen.' He thought.

Theo proceeded to head in the direction of Wormwood Scrubs and onward via Hammersmith Hospital. Rather than take the shortest route, he opted to cross the river at Hammersmith and head towards the fields of the London Wetland Centre. He aimed to use as much parkland as possible.

He followed the Putney Embankment on the riverside of the Thames. Following Putney Bridge Road to Wandsworth and onward to the common. At 9:37 a.m. He stopped at the cafe in Wandsworth Common to use the toilet and message his father to let him know he was only a mile away.

Setting off again, He followed the path towards the station, then entered the second section of the common towards Balham Park Road. Before reaching the road, there was a short section of tree coverage, Theo had a sudden and uneasy sensation of familiarity. He felt faint and light-headed. He was uneasy on his feet. Struggling to stay upright, gravity took the better of him and he collapsed onto the path. He was out cold. No one was around to witness what happened to him.

CHAPTER 13 AELIOXAR

AUGUST 9 2021 10:10 A.M.

"Our resilience and pursuit of harmony will always prevail"
Zyphorion the Enlightened.

Theo awoke, his head was hurting, and he felt disoriented and nauseated. His vision was blurred and his ears were ringing, as if he was now suffering from tinnitus. He was aware he was lying, the surface beneath him felt soft and slightly damp. He was on his back, he could make out a green light above him. But his legs burned, and so too his arms.

Sharp stabbing pains were hitting his torso in waves. His spine felt as if now, it was an electrical conduit, plugged into the mains supply. He had never experienced such an array of sensations or pain. He was lucid enough to think that he must still be in the park, on his back on the grass and looking up at the tree canopy.

He closed his eyes and concentrated on regulating his senses one area at a time. He began with his breathing, he felt his heart which had been racing, start to slow, and his breathing also began to regulate. He focused on his ears, trying to listen out for the sound of distant cars or the wind in the trees. The ringing stopped but there were no other sounds. He opened his eyes, his vision cleared and his head stopped aching. The pains he had been experiencing, began to dull before ebbing away to a distant memory.

Looking up he could see a green roof, with parallel bands of windows. He wasn't in the park. He sat up leaning on his elbows. Glancing around the room he could see he was in a large circular room. Windows covered every wall, out of the windows it was dark, the light from the room he was in blocking any detail from beyond the windows. On the far side of the room was a single door. The room was very familiar.

'Welcome Theo' a voice spoke to him, but there was no one else in the room. *'You know this room, as you have seen it before'* the voice continued.

"Who are you? Why are you in my head?"

The door opened and a tall humanoid figure walked in, they looked human, but they lacked certain details. Standing about the same height as Theo, they were much thinner, with no obvious muscle definition beneath their skin-tight green clothing. Their hands had five digits but the fingers were longer and had a pale blue colour. Their neck wasn't as thick as a human, but the shape and size of their head were similar in many ways, except they had no ears or hair. Their nose was not as pronounced with only a single nostril. Their colour is the same as their hands, a pale blue.

'This is not our true form, some of us have chosen to change our appearance, to be closer to what you are accustomed to. I am known as Baruch'

Theo stared at the alien, although it all felt familiar "I do remember this place. Twice before I have seen it, twice in dreams, or I thought they were dreams. Where am I?"

Baruch now speaking out loud "You are on one of our home worlds. In your language, we call this planet *'Genetrix-7X'*, it is our seventh mother world, located 444 of *'your'* light years from planet Earth, we know your planet as *'Terrioxia'*. This is in a part of ***'Extherix'*** you would call the Pleiades."

Theo "Extherix? And the Pleiades is a young star cluster, you must be quite a new civilisation?"

Baruch "We are very much an ancient civilisation. Much older than even your Earth. Extherix is what we call, Space or the Universe. The Pleiades are a young cluster, but we have the opportunity to seed life in this system when conditions are right."

"Seed life. Did you seed life on Earth?"

The alien appeared willing to answer Theo's many questions. "We do seed life on planets where life has not itself taken hold, where life will thrive but the conditions were not quite right. On Earth, life thrived by itself, but conditions proved to be a challenge, many times we have seen your planet taken to the brink of annihilation. Times we have intervened."

"Why have you brought me here? What is it that you want with me? Why me?"

"Many questions young Theo."

"This is my first alien encounter, so there is that'

"But it isn't your first. It is the first that you will consciously remember"

Theo was shocked by the revelation, however, he knew in his heart that what the alien was saying was true "**WHAT**?" He paused, thinking before continuing "This is all starting to make sense now."

"You are everything we hoped for, you have a brilliant mind."

"Do you want to start from the beginning? Fill in the missing parts of the puzzle."

"We are the '*Aelioxar*'. It means life bringers. We are masters of genetics, an ancient civilisation, our earliest records, stored in the '*Great Library of Aeliox*' date us to 13 Billion years. Aeliox is our first mother world. It is located in a very distant galaxy. We were guided by '*Zyphorion*', the founder of our modern Aeliox society, but many millions of years ago."

"And you have survived all this time? How?"

"Like many of the civilisations we encounter, we were once troubled by war and the pursuit of conquest, for resources, for power and dominance. First on our home world. Our continents would wage war. The different creeds vying for precious minerals. Between the periods of unrest, we would advance. We developed space travel. But, we took our wars with us. We settled new worlds only to devastate each other as we did on the continents of Aeliox. We irradiated countless worlds, all because of our petty differences. But then our great '*Ozoxar*' Zyphorion, decreed the path ahead for the Aelioxar. The '*Ozoxar*' is our elected leader. He was bestowed the title of '*Zypohorion the Enlightened*'. Revered as the most influential of the leaders in Aelioxar history. He was known for his three-eyed vision that allowed him to see beyond the physical realm, which led to many scientific and spiritual advancements for the Aelioxar people.

Zyphorion had exceptional intellect and intuition, from a young age. His third eye was unusually active, and he often spoke of visions of distant worlds and galaxies.

He brokered peace and unity amongst our people. But Zyphorion's greatest achievement was the '*Infinite Harmony Engine*', a device that harnessed the power of cosmic vibrations to provide clean energy and brought about galactic expansion. This invention revolutionised Aelioxar society, leading us into an era of unprecedented prosperity and technological advancement.

Zyphorion also played a crucial role as ambassador, establishing the '*Galactic Council of Peace*', which brought together different alien races to discuss and resolve interstellar conflicts. His diplomatic skills and foresight were instrumental in maintaining peace across our local galactic cluster."

"Just so I understand the facts, your civilisation is billions of years old. And very much like on Earth, your people were xenophobic of other cultures on your planet, you went to war with one another over small things, then in periods of relative peace you advanced, but then war would break out again. You advanced to space and took your wars with you. It sounds very much like home, except we aren't quite as space-faring as that."

Baruch "You are much more advanced than your leaders would let you believe."

"That figures. Do you use an Alcubierre Drive to warp space-time or have you discovered a way to exceed the speed of light"

"At first we used primitive propulsion, but we quickly discovered a way to harness the sub-atomic to remove the mass of a craft. With this new device, we call it, in your language, a '*quantum mass de-scaler*', it gets around, what you would know as the '*Higgs mechanism*', but does not result in the decay of fundamental particles. We could accelerate our craft to tremendous speeds, but we did not need to get around relative time due to the way the device and the '*infinite harmony engine*' interact with space-time due to it having no mass. So we used the drive for exploration and colonisation."

"So then you have resolved the relative time issue?"

"The Infinite Harmony Engine allowed us to create a time lock bubble around a craft by utilising principles of quantum entanglement which your people have not yet fully discovered and the quantum mass de-scaler, we could go anywhere in an instant with no relativity issues of time. The Infinite Harmony Engine functions at the quantum level, we could harness every aspect of physics to our benefit. We are now even able to open doorways to move from point to point, anywhere in the Extherix in an instant."

"Like a Stargate?"

"Exactly like that, although the name is not correct. We can go anywhere we want. Or bring anything we want. It is how we brought you here."

"What about time travel? And what does any of this have to do with Earth and me?"

"Time travel. That is one of the greatest mysteries. You can travel into the future by travelling at the speed of light, but you cannot return. We have the technology to do that, but we see no use for it. It is a one-way trip, it is what we used before our great expansion when we started colonisation. We have a way of going back in time, however, you can only go back as an observer, you cannot interact with the environment or change events, it is because you will have no physical form.

We first documented visiting Earth when it was a new planet, it was in chaos. Your early solar system was unstable, planets had adopted unstable orbits, and your planet Jupiter was to become a binary system sun, but it failed to achieve its critical mass, which worked out favourably for your planet. Terrioxia, Earth was impacted by another planet, your moon resulted and it was this chance impact which helped stabilise your planet, it slowed the planets spin, it stabilised its orbit around your sun. We categorised it as a potential candidate for life. When we returned, enough cometary impacts had occurred to deposit life bringing water and essential metals, Amino acids and other complex carbon chains, giving rise to life.

We sampled the life and were amazed at what we found. We left Earth, returning at intervals to understand the evolutionary process. Earth was thriving. Then it suffered a cataclysm which caused 98% of life to be lost. We implemented our close observer protocol. We built a research station on your moon and helped along some of the surviving species of flora and fauna.

When we were happy life was able to continue, we moved on once again. It was when we returned and first encountered primates, that we understood what our help had assisted in creating. We couldn't help ourselves, we made subtle changes to the primates, giving rise to early hominids. They evolved further. We intervened again and again, Homo sapiens resulted.

But issues elsewhere forced our hand, we had to leave Earth for an extended period. When we returned Homo sapiens were the dominant intelligent life on earth, they were interbreeding with other humans, creating genetic variations, incorporating DNA from Neanderthal and other humans We decided to perform a discrete exercise on a sample of the population. We injected some of **OUR** DNA into some Homo sapiens. Quite a few of our test subjects did not survive as our DNA is different to humans. But after countless trials, we succeeded. Only a few thousand Homo sapiens had our DNA integrated with their own."

"So the alien abduction stories, they are true? It was your species" Theo was both amazed and shocked. He considered his education, his recent master's degree and his upcoming doctoral study of Archaeology. Was that now meaningless? Human history was all wrong.

"Yes and No. I will explain more soon. I will continue.

When we next returned, Homo sapiens thrived, but the other human species did not, they had failed to adapt. Sapiens earned our respect. We were able to track our genetic subjects' offspring. They were still in numbers but were not integrating well with other sapiens."

"How could you track them?'

"Within the genetic code that we implanted, we placed some tracking code utilising a quantum entanglement principle, it's how we found you, Theo. We introduced ourselves in a similar way to how I am introducing myself to you now. We shared some of our knowledge and then left.

In your culture, you would know of those people as Atlanteans."

"**HOLD ON A SECOND!**. Atlantis was real? And just to back up a few chapters, your people are the explanation for the missing link. Humans effectively did just appear out of nowhere!" Theo was excited by the revelation. Here he was with the answer that academics had been struggling to solve for generations. But realising he had no proof. He couldn't go home and reveal the truth, he would be ridiculed, ostracised, losing all credibility.

"There is a lot more. We are the reason for your human evolution and history."

"I am all ears" he was mesmerised by the story, anxious to learn more.

"Atlantis was thriving, they were a peaceful yet advanced civilisation. But then a comet hits the northern continent and brings a cataclysm. Atlantis is destroyed. Almost all of the Atlanteans are killed. We return to earth learning of this and instruct the survivors. We tell them they can not live isolated from the rest of humankind, they need to integrate, share their knowledge and wisdom, teach the meaning of space and warn of the '*snakes*' from above. We teach them how to use the '*gyrotron*', to harness millimetre wave drilling. We loan them some of our technology. We indoctrinated them into stories of gods, of floods, of pestilence and instructed them how to construct more primitive versions of the Infinite Harmony Engine.

They carry out our wishes and start to build what to you would be neolithic structures across the world, telling stories of gods and great serpents of destruction coming from Orion's belt and Sirius.

With our assistance they built great pyramids around the planet which served as primitive infinite harmony engines, they could focus solar and stellar energy by way of harmonic frequencies allowing for elements to be altered by fusion or fission, chemicals to be created or altered to assist in the advancement of their society.

But wars raged on, the climates changed and the technology was lost to time. We removed all of our devices and disabled the infinite harmony engines, hiding their purpose. They would stand as warnings to other space-faring civilisations that Earth was under our protection.

Our surviving humans dispersed around the Earth, integrated and lived with other humans, carrying one secret that they passed on to their offspring. Some of them began to exhibit an unforeseen consequence of the Aelioxar DNA they carried. You will know of these people in your myths and religious teachings. Goliath, Sampson, Jesus, Achilles, Plato, Isaac Newton and many more.

The environment on earth, the ultraviolet radiation, natural gamma radiation, and exposure to the conditions over time, activated various genetic traits in the Aelioxar base pairs. Giving rise to what would be considered godly abilities. Great strength or speed, the ability to heal by touch, manipulation by thought or the ability to read another mind. The ability to control objects with the mind. Every account in human history which was not a hoax is a manifestation of the Aelioxar base pairs being partially active.

Religion arose on earth because we wanted to unite humanity in a belief, to give them purpose, direction and most of all fear. We are the reason you have a bible or other religious text. We did not foresee that it would end up becoming a reason for war, for killing and destruction.

During the Middle Ages and until quite recently in your history, people have been accused of being witches or clairvoyants, and some were executed. They were unfortunate to have had our DNA activated. What we intended to be a blessing was in the end a curse for many people. Some unfortunate people, spontaneously combust, and that was our DNA undergoing a mutation. For the past 10,000 years, we have observed.

We have on occasion carried out tests, to try and fix our error without success. Slowly the number of our humans dwindled, to a few hundred spread across the earth. It was when your mother and your father conceived you, did the miracle truly happened. Both your parents were carriers of our genetic code. Your mother was a recessive carrier and your father was a dominant carrier, he had active traits.

We took your mother and carried out a test on her, early in her pregnancy. We determined that you were the first viable human to carry our DNA to its full potential. We injected your mother with a catalysing compound which when absorbed into your body would initiate a cascade of genetic activation.

You were born with an exceptional mind, as you grew older, your intellect advanced faster than your physical maturity. Eventually, your body would catch up. You developed speed and strength.

We then '*took you*' and implemented stage two of the catalysing process, this would activate all the Aelioxar base pairs, except for various genetic instructions. This gave rise to a limited version of your enhanced speed, strength and perceptions.

Today we initiated the final catalysing process, which will trigger the remaining DNA base pairs. That is why when you woke a short while ago, you were in pain and felt disoriented."

Theo could feel his anger build, he was conflicted, he loved that he was fast and strong, but at what price?

"I am sorry, but your species has interfered in the entirety of human history, we have been one gigantic experiment and you call yourselves enlightened? And then if that is not enough, you are the reason my mother died? You caused her death!."

"We are the reason your species lives to this day, we are the reason you live. We are sorry that some of our choices have not had the intended consequences, but as you will soon see, we have more than made up for it. But please listen, Theo, there is a lot more."

"I can't believe this. **MY LIFE IS A LIE**." He was angry, more so than he had ever experienced before. But it was more than just the revelation, it was the manner of the reveal, Baruch didn't show any emotion, their voice was monotone, lacking any personality. The delivery was so matter of fact "I am just a walking talking human petri dish"

"I see you need a break. Do you require some refreshments or perhaps some rest?"

"A **BREAK**?" He paused. Closed his eyes and controlled his breathing, and slowly he calmed "I take it my father knows none of this. What about my Granddad Levi? What did he know?"

"I will answer your question in good time. Please. I will stop now and leave you to consider all I have presented. By the window to your left there is a device, ask it for whatever you desire and it will provide it."

"You have got to be kidding me. I am still mad at you all"

Baruch exited the room. Theo stood and walked over to the right-hand side of the room and peered through the window and as he followed the arc of the glass, he could see a slight glimmer of light rising on the horizon. As he continued to watch, a second brighter light began to appear on the horizon. It was the binary suns he had seen in his dreams.

CHAPTER 14 EVENT

AUGUST 9 2021 11:00 AM

"Things do not happen. Things are made to happen."
John F. Kennedy Sept. 25, 1963.

Theodore was getting concerned. His son should have arrived a while ago. His last known location was the cafe on Wandsworth Common. Calls to Theo remained unanswered and messages were shown as undelivered, suggesting his phone was off or out of power. The tracking app, that Theo had consented for his father to use, hadn't updated from his last known position.

While he knew his son could take care of himself, he did not like the idea that he would have to.

Theodore speaking to his wife "I am going to take a walk, see if I can locate him."

"OK. You take care of yourself. See you soon"

Theodore exited the building and proceeded in the direction of his son's last known position. It was a hot Monday morning, only a few wispy white clouds dotted what was otherwise a clear blue sky.

Heading down Tooting Bec Road, he joined the common at a cycleway and crossed through the parkland before exiting onto Bedford Hill. Theodore pulled his phone from his pocket and called his son once again, but still no reply. He opened his maps app to check his location in proximity to Theo's last known position, he was nearing where he wanted to be.

He cut down Elmfield Road and across Balham High Road and onto Balham Park Road. The whole journey took a little under 20 minutes. He slowed as he entered the common land behind the park road. There were a couple of paths Theo could have taken, he would need to walk each of them if he had indeed taken this exact route. It was like trying to find a needle in a haystack.

He could sense he was on the right path and that he was getting close. The bond that he and Theo shared transcended rational thinking. He knew his son was still alive, he knew he was safe, he just didn't know where. It was only after a few minutes of walking down a second path that Theodore had found what he suspected.

The grass looked scorched, a circular ring, approximately 3 meters in diameter etched across the path, either side pale yellowing grass, as if it had been bleached by some otherworldly device. Looking up to the canopy above, the trees were showing a similar appearance. The leaves no longer a dark green, would be more familiar to autumn with their yellow or orange tones.

Theodore was certain that his son had experienced another '*event*', there was nothing more he could do. He would have to hope that Theo was ok.

He pulled his phone out and messaged John.

'Theo missing. Suspect another event. Location ///inform.zips.noble same signs as before. Nothing more I can do now, worried this is different to the other times. Heading back to Streatham Hub. T'

Within moments his friend responds.

'Another event? I'll take a look. Stay strong my friend. I'll try and catch you this evening. John'

Anxious Theodore heads back to the hub.

CHAPTER 15 REVELATION

AUGUST 9 2021 11:00 AM

"We can't help everyone, but everyone can help someone."
Attributed to Ronald Reagan 1964

Theo continued to look out the window as he moved to the left side of the room. At the end of the glazed expanse, he noticed the screen which activated as he approached. It was displaying some strange symbols. There were no buttons, no obvious sign of how to interact with the device.

'How about I just ask it, maybe it is that simple.'

"May I have a glass of iced water?" Theo asks aloud

Nothing happened, no lights, no noises, no change to the display.

'Perhaps it's touch screen' he pressed one of the symbols on the screen, but nothing happened.

'I'm sure if Baruch intended me to use this contraption, then its function must be intuitive. How do I ask it for a glass of ice-cold water?'

The device at that moment activated, and the display changed to show what appeared to be a progress bar, continuing to display strange-looking symbols. A shelf emerged from beneath the device followed by a pale blue column of light, as if appearing from no obvious source. Within a second the light was gone and in its place was a transparent vessel of Iced water.

"Ok so it works via telepathy, of course it does, pretty neat. But if I speak what I want, aren't I also thinking it?..." He paused for a moment "I guess this device identifies specific electrical impulses in the brain, recognising speech-based signals located in Broca's area of the frontal lobe and maybe the Cerebellum which coordinates the muscle movement for speech. And I have just realised I am speaking out loud" Theo chuckled to himself.

'This is one weird day. I would like a golden delicious apple'

The device activated once again, however, the light on this occasion was green, and there on the shelf was a golden delicious apple. Theo picked it up, felt it, tossed it into the air and caught it.

'It feels like an apple, it weights like an apple, it looks like an apple'

taking a bite

'It tastes and smells like an apple. But is it an actual apple? Or is it an artificial construct of an apple'

The device activated and began to talk.

"The apple you requested while not grown or cultivated like the fruit on your planet, is indeed an apple. We use the genetic profile from the specimen apple and with its chemical composition, synthesise an exact version. It is identical to the cellular level of the original apple which was coded. It has the same nutritional value and chemical energy of a cultivated apple"

Theo "Absolutely amazing." He continued to think of another question

'What name is given to this device? Are you able to create these objects using the Infinite Harmony Engine?' The machine again answered

Device "This device is known as the '*Quantum Nexus Forge*'. In answer to your question, Yes. The core is based around the Infinite Harmony Engine, the vision of Zyphorion the Enlightened. It focuses particles at a specific harmonic resonance and specific frequencies. Utilising '*extherix*' energy and matter. It converts and structures one form to another."

'How do you create the object? You must utilise some form of a matrix or scaffolding in which the matter is layered and applied?'

"Yes. We utilise quantum field induction in the 4th and 5th dimensions to create a photonic matrix held by the weak and strong forces and the magnetic force. By applying specific frequencies, we can manipulate atomic bonds and mass. When the object is constructed it is transitioned to the 3rd dimension. The exact mechanism cannot be shared with you."

'What if the requested object is not known to you?'

"We will compile a virtual construction based on neural instruction. If sufficient neural instruction exists we will create the object. If sufficient instruction does not exist, we will not."

"This is amazing. Almost like how the device works when they '*Boldly Go*' "

Theo's attention was drawn back to the window, in the time he was focused on the device, he had missed the full binary dawn, the dual suns were now completely over the horizon bathing the amazing city which extended out in front of him in the most extraordinary patchwork of light and shadow. He was witnessing what he could only describe as rainbows cascading across the sky, splitting from their usual full spectrum into individual arcs of colour. As if the air was dense like glass prisms, providing the surreal spectacle. It was as if he was in a dream.

Gazing out of the window, he tried to determine the function of the city there appeared to be no obvious purpose to the buildings, they varied in size only. Their construction was uniform in material and colour, which appeared as a dark grey metal with no obvious windows. It was as if planning was restricted to one design type, which could only increase in scale and no other characteristic.

There were no signs, no symbols. They could be homes or offices, military installations or schools.

Within the confines of the city, he could see no gardens or parks, no streets or roads. No vehicles or aircraft. No people, birds or indeed any other animal.

In the distance, however, he could see waterfalls, lush forests but not limited to greens, reds or browns. The trees from his vantage point must be in the order of hundreds of metres tall, with thick trunks transitioning to deep anchoring roots providing a firm foundation. Behind the forest were mountains.

Theo spun around as he became aware of Baruch re-entering the room, but they weren't alone. With them was another being, they didn't look like Baruch. They stood 7 feet tall, and their skin while initially green, changed, with a fluid-like motion, shifting as if it were a chameleon. They appeared to be wearing the same clothing as Baruch, except it was translucent allowing for the shifting skin tones to remain visible.

They were thin with long skinny legs. Their arms were long, except, for a joint which would be the elbow on a human, the limb branched. They had two sets of forearms leading each to a wrist with long fingers which numbered four and seven respectively on the hands. With One and two thumbs respectively.

Their neck was long and thin which supported their head. The proportions were odd. Their head was maybe 50% larger than it should be for the size of their body. Oval in shape, there was a protruding chin, above which there was no mouth and a flat nose with a single nostril. Above the nose, Theo counted seven eyes. Two of them were positioned where they would be on a human, with a third slightly larger eye middle of the forehead like an image of a cyclops. To the left and right, symmetrically positioned near the temples were two smaller eyes bringing the total to seven. They were all black with no obvious pupil, iris or white of the eye. They looked remarkably similar to the eyes of an arachnid.

Like Baruch, they had no ears or hair.

"This is Exi-zox. I thought it would help you if you witnessed one of our natural forms. She is a type of Aelioxar from our western continent on Aeliox. She differs from other Aelioxar in that she has seven eyes, the

Aelioxar from our eastern and southern continents have three eyes. Those from our southern continent do not possess the ability to camouflage skin. We all have four limbs at our second articulated brachium joint.

Zyphorion the Enlightened was from our southern continent, he had a powerful third eye. Baruch turned to Exi-zox who bowed slightly and then left the room.

"I see you have had success with our energy matter device"

"Yes. It's quite remarkable. I assume it works via a sophisticated AI interface."

"Yes, in part. But I cannot go any further into detail"

"That's ok. I notice you mention that Exi-zox is a female. I didn't want to presume, but what gender are you?"

"I am also female. Like almost all intelligent lifeforms we encounter, we are binary, we have a male and a female. Like your human biology. However, we have eradicated biological errors, for many thousands of generations now, and we have not seen a hermaphrodite or an agender individual born. They are either male or female"

"What about those born as male but identify as female, or vice-versa, or those with no clear gender identity?"

"Ah yes. They are purely constructs of your society. It is part of a greater explanation that I may come onto later. We don't have such problems in our society"

Theo is quite taken aback by Baruch's choice of words "Problems in our society? Peoples beliefs? Their right of choice, of expression, of belief. To you they are problems?"

"Do not concern yourself with such inconsequential issues. You have much to learn and time is pressing on."

Theo now quite irritated "So why am I here? Come on then? Tell me what plans you have for me?"

Baruch stood tall, their face displayed signs of what Theo interpreted as anger, he could feel Baruch radiate pain and loss, for the first time, Baruch had allowed emotion and feelings to show "Theo Newton. You need to remember, that we have existed for billions of years, and we have amassed a wealth of knowledge and understanding. WE HAVE WITNESSED HORRORS. DESTRUCTION. VIOLENCE ON A SCALE THAT YOU COULD NOT COMPREHEND. YOU DO NOT KNOW WHAT AWAITS YOU. OUR CHILDREN.." Theo backed up from Baruch, he was overwhelmed with the intensity of history, of emotion flooding from the alien. Theo fell to the floor, his hands covering his ears, his eyes as tightly closed as he could manage. Baruch invaded Theo's mind, sharing an eternities worth of the Aelioxar's history in seconds. It was too much for Theo, he screamed out "**STOP**"

Baruch bowed their head in shame, and the emotional attack stopped. "I am sorry Theo. Forgive me, but **YOU** are '*The One*'."

Theo's tears streamed down from his eyes. He slowly recovered his breath and his heart which had been racing quickly came to normalise, still panting from exhaustion "No. Don't apologise, I see now" he was on his knees, looking up towards Baruch who looked frail and very much afraid.

"I have to ask. Why me? Somewhere in all of that pain and emotion, I believe you told me. But there was so much."

"Theo. When we visited your world after the great cataclysm of the period you call the '*Younger Dryas*'. We realised how fragile your planet, Our children of humanity was. We had forgotten how dangerous the Extherix was, we had developed tools to keep *us* safe. But humans were still young and fragile. That is why we shared the Infinite Harmony Engine and it is why we shared our DNA. We set in motion a series of events that would take thousands of years to be realised. We wanted to birth a human that would be the embodiment of all of our defensive tools so that humanity would have its own protector. That would guide and when the time came, save humanity.

What I am saying Theo, is you have abilities now that even your most gifted fiction writers could not perceive. When I say you are '*The One*' I mean that. You are the only one, we will not repeat, we will not create another. You are the one who will have to make some choices, very difficult choices. You are the one who will be challenged. You are the one who will represent all life on Terrioxia - Earth. You are the one who will defend it."

Theo nervously laughed "So what I'm like a superhero or something? What if I don't want to be? If I choose not to be?"

"You can choose what you wish. If you turn your back on this gift, you have that right. But I, we the Aelioxar believe you will embrace our gift. The term super-hero does not quite cover the scope of what you can do"

"I don't feel any different, maybe a little tired. If you have given me '*a gift*', I don't know how to use it. What is it I can do exactly?"

"It will take time. The final process was only initiated today. You are still undergoing the final stages of the change. The Aelioxar DNA or rather, the synthetically modified Aeliox DNA is still activating, you cannot leave this room until the process completes. As for what you can do. What would you like to be able to do"

"Is this like three wishes from a genie kind of deal? Or is it more literal? Such as can I fly? Defy gravity? I guess I will be fast and strong. These are the reasons I am a great athlete and have a great mind. Isn't it."

"Yes. Your body began the process in the womb of your mother. You were already enhanced at birth. Your doctors detected some traces of your alien DNA, but the samples themselves began to adjust giving inconclusive or contradictory results. Your body also adapted and was able to shroud its uniqueness in a veil, further tests prevented its detection. If they were to try and sequence your genome, they would find no trace of the Aeliox base pairs."

"I still have human base pairs though? I still have Adenine-Thymine and Guanine-Cytosine base pairs?"

"Yes. Your body is still 98% human base pairs. However, 2% is different. You will be aware that in humans Adenine always pairs with Thiamine and Guanine with Cytosine. The Aelioxar DNA doesn't have such a pairing system. Your new base pairs can mix to give you new traits. You now have four additional bases.

Each of the new bases, can pair with themselves or pair with another base, they can even pair with your human bases. Even the direction of the base pairing creates a new trait. For example, in your human DNA, the order that Thymine and Adenine pair makes no difference, it could be T-A or A-T, however, since the Aelioxar bases go beyond hydrogen bonding and incorporate at the quantum level, your biology is less limited. As such you have 32 new base pair combinations, whereas previously, you only had 2.

Each new combination can give rise to extraordinary traits. Your new bases are '*Zirconine, Vitronine, Spectrine and Quantine.*' At the heart of each base is an element unknown in your world.

Zirconine which protects against regenerative overload. With the enhanced healing that your body is now capable of, you could have suffered from regenerative overload. Your cells could over-divide in response to injuries, leading to unwanted growths or detrimental mutations. This base prevents this from happening. *Zirconine* when paired with itself gives your body an impenetrable skin."

"So I am bulletproof? What about fire? Explosions?"

"Yes. You could sit at the centre of a fission explosion and your molecular structure would be unchanged. I will explain in a moment, but you will feel better for it"

"Sorry? I will feel better for being in a nuclear explosion?"

"Yes. The *Zirconine* base as I stated, would grant you rapid cellular repair capabilities. But in you, it continuously regenerates cells to prevent bodily harm, it also assists in the absorption of radiation, channelling it and storing it like a battery. This gives you your almost boundless energy"

"So I am like a Lithium Ion battery which cannot be pierced?"

"In a very simplified and under-specified way, yes. Then you have *Vitronine* which gives superhuman stamina, however, you are still prone to rapid energy depletion. Without sufficient energy replacement or rest, your enhanced metabolism could consume vital reserves, leaving you weakened, *Vitronine* will allow for conservation of energy by reducing metabolic processes, this can be likened to a free diver when descending to extreme depths with no external oxygen tanks. When *Zirconine* is paired with *Vitronine*, the combination is what recharges your body and stores the energy you are exposed to.

To explain, when you are in a highly active state you will burn through your energy reserves very quickly, you could fatigue and therefore struggle to continue in that state indefinitely, however, if you are exposed to high energy levels such as radiation from a star; gamma radiation, ultraviolet or infrared, then your body can keep replenishing your energy, potentially, at a rate faster than you are using it, in this instance you become stronger, the Vitronine is what provides this stamina. If you are not able to recharge as you burn your energy with no replacement source, you may pass out. Be mindful of this Theo, as this is your weakness, but energy is in abundance everywhere, remember this is how our Infinite Harmony Engine works."

Theo was beaming, he couldn't believe what he was being told.

"This is incredible. My body doesn't defy the laws of physics. How much energy can I store?"

"The laws you know or think you know. Your science is wrong in many areas, I would not dwell on that. Your body has the energy of a star."

"I am sorry, What! What the hell kind of active state would I need to be in to deplete the energy of a star? Am I going 'one on one' with Blackhole or something?"

"For now, all I will say is, there will be encounters which your people could not possibly begin to imagine"

"um.. okay. I think."

"Fear not Theo. I must continue. There is much you need to know.

Next, there is the base pair of *Spectrine*. You have been gifted with incredible sensory abilities, from a young age, you have been able to read the minds of people close to you. This is the *Spectrine*, it enhances neural conductivity and sensory input. However you need to learn how to control your enhanced sensory abilities, they could lead to sensory overstimulation.

Everything you experience will be more; noise, lights, or odours. They could become overwhelming, causing disorientation or pain. In time you will be able to tune your mind to focus on specific inputs, and you will learn to instinctively react to those inputs which you are not consciously focussed on. *Spectrine* will allow your senses to navigate space, detecting vibrations and changes in the cosmic environment that will guide you.

We will teach you. Unchecked your nervous system could be overloaded with pain. However when *Spectrine* is paired with *Zirconine*, it acts like a damper to pain, you still experience incredible sensory input, and you will still feel a level of pain, but this will be greatly diminished. A bullet hitting you will feel like a slight tickle. You will still experience pleasure and the sensations that come with it.

"So I have a kind of second sense? An awareness beyond what could be considered tangible"

"You could describe it like that. The next base is the one which gives you your greatest abilities, it is the one with which we are most proud. *Quantine* will give you quantum tunnelling capabilities, through a series of regenerative bonded quantum dots. We call the '*Quantum Nexus Heart*'. Giving you the ability to manipulate quantum fields, be aware, that this power is at the Quantum level, its misuse could cause quantum instability, leading to unpredictable effects at the molecular structure such as unintended teleportation, atomic annihilation or dimensional decay.

You will be able to create a quantum field, creating such a field will allow you to manipulate matter, you will be able to move at the speed of light without relativistic time issues, you will be able to defy gravity, and more accurately, you will be able to both generate an anti-gravity field and when needed, your own gravity projecting the fields as you wish. *Quantine* will allow you to teleport anywhere, remember, if you use this ability to go back in time, you will be an observer only. Never use this ability to advance to the future, as when you return you will only be an observer until time catches up.

"What you describe could be considered weird science fiction, quasi-science, but this is all possible? And I can do all these things?"

"Yes, Theo. You will appear as a god on Earth, as we did each time we visited Earth and other worlds"

Theo was in a state of amazement "This is incredible"

"With *Quantine*, as I mentioned, you will be able to manipulate matter. What you can do is down to you. But we call this manipulation the '*Etheric Surge*'. It is an ability that allows you to tap into this all-pervasive energy and force in the *Extherix,* to manipulate energy and matter. This could manifest as telekinesis, energy manipulation or even the altering of the fabric of reality at a quantum level. You will be able to sense and interact with the life force of living beings, influence emotions and thoughts, or traverse different planes of existence."

Theo "You mean dimensions?"

"Yes. But also at an almost spiritual level"

"You mean such as an afterlife, to be able to speak to the dead? Or God?"

"In a manner of speaking. There is no god. There is no afterlife. When a sentient life form dies, the electrical activity in their body ceases to be. Their life force or what you call their soul, ceases to be and they die. However, there is an enduring essence, a memory, that can survive in the DNA of the departed. You can interface with this memory."

"What will that tell me? I don't understand what that could do or how it will be of benefit!"

"Powerful memories, the character and essence of the person is coded into their DNA. Those memories can be passed to their offspring and remain hidden in their DNA. There it can lay dormant, throughout generations. It is how your dreams were so vivid. You were reliving memories of your ancestors by reading the stories encoded into your DNA. Some memories are lost, replaced with other stories."

"Oh my! This is remarkable. I would never have considered that DNA could hold a story, could hold memories. Just from an archaeological and paleo-anthropological point of view, it could rewrite human history. I guess this is how people believe they have a past life?"

"Yes, a past life is an individual reading the most powerful of memories stored in their DNA.

There is one more detail I **MUST** tell you before I can let you rest. I mentioned that we instructed the early carriers of the Aelioxar DNA to keep their secret. That is not quite accurate.

We told them to pass the story down to their male heirs when they reached adulthood. We bestowed the title of '*Order of the Etheric Veil*' onto them.

This order has endured since your ancient times. They are the keepers of these most profound secrets, the protectors of knowledge that, if misused, could lead to their end. Membership is by lineage and not merit, with each member sworn to uphold the order's principles.

They operate in the shadows, influencing events from behind the scenes, to ensure the stability of the world and the safekeeping of the knowledge of the '*Etheric Surge*' and our involvement.

When you are returned home, you will likely be contacted by a member of this group. They will be your aides, your confidants, your knowledge keepers."

"*Order of the Etheric Veil*? Do they possess abilities like my father?"

"Some of them have a genetic trait which is active, others do not. We have kept in communication with '*The order*'. Until recently, some Aelioxar lived on earth, living as humans. They prepared '*The Order*' for your arrival. Some of them were tasked with the preparing of you"

"HOW exactly did they prepare for me?"

"Once we had identified that you were conceived, we set in motion the events to allow for your enhancement and activation. I explained the catalysing procedure. The '*Order*' were involved."

Theo asked Baruch to leave. He needed to process the information alone. He knew he was different. Growing up he knew he was special. He suspected so much on many occasions. But while he may have joked he was an alien, in his wildest imagination, he never expected this.

He considered human evolution. The Neanderthal, Homo heidelbergensis, Homo erectus, Homo sapiens. He considered what his predecessors in paleoanthropology had been striving to solve with evolution, the dispersal of the species across the planet, their behaviours, social interactions, the rise of belief systems, art and language.

Not for a moment would it have been hypothesised, that humankind would be the direct result of extraterrestrial involvement. Any archaeologist or anthropologist would have been condemned and ridiculed, thrown out of the discipline, and their respect lost forever.

Theo *'I am an idiot. Why did it not occur to me earlier.'* Realising that he may not be able to class himself as from the species Homo sapien. He was a species of the genus '*Homo*', that much he could be sure, but '*sapien*'? He was wise and knowledgeable, which is the literal meaning of '*sapien*', but he couldn't be considered of the species Homo sapien. He needed a name for the new species he represented.

He considered it further, could he consider himself in any of the seven classifications of biological life? He came to the decision that he could. But he was not Homo sapien, for the moment he would consider himself to be 'Homo pars-deus' meaning 'Man is part god' or 'Homo pars-aeliox' meaning 'Man is part Aeliox'. While there were other humans, with a similar genome on Earth, they would not exhibit anywhere near the same degree of superhuman ability. Would they fit into the same classification as himself?

CHAPTER 16 GRIEF

SEPTEMBER 10 2021

"Every time you were convinced you couldn't go on, you did."
Anonymous

Theodore had not seen his son in over a month. There were no signs of his whereabouts. John filed an official police missing persons report on behalf of his godson. Theodore was now suspecting the worst and was grieving.

CCTV footage was reviewed and Theo's route was confirmed. He was seen entering Wandsworth Common, the text message to his dad confirming a connection to the cellular tower near the park, the timestamp of 9:37 a.m. matching the footage at the cafe.

The footage further identified Theo entering the second part of the common back of Balham Park Road. The Police went door to door, asking the owners of the properties backing onto the common if they had security cameras. It was after speaking to one resident that they became aware of wildlife monitoring equipment that had been installed by a local animal charity.

The police discovered a network of motion-activated video and still cameras placed around the common with several orientated to capture various angles of Theo's last known position.

The charity cooperated and released the footage to the police. What was discovered defied explanation! While some of the closest still cameras exhibited signs of electrical interference resulting in some malfunctioning devices, others recorded images with typical signs of radiation exposure, the pictures did show Theo, but there was too much 'snow' on the image to provide any clear indication of what occurred.

But there was one high-definition video camera with tracking. It captured Theo entering the common and running away from the camera. It then clearly captured Theo slowing his pace and putting his hands to his head as if he was experiencing some pain before he staggered and fell on his back landing on the grass. The video began to distort and blur, but the evidence was there. A blue shaft of light was seen, perhaps three meters in diameter, it enclosed Theo, its source not apparent. Lasting no more than a couple of seconds, before the light began to fade, Theo was no longer anywhere to be seen.

The video was sent for a more detailed forensic examination. Theodore was informed by John of the video's existence and sworn to secrecy by his friend about its contents. It was now considered a national security issue and was confiscated by the security services. Those officers aware of its content are made to sign a non-disclosure agreement.

John felt for his friend. The evidence while inconclusive of any known intervention, clearly showed Theo disappearing at the will of some otherworldly force.

Theodore knew his son was special, his achievements both academic and athletic proved so much. But he didn't know why. He had his suspicions, ever since his beloved encountered the mystery in Broadacre Park, he had been overly cautious but had allowed this mystery to spark an intrigue and a longing to know more. From John's description, the events in the common matched the previous encounters, from that of his late wife to the event on Hampstead Heath. The first encounter resulted in his wife being taken from him. The most recent was his son.

Louise didn't know how to console her husband. She could only comfort Theodore. She didn't know what to say, what would help. She was present when John shared what he knew with Theodore. She had been confided in with the entire story, also sworn to secrecy.

The media, on hearing of Theo's disappearance, ran a series of stories claiming he was ashamed of his cheating at the recent games, that he was embarrassed to face the public, he wanted to hide. The stories turned more sinister claiming that he was murdered or that he had ended his life. Theodore was once again hounded by the media, several vans parked outside his home for days on end. It wasn't until John managed to secure a dispersal order that the media moved on. The wild stories abated, but the legacy of Theo appeared beyond ruined.

On the 10th of September, Theodore was at home alone. Louise reluctantly went to work to meet with some potential donors to the charity. Theodore insisted she go.

He sat in his late father's rocking chair, positioned in the bay window of his front room. Its creaky rhythm a comforting echo of memories. The room was dimly lit, the curtains partially drawn against the world outside.

His once well-groomed beard now bore streaks of silver, a testament to the weight of grief he carried. The parting of the curtains framed just enough of the view of the quiet London street, a bleak September day, raindrops tracing delicate paths down the glass. Each droplet blurred the world beyond, much like the tears that blurred Theodore's vision.

He strained to see any sign of his son returning. But the street remained empty. The ticking clock on the mantelpiece seemed to mock him, measuring out the days since his son disappeared.

The rocking chair smelled of old wood, faded memories, and the faint scent of his son's favourite cologne. Theodore's hands clenched the armrests, knuckles white against the worn fabric. He whispered his son's name into the silence, hoping it would reach him wherever he was. Outside, the rain continued its gentle descent, as if weeping alongside Theodore.

Theodore, retraced each moment of Theo's journey home in his mind, hoping that something would occur to him that was previously missed. At that moment, his mobile rang, as if screaming at him for attention. He looked at the screen '*Unknown number*' he silenced it. The remote intruder stopped their assault on his peace after 10 seconds. Then it rang again. And again.

The persistence continued. Theodore couldn't face another member of the press, invading his privacy.

'*But what if it wasn't the press*' he thought to himself '*What if it's Theo or about Theo*'.

On what seemed to be the Nth occasion the phone rang he answered

"**What**?" Theodore was blunt and angry.

It was a female caller, the voice seemed familiar, but he could not recall who it was "Mr Newton. Thank you for answering. I need to meet with you"

"**Who is this? Do I know you**?" He was shouting at the caller.

"We have met once before, a long time ago. You may not remember me, I am sorry, but I can not tell you who I am, at least not over the phone. Please meet with me." The lack of detail irritated Theodore.

"**What is this about? Why won't you tell me who you are?**"

"I can't risk it. The phone isn't secure. I don't have time. Meet me on her bench. 6 p.m. this evening. Don't bring John, don't tell him." The call hung up.

Theodore stared at the phone, the call lasted 32 seconds. The caller sounded scared as if by calling Theodore, they were putting them both at risk. '*She mentioned not to tell John.*' He thought. Why shouldn't John know, he was a friend, he trusted him.

In the past six years, John had excelled in the Metropolitan Police, and having Joanne in his life had lifted him, her love and support for her husband being the missing piece in his life.

He was promoted from Detective Chief Inspector to Detective Superintendent and very recently to Detective Chief Superintendent. While he made no secret of his desire to work for the '*Special Branch*', no opportunity had arisen, instead taking a position of responsibility in the North London Boroughs of the Metropolitan Force. Theodore considered this for a moment.

'John wouldn't have sought authorisation to have my phone tapped. He wouldn't do that.'

Dismissing John having any disloyal involvement in the investigation into his son's disappearance, he still felt uneasy, his gut was telling him that maybe he should agree with the caller's request. Buy what about Louise? What excuse could he give for why he wasn't at home when she returned this evening? Should he tell her? If his phone was tapped, he would have to be cautious about what he could say.

It was only five past nine in the morning. He would have plenty of time to consider his actions, too long, if there was one thing that was beginning to irritate Theodore, it was waiting. Everything in his life was now about waiting, time seemed to be drawing itself out.

For the first time since his son's disappearance, he used his home gym. He showered. Looking in the steamed bathroom mirror he caught a faint glance at his reflection. Wiping the condensation from the glass, he noticed the grey in his beard and his hair.

'This will not do. Theodore, you are a disgrace. Get a grip man. You know Theo is alive. You know it. You still sense him'

Theodore couldn't explain the feeling he had, he often dismissed the gut sensation, his emotion and logical thought overriding the better of this intangible sensation.

He dressed and at a little after 11 a.m. left the house. He took the short walk to the end of his street, turning left he continued down another avenue, before crossing the road at an adjoining street and proceeded to head towards the main street of Dunthorpe. A little over a 7-minute walk, he entered the barbers.

The shop was simply decorated. One wall was covered with a large mirror with several barber chairs positioned opposite. In front of the chairs and beneath the mirror was a bench with several sinks. Reggae music was playing out of a small hi-fi system in the corner of the room. The shop was empty except for a solitary figure sitting next to the speaker drinking from a mug.

"Bill. It would seem I am ageing a little prematurely"

"Now Theodore, you know I don't like Bill, it's William, you mind yourself now. But man, It is good to see you." William spoke was a thick Jamaican accent. A short thin man, perhaps 65 years old.

"Sorry. You know I can't help myself"

"I am so very sorry for what has happened to your boy. If Levi were here now, he would be out there leaving no stone or blue land crab unturned. Take a seat boy. If you were here earlier. Ooh man, what a wait you would have had" he laughed

"Thanks, William"

"Now let's see what we have here." He let out a distinct laugh, quite musical "Ooowhooo Man. I can trim your beard, and hide those grey hairs. Now what about your head? Got some great hair dyes if you want?"

"I don't think that is needed, William. Just a trim if you don't mind."

The pair talked, although in the main it was William, for over an hour, mostly about what an amazing man Levi was and how Theo's recent performance should be celebrated and commended by a statue. Theodore agreed, he couldn't think of another statue of an athlete anywhere in Britain, but there must be.

After the trim and long chat with William, Theodore started reminiscing about the good times with his dad. This spurred him to visit the local grocery store to grab a few items. He was going to make a recipe his dad would make at least once a week, mutton, plantain and fried okra curry.

Leaving the grocery store he intended to head straight home, but he had another one of his gut feelings. He stopped, not realising he was blocking the doorway to another shop.

"Excuse me" a voice abruptly called out "Do you mind moving, I am in a hurry"

"Sorry" he replied as he took a step forward, the lady he had momentarily inconvenienced, tutted under her breath as she rushed out to her car which had been poorly parked outside. The front right wheel mounted onto the pavement, while the entire rear end of the vehicle blocked at least a third of the narrow roadway.

She hopped in and without checking any mirrors or indeed putting on her seatbelt, she floored the German hatchback, dismounting the pavement with a crunch of her front suspension, narrowly avoiding a head-on collision with a van coming in the opposite direction.

"The hell is her problem" the driver of the van could be heard shouting. Theodore, while witnessing the incident, had no problem believing it, it was, after all, a very appropriate behaviour for the make of car she was driving.

He turned and looked up at the signage of the shop he was in front of, '*Nicholsons Newsagents*'.

He went in and without giving it any thought, found himself at the lottery stand, he instinctively filled out a line of numbers and took it to the counter. Paying he shared with the assistant that he had never played the lottery before and was wondering why he decided to start now. They responded "Good luck" before heading home.

Upon arriving, he got straight to work in the kitchen. He would leave the curry to finish in the slow cooker. It was now just after 1 p.m. He stood in the kitchen wondering how else he could pass the day before his clandestine meeting at 6 p.m.

'Kitchen, it could do with a tidy. Rearrange the cupboards' Theodore set to work, emptying, cleaning then resorting each storage compartment. When he was done, he vacuumed and mopped the floor. He moved onto the hall, the living room, the stairs and the bedrooms, although he left Theo's room as it was. Finally tackling the bathroom. Six bags of clutter ended up in the rubbish when he was done. It was half past five.

He hurriedly wrote a note for Louise.

'Hi babe.
Did lots of thinking today.
Had positive thoughts. Certain he is ok.
Did some cleaning and went for a cycle.
I had to snap out of this self-pity.
Love T'

Grabbing his bike, he headed toward Broadacre Park.

Upon arriving at Isabella's bench, he flicked out the kickstand on his bike and sat down, glancing at his watch it was five to six. He looked towards each direction of the path, there were a few people about, some runners, but in the main dog walkers.

Turning to look back towards the entrance of the park, he was startled, by a woman now sitting next to him.

"Woah, I'm sorry, I didn't see you sit, startled me there."

"No, I apologise, that was my fault, I am glad you could make it Theodore"

"You are the caller. Do I know you?"

"We have met before, over twenty years ago in fact"

Theodore stared at the woman, she seemed familiar, but he couldn't place her.

"You don't remember me, do you? That is good. My name is Katherine Williams. Dr Katherine Williams. I was the.." Theodore interrupted her

"You were the registrar when Isabella was admitted to the hospital. If I remember didn't you resign?"

"Very good Theodore. Yes, you are correct"

"What is this about? And why the cryptic call this morning?"

"I don't have long to explain. Your son is safe, he will be returned to you very soon. I can't tell you how I know this."

Theodore looked at her shocked. He considered trying to restrain her and call the police. But what if she was holding Theo, he couldn't risk it "**What**? Where is he? Who has him?"

"I really can't say. Theo will explain it all to you when he returns. It is usually the father telling the son, but, well this is a very unique set of circumstances, Levi, your father's loss was upsetting to us all." Theodore could feel his emotions build, all of the grief he had ever felt trying to surface.

"**My father**? What has my dad got to do with Theo being missing for over a month? Who are you? You are not just a Doctor are you?"

"I am sorry. I really can't say any more. Take this"

She handed him a card with a name

'Theo R Derotev'

"Find this man, get yourself a burner phone, when you locate the number, use the burner to contact him, do not register the phone with your details. You must preserve anonymity. He will know who you are. He will expect you."

"Can't you give me his number? Why the mystery?"

She stood, beginning to walk away then stopped, with her back still to Theodore she responded one last time "It's all on the card"

He stared at the card, turning it over and examining it, he ran his finger over the surface but couldn't identify any extra features.

He looked up shouting "I don't understand", but she was gone.

'This is all damn peculiar' he thought to himself. He put the card in his trouser pocket, before, climbing back on his bike, if he was quick enough he could see where she went.

Pedalling in the direction Katherine went, he reached the entrance to the park, scanning the adjoining road for the mysterious woman, but she was nowhere to be seen.

'The hell' he thought, *'There is no way she could have got out of the park before I could catch her, even if she ran'*

#

By the time he had returned home, Louise was already there. He opened the garage, closing the garage door behind him. He hung the bike on the wall before he entered through the internal garage door and into the house.

Louise was sitting at the kitchen table working on her laptop

"Hi beautiful" he leaned over and kissed her, as he was about to pull away, she gently placed her arm around the back of his head and continued to kiss her husband, before releasing him.

"You cleaned. You trimmed your beard. And your hair."

"Yeah. I have had a really bizarre day."

"And you cooked, it smells amazing. How was it bizarre?'

"Are you ready for dinner? It's a recipe my dad made every week, Mutton, Plantain and Okra Curry."

"Please. And tell me about your day?"

Theodore microwaved a pouch of rice before serving up dinner. He started to explain the cryptic call, then the even more mysterious encounter with the doctor.

“Show me the card,” she asked

Theodore pulled the card out of his pocket and handed it to his wife.

Examining it for a moment “Theo R Derotev. Another Theo! Coincidence? The surname seems Russian, Eastern European at the very least. Maybe they are former KGB?” Turning the card over, the reverse side was blank. She continued “Plain white back, can’t feel any texture. Maybe it has invisible ink?”

“I thought about that. But given what she told me, the way she behaved, the absolute secrecy, would she use an invisible ink? I’m joining the dots here, but she didn’t want John involved, I can only assume because he is Police, which suggests she also doesn’t want them to see this card. Forensic analysis could reveal an invisible message. Or am I thinking too much into this?” Usually, he enjoyed a mystery but not when it involved his Son and perhaps his Dad. What he needed was for his wife to show support and join him in the investigation. He wasn’t let down.

“Not at all, I think that is a reasonable assumption. But you trust John, don’t you? And this is about Theo. What is in your and his best interests? Maybe you should ask for John's help!”

“Perhaps. But I do like a mystery. If I can figure out what is on the card by myself then, the fewer people who know..”

His wife was quite shocked by his statement, if she knew him like she thought she did, he only had what was best for Theo at heart “The fewer people who know? You are starting to sound like this is some conspiracy. That at the very least, suggests the Police are involved.”

“Isn’t it though? She called me multiple times from a withheld number. Told me to keep everything secret, but couldn’t tell me anything specific. Tells me Theo will be home soon, but to contact this ‘*Derotev*’ using a burner phone. The only reason you use a burner is to stop being traced. If not the police then who? Does this not all sound like some kind of conspiracy?”

"When you summarise it like that. But up until this morning you were grieving. You were an emotional wreck, are you thinking straight? Maybe you are letting your emotions take control of you. You could be being played? Someone could be manipulating you!"

"To what end? How does a woman, a doctor no less, tie into this manipulation?"

"Okay. Let's just stop and think about this rationally" She pulled forward her laptop and lifted the lid. "Where should we start? Hmmm… how about a web search?" She loaded her web browser and began typing the name into the search box.

The page loaded

It looks like there aren't many great matches for your search.

Try using words that might appear on the page that you're looking for. For example, 'cake recipes' instead of 'how to make a cake'.

There were a few pages suggested but none of them appeared related to the search term. Theodore suggested trying the surname only. Louise highlighted everything but the surname and pressed delete, then return.

The page loaded

You're seeing results for Derivative.
You originally searched for Derotev.

She clicked on Derotev, reloading the search. Again the results were unhelpful. Adding back in his first name only, once again the results did not yield anything of any significance.

“This is quite strange. I would have expected something for the surname at least. Try Dr Derotev or Prof. maybe Professor”

She tried all permutations of title she could think of, with no successful results.

“I can only assume Derotev is not a surname. Maybe it’s a place? But surely that would have been brought up in the results. I’ll give it a go.” She clicked on the ‘maps’ link and entered the surname as a place search.

‘No matching places found’

“Maybe we are looking at this from the wrong angle. What if it isn’t a name?”

“Didn’t she say find this man?”

“She did. But what if it’s not a man, what if it was just her way of getting me to call the number.”

“But there is no number. At least nothing obvious.”

“I know. I know” his frustration was all too clear

“What if it’s an anagram or acronym or a code?”

“OK. Let’s give that a try. Let’s start with an anagram. Search for an anagram solver”

“Got one.” She proceeded to enter all 12 characters with no spaces. The results weren’t anything obvious.

‘Hoovered, Overdoer, Overrode, Retorted, Reverted, Revetted,
Tethered’

“They are all only 8 letters. 4 short. I don’t think it’s an anagram. Not a clear one.”

“How about an acronym then? But the letters could mean anything. She stared at the name. It might be nothing but the first part of the name is ‘*The order otev*’ Maybe it could be that simple?”

"Maybe so. Or maybe we are wasting our time. She said the number was on the card. THIS IS SO FRUSTRATING" Theodore yelled.

Louise exclaimed "The order of the ev! What is the EV? Maybe you are right. What do you want to do next?"

"I'll pop out tomorrow morning. See if I can get a pay-as-you-go handset and a SIM card. A black-light or UV light would be good also."

"A UV light?" She exclaimed

"If it's written in invisible ink, wouldn't a UV pen be a possibility?"

"My electric toothbrush has a UV light, which helps to spot plaque before and after brushing. I'll go get it." She headed upstairs to get the tool. Meanwhile, Theodore took her place at the laptop. He tapped on the table while he thought, something came to him and entered another search phrase.

'Common forms of secret code'

There were thousands of search pages. He clicked on the first result. It was a website that described common types of cryptography. The first one suggested the substitution of the alphabet order for the order of letters on a qwerty keyboard. A being replaced with Q and E with T and so on. He opened the word editor and typed in the name on the card. Louise returned with her toothbrush.

"What are you looking at now?"

"Cryptography and cyphers"

"Do you not think we may be taking all of this a little too seriously" Theodore glared at his wife, she read the meaning of his look "Sorry Darling. I know, this is for Theo. She kissed him on the cheek. Fancy a cup of coffee?"

"Please. The first cypher I tried, converting the name on the card, came out as *'EPCI D MCDIECW'*, gibberish! Guess that's not it. Where is the toothbrush?"

"Sorry, here" She handed the brush to Theodore who pressed the button to activate the UV light. Then proceeded to run the beam across the front and back of the card. Without any success.

"I don't know, maybe it's too bright in here?"

"I have an idea." She left the room, returning with a thick tartan picnic blanket. She pulled the laptop away from Theodore "Lean forward" Theodore did as she asked as she covered him in the large blanket "Better"

"You won't believe this" he exclaimed lifting his arms so the blanket fell behind him, "most of the letters are circled, everyone except the OT of Derotev."

"Are there any numbers?"

"No."

"So we aren't much further forward are we?"

"I do not know. But at least it is something"

"Score!" She smiled curling her upper lip and causing her nose to wrinkle as she does when she is being cheeky.

"Where is that coffee?"

"Okay, it's coming. So what is next Einstein? How many characters were circled"

"That makes ten"

"Most phone numbers are ten if you ignore the leading zero"

"You are right." Theodore exclaimed "They are. Not sure how that helps us, however," He mimicked Louise by curling his upper lip in his attempt to copy her smile. She threw a tea towel at him before handing him his cup of black coffee. "I don't know. I feel we are onto something but I don't know what." He put his head in his hands. After a few minutes turned to Louise with a grin on his face.

"Louise, this may not work, but I want to try something. Here" he held out the card for Louise to take. "Ok. Just hold it'

Theodore closed his eyes and concentrated. A minute went by.

"Is something supposed to be happening? Do all the lights need to be on for the flickering or something?"

"Damn. I was sure that would have worked."

"You tried to remote read the card, didn't you? How would that work exactly? You know what the card says"

"I know. I know. I thought that maybe I could have seen what the meaning of the card was"

"It's seven-thirty. I think maybe we should call it a night with this game and maybe invent another game of our own?"

#

The next morning Theodore was up early. When Louise came down, she wasn't at all surprised to see her husband sitting at the laptop.

"Let me guess. Cryptology? Cyphers? Codes? How about use your voodoo and predict the lottery numbers" she chuckled.

"Lottery. I forgot. Grab my wallet, I bought a ticket yesterday for last night's draw"

"I didn't think you did the lottery!"

"I don't, or I didn't, this is my first ever try"

"Coffee?" She asked

"Please. So you were right. I've been looking at cryptography, specifically cyphers where numbers are represented by letters. There are a few different systems, I thought it was a sophisticated substitution cypher. But nothing seems to be working. I'll pop out soon and grab a burner phone from the Mobile store on the high street"

"You not want any breakfast? I'm going to have some toast and jam."

"That will do me. OK, I'll stop there. Had enough research for the moment. Let's check this lottery ticket."

Theodore loaded the lottery website and checked his ticket.

"First attempt at the lottery and I have won £56.70. That should pay for a cheap burner phone at least. I got four numbers and one-star number."

“Wow. Can I say how impressed I am with your clairvoyant skills? Well Done” she let out a squeaky laugh.

“Do you mock me?” He stood and embraced his wife.

“We could do with a lottery win. I don’t think the meeting went too well yesterday”

“Sorry. I forgot to ask. That bad? I should have been there.”

“I can always donate another couple of hundred thousand. But we have time yet. Did they give any reasons why?”

“They didn’t give a no. It’s just a feeling I had. They were asking lots about Theo. I think that while he is missing. He is kind of a liability”

Theodore looked at his wife in disbelief “God’s sake man. These people make me sick. It’s all about optics and opinion. Association and fallout. What about doing the right thing, because it is the right thing to do”

“I know. We will get there. But maybe we need to consider sticking with the four hubs for the moment. With the funds we have, that will see us through the next couple of years. It’s the smart business move.”

“You are the CEO. You make the strategic decisions.”

“But it is your vision. We make these decisions together. Now eat your breakfast like a good boy”

After his morning shower, Louise dropped Theodore in Dunthorpe town centre before continuing to work. He had arrived too early for the shops to be open and again he found himself having to find ways to pass the time. Across the road from the Mobile Store was an independent coffee shop and roasters, he crossed the road and entered. The smell of freshly ground coffee was intoxicating. He ordered a large americano with a slice of toasted and buttered teacake, before taking a seat next to the window.

‘Not the worst way to pass the time’ Glancing at his watch, he had a little over 30 minutes to wait.

The waitress came over with his teacake and asked if he minded if she popped the TV on. Having no objection, the girl flicked the remote and the flatscreen TV on the wall next to the doorway came to life. The local news channel was currently broadcasting, muted but with subtitles.

Theodore took a sip of his coffee *'Wow, this is an incredible coffee'* he thought *'nutty, with notes of caramel, chocolate and the slightest hint of cinnamon'* He stood and went over to the counter and asked the server if they happened to sell packets of the coffee beans. He was delighted to find out, that not only did they sell the coffee, but they offered a subscription service with local delivery. He asked to speak to the owner and after a few minutes of negotiating, he had agreed to a trial, whereby the local coffee shop would supply the beans to the DexBox hubs.

Theodore returned to his seat and took a bite of his teacake. Glancing up at the TV, the news was reporting on a local lady who had been involved in a head-on collision, she, unfortunately, did not survive the crash as she had not been wearing her seatbelt. By all accounts, the description of the victim and her car matched the woman who he had the encounter with the previous day.

'It's a shame, but If you don't take precautions and abide by the law, these things happen' a chill ran down his spine *'Karma. No. She didn't deserve that.'* He remembered that he had to cash his lottery ticket before buying the mobile. He thanked the staff at the coffee shop before taking the short walk to the newsagents to claim his lottery prize, dropping the loose change into the charity pot which was raising funds for sickle cell awareness.

Back across the road, he arrived at the mobile store, just as it was being opened. A slightly rotund man maybe mid-twenties stood at the door "Can I help you sir?"

"Yeah, I am after a basic phone, for my dad, he is getting on, he can't be doing with touch screens, you get me"

"Yeah guv, like me gran, she is the same. Old people innit. Take a look at these. What kind of Reddies are you talking?"

"A pony. Max, a bullseye"

"I got you guv. This one is Chinese innit. Its three tenners"

"Anything bargain basement?"

"Na man. Most of the gear is well pricey. You get me?"

"I'll take it." The assistant directed Theodore to the till, he removed the cash, that he had just claimed from his lottery win from his pocket and counted out thirty pounds

"Na man. Its card only innit."

"Card only? For a cheap phone?"

"Yeah, man. Sorry, it's the rules, bloody feds man"

Theodore gestured that he wasn't going to bother and left the store. *'I have to stay smart here. Can they track a card purchase to the phone? I don't know, but, I have to stay smart. OK. Theodore, think. Where can I get a phone with cash?'* He looked up and down the main street and noticed a sign several shops down. *'That might work'* he thought as he proceeded to head to the store he had spotted. On entering, he noticed the main wall was floor-to-ceiling of locked glass display cases with various second-hand electronic devices.

Spotting some mobile phones, he moved towards the display case.

"Excuse me." Directing his attention towards a skinny teen behind the secured counter. The boy entered the shop via a heavy security door.

"Yes. Can I help"

"Can I buy that phone" he pointed to an old push-button mobile phone which was very similar to the model he used to own "Can I pay cash?"

"Yeah, we prefer cash"

"Great. Do you happen to sell sim cards?"

"We only sell the '*Atmosphere*' network sims"

"That will do, can I buy a tenner top-up with that?"

"Yeah, we do that also. All cash"

"That's great"

The assistant processed the sale, applied the top-up and put the SIM in the phone before starting the SIM activation process.

"Thanks. You have been a great help. Here take this for yourself" Passing an extra twenty pounds over to the teen.

"When you are done with it, you can always pawn or sell it back to us."

"Thanks. I will bear that in mind"

Walking back home, Theodore couldn't help thinking how the times had changed. He would never have thought, that one day, he would find himself having to buy a second-hand mobile phone from a pawn shop or even avoiding having to use electronic payment methods. He wasn't a criminal, he was certain neither was Theo and yet, here he was, behaving like one, he still didn't know what came over him in the mobile shop, trying to act all gangster. Louise would kill herself laughing when he told her.

Back home, he made himself a coffee with the beans he bought and sat at the kitchen table, once again staring at the business card. *'Ok, so it's 10 characters.'* He picked up the mobile phone he had just bought and looked at it. *'What the hell Theodore'* He held the power button on the keypad and powered the phone off. Talking out loud he cursed himself "You have to be smarter than that. Idiot" realising that the phone would be connected to the nearest cellular tower. Once he discovers the number to ring, he doesn't know if it is being monitored. In which case if it's being tracked, so too will the calls made to that number and so his location potentially triangulated. Was he being paranoid? Should he make himself a foil hat? This wall is all getting too surreal.

He pulled out his mobile phone and typed out a message to John

'Need to meet. Not in a good place. Would be good to talk. Let me know when you're free. T'

Theodore conceded that his behaviour was irrational and that he trusted John. He couldn't let himself be manipulated even if it was to discover what happened to Theo.

He didn't get an immediate reply, why should he, John was a senior member of the Met Police. But he knew he would reply eventually. Theodore was back to twiddling his fingers.

He spent the next couple of hours in his gym. Mixing free weights with cardio and callisthenics. Finishing with some sparring time with the boxing bag.

About to take another shower, his phone rang, it was John

"Thanks for ringing" Theodore exclaimed

"Are you OK? I am concerned for you"

"I am about to grab a shower, but, are you free, would be good to catch up, I need a familiar face."

"I do have some officer appraisals scheduled for the next couple of hours, but I am free after three. I can come to you if that's easier."

"Perfect. Thanks, John. See you then" the call disconnected.

#

Theodore was sitting drinking another coffee, in the bay window when John pulled up in his unmarked Jaguar. Theodore stood, mug in hand and went to greet his friend.

"Thanks for coming. Do you want a coffee? I've just bought this today and it's incredible"

"Sure. You are looking well. Kind of took me by surprise. I was expecting you to be wearing sweats. But you are looking good"

"Yeah sorry. I will confess. I have brought you here with false intentions"

"Theo? Is he back" John looking for signs of his return.

"No. But this does have to do with him."

Theodore spent the next few minutes explaining the events of the previous day and his paranoid behaviour to his godfather. John didn't interrupt. He pulled his notepad from his pocket and wrote a single line.

'Turn off your mobile'

John did the same.

In a hushed voice John began to explain "Sorry Theodore, you aren't paranoid. Our phones are listening to us. I am glad you brought this to me. I have to be very careful what I say, they are going to want to know what I have said to you and why my phone is off. But since the video footage of Theo disappearing was confiscated, I have learned that It has been passed over to a US agency. I don't know who they are, or what they are called. But I am certain they are watching us."

"**Shit. For real**?"

"Afraid so. We, or as far as I know, The Met does not know who this Derotev person is or what the number is. I have heard the name mentioned, but I am not familiar with the context of it, but then I am not Special Branch nor do I have privy to some of the counter-terrorist briefing notes. There is a lot of compartmentalisation in the Met, the left hand doesn't always know what the right hand is doing"

"It's ok. I appreciate you being here"

"All I can suggest is if you work out what the number is. Make sure you are out in the countryside when you ring. You will want to try and hide your steps, and keep yourself from being tracked. Paying with cash is a start, that was a smart move. Hell, maybe treat Louise to a weekend away, take the Eurostar to the continent. Make the call from there. Make it harder for the Americans. But don't do it in London. There are too many cellular towers and too many cameras. Watch your back. In the meantime, I will ask Joanne about this Dr Williams, what she can remember about her."

"Thanks, John, I know how much you are risking your career with this. If you do get caught out. I always have a position for you at DexBox as a director. Your experience of knife crime and gang culture would be invaluable, if you can't make a difference in the force, then you can make that difference with us"

"I have been thinking about that myself. I have a great pension now. But the bureaucracy and the politics in the Met can be too much. I may take you up on that one. I have to go. But heed what I said and take care. I catch up with you soon."

The pair hugged it out before Theodore escorted John to the door. He had more of an idea of how to proceed. But was no further forward in discovering what the number was he needed to dial.

CHAPTER 17 THE ONE

SEPTEMBER 15 2021

"I did not ask for this. But the burden is mine.
It would be irresponsible of me not to make a difference when I have the ability in me, to force it"
Theo Newton ***'The One'***

Theo had completed his training. It was quite disconcerting, that he needed a manual to understand how to be, *him*. Or rather, how to be the new him, *'The One'*, the person who was, unlike any other person, in the entirety of human history, to have an ability to make change on the scale, impact, impression, that he could.

Sure, there had been individuals in history, who exceeded their mandate, forcing horrors on the world, or promised imperial expansion and delivered it, beyond their wildest expectations. Even historical religious idols could not compare to what Theo as 'The One' could achieve.

It was down to him. He possessed superhuman abilities, but even to him, that did not fully capture the scope of what he could do, it would be more accurate to describe him as a *'god'*. In the way that his name, *Theo*, essentially meant *'god'*. Just another twist in his destiny which to him felt, pre-planned.

Baruch met with Theo one last time. She explained that the Aelioxar had pressing issues of defence on their home worlds. As such, they weren't turning their back on their children, the human race on Earth or the other planets with which they sprinkled their design. Theo was their appointed guardian. He would watch over Earth and when needed, he would be there to protect it.

Baruch gave instructions, providing the necessary evidence, and convincing Theo of what was happening at home. These would become his primary objectives when he returned to Earth.

But they, the Aelioxar, were unaware that there were other events taking place. Events that only Theo could deal with. Events so horrific, they could not follow judicial process or military intervention. Some world leaders were complicit in the deception that was unfolding.

"Theo you are ready. Trust your ability. Remember you are '*The One*', the only one, if you fail, Earth '*may*' go on, and humanity '*might*' go on, but we will not be able to steer its future. We can no longer continue influencing its direction. We will return, but only if you succeed."

"I did not ask for this. But the burden is mine. It would be irresponsible of me not to make a difference, when I have the ability in me, to **FORCE** it."

"Remember. You are virtually indestructible and unbeatable, you are both an unstoppable force and an immovable object. But be mindful of your energy. When you are at your weakest, you are at your most vulnerable. Remember if you seek guidance, you can jump to this location. We won't turn you away, but it will leave you drained and the Earth will be defenceless. '*The Order of the Etheric Veil*' will be your council"

"Thank you, Baruch. I hope one day we will meet again. What do I call myself? My superhero name?"

"Do you need such things? I will place you somewhere remote, where your arrival should go unnoticed. Good luck and farewell Theo Newton"

With that Baruch activated the star jump, teleporting Theo in an instance across the 444 lightyear distance to Earth.

A blinding blue column of light appeared, as if from nowhere, just as quickly as it appeared, it began to fade, leaving just the faintest of an electric blue glow.

Theo found himself standing in a field of wheat stretching out for miles in every direction. The crop in a twenty-five-metre circle was flattened and scorched. He surveyed his surroundings. It felt warm, his senses were telling him he was located in the northern hemisphere, the USA. He could feel the magnetic lines of the planet, the faint vibrations of Earth, the warmth of the sun, and the fresh air filling his lungs.

His attention focused on a worker bee, while over 50 metres away, his incredible vision could see the insect, the motion of its wings, its struggle against the buoyancy of the air and the haphazard eddies of the current. As he stared, he focused his thoughts on calming the airflow, granting the creature a smoother path on its onward journey. For a moment he felt like he knew where it wanted to go and he made it so.

Theo leant back and closed his eyes, facing the direction of the sun. He soaked in the moment, before opening his eyes as he began to rise into the air. As he ascended he slowly rotated, taking in his position and the landscape that stretched out before him. He stopped rising when he reached one hundred feet. He was in the state of Montana.

Before he left Genetrix-7X, the Aelioxar had created an indestructible super-suit for him. Crafted from material exotic to earth, It would act as a catalyst, enhancing the rate he could absorb surrounding energy, it was an extension of him, but would not define him.

Black in colour, it closely resembled a carbon fibre material, embedded with silver metal threads, when excited these veins, would glow blue and serve as conduits for his innate abilities.

As he moved and if he willed it, the suit would reflect light and he would shimmer with a pearlescent lustre of black, silver and electrically charged blue.

The suit's nano fibres, able to be rearranged with a thought, locking into a rigid lattice for defence or loosening, allowing fluid movement for close combat. The nanofibre tech self self-repairing and adaptive.

On the chest was a silver oval shape, resembling the letter O, which some would associate with 'The *One*'. Embedded with the same nano threads of the metal fibre. Crossing through the oval, on the vertical from beneath his chin, down to his abdomen was a silver blade, resembling that of a sword, not as polished as the oval on his chest, also threaded with metallic nanofibres. Elsewhere on his suit, there were more obvious silver embellishments contouring around his muscles, making his physique more obvious, the same metal threads interwoven to maximise the visual spectacle and sheer awe that their excitation would deliver to anyone who would bear witness.

At the back of the suit and beneath his head, was a hood, not a cape as you would expect superheroes to sport. When he raised the hood onto his head, he could will the suit to either morph the hood into a mask or cloak his suit to an observer, who would then see Theo wearing Jeans and a plain black hoodie or if he chose, he could manipulate the suit to display anything he wishes.

Floating at the minimum level of radar detection. He noticed a diner approximately 10 miles away to the southwest. Leaning forward, he tipped his body into a horizontal position and willed his body to fly towards the diner, he dropped his altitude slightly until he was within a couple of hundred metres of his target. He dropped to the ground just behind a fence.

'Cool. Ok. Let's try invisibility.'

With a simple thought, he vanished. He leapt the fence and jogged towards the road on which the diner was situated. He waited at the side of the road, still invisible, until a 16-wheel lorry which was on its approach got closer. He walked into the road standing in its path.

'Ok, then, intangibility'

He found he was bracing himself for the impact of the multi-ton lorry, which for any human would be the natural response if finding themselves too late to move out of harm's way. The lorry continued on its course, Theo standing his ground, he passed right through the vehicle, coming out the other side unscathed.

'Wow, what a rush. I need to get over that, I don't need to brace'

He looked around before heading towards the diner. He moved to a sidewall, next to the car park of the diner and made himself visible once again. Flipping up his hood, his clothing changed to jeans and a black hoody sporting the Bobcats team logo of Montana State University. Making his way round to the front of the building he entered.

The bell above the diner door jingled as Theo stepped inside. The air smelled of frying bacon and old coffee grounds. The worn vinyl booths were mostly empty, except for a few grizzled locals hunched over their mugs.

Theo, standing 6 foot 6 inches tall, with an athletic and muscular build, felt the weight of their gaze. His skin was a canvas of sun-kissed brown, and his eyes held the wisdom of generations. He'd hoped for a bite to eat and a hot cup of coffee, but the diner's atmosphere turned icy.

The waitress, a stout woman with a name tag that read 'Marge' glanced up from behind the counter. Her eyes narrowed as they swept over Theo.

"We don't serve your kind here," she said, her voice sharp and cutting.

Theo's heart sank. He had faced prejudice before, due to his intellect and ability, but this was different. This was Montana

'The Big Sky State, where the mountains stood tall and the rivers ran wild'.

He had heard stories of remote towns, intolerant towards people who, in the local's opinion 'didn't fit'.

Ignoring the stares, Theo squared his shoulders. "I just want a coffee please" he replied.

A man sitting at the counter, a rancher with a weathered face, spat into his empty mug. "Coffee's for real Americans." he sneered.

Theo replied that he was British, just passing through and would very much appreciate a cup of coffee.

"You're not welcome here" another voice chimed in. A trucker, his cap pulled low, leaning against the jukebox.

Theo met Marge's eyes. "My kind?" he said softly. "We're all just trying to find our place." She hesitated, then turned away.

Theo took a step towards the counter "Marge, that is your name. Any chance of that coffee please?" She ignored him.

"Are you deaf and stupid? She said your kind ain't welcome here." The rancher stood glaring at Theo.

"I don't want any trouble. I get the point." he turned and headed back towards the door, but before he was able to pull the handle to make his exit, a glass beer bottle shattered against his head. Unfazed he continued to pull the door open. The rancher stared at the trucker who had thrown the bottle, shrugging his shoulders, the trucker stepped forward.

Theo "I wouldn't if I were you. I will let you have that bottle. But don't think for a minute that I won't put you on the ground."

Trucker shouted "Hey Al, you heard the brass coming from this douchebag"

Al stepped out from the kitchen, a giant of a man, wearing a stained white shirt and a cigar hanging from his mouth.

Al "I heard. Threats to my loyal customers are not welcome here. You apologise now and while you're at it, you can buy him another beer."

"Pardon? It sounded to me like you think I should apologise. For being assaulted! I'll tell you what is going to happen here. I am going to walk out this door and leave. Just consider this to be the luckiest day in your life" Inside Theo was raging.

The last time he felt so angry was in front of Baruch. But his time with the Aelioxar had taught him control, he didn't need anger, instead, he learnt to focus his emotion towards understanding and compassion, in this case, he pitied them, just like he pitied a rabid dog, who knew no different and couldn't control themself.

He exited the property and turned left towards the car park where he had earlier noticed a gas station. Before he was able to get halfway across the forecourt he felt another bang against his head. Looking back he could see a spanner rebounding toward the ground, the outstretched arm of Al standing next to the trucker.

Their expression was painted with a look of disbelief.

"Sorry, should I have said ouch? Just a moment.." Theo lifted his right hand to his head gently rubbing it "Ouch, that hurt you bully"

"You mock me?" The diner cook began to march towards Theo, picking up his pace as he got closer, when he was within a couple of meters, leaping into the air, he pulled his arm back, creating a fist with his hand and swung his arm in an arc towards Theo's face. However, Theo took a step back, the man missed his aim, his momentum too great to restore balance on his landing foot, tripping, he face-planted the gravel ground, his face, the cheese on a grater. He skidded to a stop. Groaning the man rolled onto his back, his face lacerated from the impact.

"It is quite rude of you. I would, at the very least, expect a postcard after your trip" Theo mocked the man.

The trucker looked at Theo in disbelief as he walked towards his big rig. Theo ignored the man before continuing towards the gas station. The doorway was blocked by a scrawny-looking man holding a wrench. "You are not welcome here" the man exclaimed before spitting a mouthful of chewing tobacco on the ground, narrowly missing Theo's feet. "You ok Al?' The man continued.

Al groaned "I think he broke my nose."

Theo without looking, was aware that the trucker had tucked a handgun into his trousers and was now holding a shotgun. He turned and looked towards the now-armed man. Al had got back onto his feet and was scurrying back to the diner.

Theo watched the trucker closely, but there was still the gas station attendant with the wrench, Theo invoked a mental connection with the man *'Go back into the station, close the door and enter the backroom'*, just as Theo wished, the man responded to the voice in his head.

The trucker looked dumbfounded, why did his ally disappear? In a moment of panic, he pointed his shotgun and fired. The shot roared out of the double barrels. As the pellets neared Theo, time slowed, and his powers surged.

Theo reached out, his fingers grazed the suspended shot. Time was standing still. He proceeded to pluck them from the air, their metallic edges felt dull against his skin. Then, as time resumed its flow, Theo stepped towards the stunned trucker, extending his hand.

"Here," he said, offering the pellet's back. The trucker's eyes widened. Glancing down at the shards of metal in his hand, the trucker dropped the shotgun and pulled out the handgun.

Shaking he struggled to maintain an aim on Theo. As much as he tried, he couldn't pull the trigger. Theo had fused the firing pin, locking it permanently into a deactivated state. The trucker feared for his life, in what he considered his last moments, a flow of warm liquid coursed down his leg, revealing a large wet patch on the crotch of his jeans.

Theo "You may need to change those" Our hero, without laying a single finger on any of the intolerant men, walked away.

Once out of sight, he surged into the air, a blue glow emanating from his suit, accelerating beyond the sound barrier. A sonic boom followed, the thunderclap radiating outward, shattering the windows of the diner in his wake. As he climbed higher he passed Mach 2, Mach 6, and Mach 12, and within seconds of leaving the ground, he had punched through Earth's atmosphere.

The blue faded to black, stars began blinking into view. In less than ten seconds of leaving the xenophobic diner in Montana, he had crossed the continental USA, followed by the Atlantic Ocean and finally, the British Isles came into view beneath him. Altering his angle, he dived earthwards, London his destination, the quantum bubble he generated in front of him, countered the normal effects of atmospheric reentry, there was no fireball, and no one would observe him on his ultrasonic approach. Theo rapidly reduced his speed, holding out his arm, a pulse rippled from his hand, dissipating the sonic wave which had now overtaken him, he didn't want his arrival home to be announced with another sonic boom.

Hovering twenty thousand feet above the ground, he considered if he was visible to radar. He didn't think of the question when he was discussing flight with Baruch. After giving it some thought, he rationalised that he was not visible, he was fully stealth-capable, if he wanted to be, although, he thought.

'I could have a bit of fun with foreign military jets if the situation ever presented itself'.

After more than 35 days away, he was finally home. He hadn't chosen this future for himself, but it was his destiny, now *'IT'* was on him, and he had accepted that now. He was actually enjoying it. Still hovering over London, again, he went invisible. It was just after 4 p.m. when he made the slow descent towards his house, gently landing in front of the door to his home. What a story he had for his father.

THEO NEWTON WILL RETURN IN BOOK 2 of the serial

DECEPTION

EPILOGUE

"Get the commander, I have confirmation of an energy signature, picked up by one of the G.A.R.D Satellites. Hurry"

The large open planned room was frantic with activity, a woman dressed in military uniform raced towards a door located to one side of the high ceiling room, her shoulder epaulettes marked with two chevrons crossed by what appeared to be a delta wing shape.

The room was laid out like it was a mission control centre, preparing for a space launch. Several rows of booths had operators working at computer terminals with large computer monitors, the displays varied from radar projections and live feed satellite imagery to the more unusual, with representations of what appeared to be live monitoring of energy waves, lidar images, gamma and magnetic fields.

At what was to be the front of the room, were multiple massive display screens, almost filling the wall with live feed information. Some of the screens were cycling through what the operators were observing on their displays, while what appeared to be the main focus of the larger display area, pictured a representation of the solar system, the planets as far out as the dwarf planet Pluto were pictured, however, the displays also indicated multiple monitoring satellites orbiting the systems 8 planets, as well as what could only be described as a fleet of other '*craft*' randomly dispersed.

Another display gave a computer representation of Earth, the background to the image was flashing red with a red circled '*X*' positioned over the planet indicating the detection of something. The words '*ENERGY PROXIMITY DETECTION*' flashed repeatedly.

A voice shouted over the noise of the room "Is it London?"

The man, accompanied by the two chevroned woman, was also dressed in military uniform, his epaulettes were different, they were clearly of the rank colonel. On the breast pocket of his uniform, was a US military badge with the same delta wing image at the centre, as on the epaulette of the woman.

The Colonel looked at the large display boards as he hurriedly walked towards the man who had requested the commander.

"Is It London?" He repeated.

"No Sir. The energy signature is coming from Montana."

"Technical Sergeant. Did you say, Montana? As in Montana, here in the USA?"

"Yes sir, that is correct"

"Show me." The operator adjusted the resolution of the image of Earth displaying the red circled cross. He pulled in on the indicated spot, zooming closer and closer.

"Chouteau County Sir, close to Loma."

"Have you double-checked Technical Sergeant Harris?"

"Yes Sir. Colonel Bellamy, If I may."

"Continue"

"The energy signature was off the scale, the highest readings so far. Those we registered in London were in the order of three to four petajoules. Sir, this one is in Montana. It was one thousand petajoules. That is One Exajoule Sir"

"My God. How long ago are we talking?"

"10 minutes Sir."

"Thank you, TS Harris. Carry on."

The Colonel returned to his room. Without even sitting he picked up his phone and pressed a button, after a couple of seconds the call connected

"Sir, this is a Colonel Bellamy, Space Command Monitoring Station. You requested to know when we had another energy event. Sir, we have just recorded one." The colonel listened to the voice at the other end of the line, replying "10 minutes. Near Loma, Montana. Sir, it was One Exajoule." He replaced the receiver.

ABOUT THE AUTHOR

Mark P. Smith is passionate about science, both factual and fiction.

His love of science ranges from Archaeology to Theoretical Physics, while his enjoyment of SCI-FI covers all genres.

He lives in the North East of England with his family and Labrador called 'Luna'. He studied in York attaining a degree in Geography with Applied Environmental Science.

Printed in Great Britain
by Amazon

45124136R00136